⟨ W9-ASO-676

ROBERT S. GOLD is a member of the English Department at Jersey City State College and has taught at Queens College and New York University. He edited *Point of Departure* (available in a Laurel-Leaf edition) and is the author of *A Jazz Lexicon*.

LAUREL-LEAF BOOKS bring together under a single imprint outstanding works of fiction and nonfiction particularly suitable for young adult readers both in and out of the classroom. Charles F. Reasoner, Professor of Elementary Education, New York University, is consultant to the series.

ALSO AVAILABLE IN LAUREL-LEAF BOOKS:

POINT OF DEPARTURE: 19 STORIES OF YOUTH AND DISCOVERY
edited by Robert S. Gold

GREAT TALES OF ACTION AND ADVENTURE
edited by George Bennett

DEAR BILL, REMEMBER ME? AND OTHER STORIES
by Norma Fox Mazer

LITTLE VICTORIES, BIG DEFEATS *edited by Georgess McHargue*

IN NUEVA YORK *by Nicholasa Mohr*

ARRIVING AT A PLACE YOU'VE NEVER LEFT *by Lois Ruby*

STEFFIE CAN'T COME OUT TO PLAY *by Fran Arrick*

THE CHOCOLATE WAR *by Robert Cormier*

I AM THE CHEESE *by Robert Cormier*

THE DISAPPEARANCE *by Rosa Guy*

STEPPING STONES

STONES

AN ANTHOLOGY

edited by
ROBERT S. GOLD

J 808.831 S453s 1981

Stepping stones NOV 1 3 '12

for Eva Gold

Published by
Dell Publishing Co., Inc.
1 Dag Hammarskjold Plaza
New York, New York 10017

Copyright © 1981 by Robert Gold

All rights reserved. No part of this book
may be reproduced or transmitted in any form
or by any means, electronic or mechanical, including
photocopying, recording or by any information storage
and retrieval system, without the written permission
of the Publisher, except where permitted by law.

Laurel-Leaf Library ® TM 766734, Dell Publishing Co., Inc.

ISBN: 0-440-98269-3

Printed in the United States of America
First printing—April 1981

ACKNOWLEDGMENTS

"Manhood" by John Wain: From DEATH OF THE HIND LEGS AND OTHER STORIES by John Wain. Copyright © 1966 by John Wain. Reprinted by permission of Viking Penguin Inc.

"A Lot You Got to Holler" by Nelson Algren: Reprinted by permission of Candida Donadio & Associates, Inc. Copyright © 1947 by Nelson Algren.

"Total Stranger" by James Gould Cozzens: Reprinted from *The Saturday Evening Post.* © 1936 The Curtis Publishing Company.

"Indian Feather" by Thomas Mabry: First published in the *Sewanee Review*, 60, 4 (autumn 1952). © 1952 by the University of the South. Reprinted by permission of the editor.

"Samuel" by Grace Paley: From ENORMOUS CHANGES AT THE LAST MINUTE by Grace Paley. Copyright © 1968 by Grace Paley. Reprinted by permission of Farrar, Straus & Giroux, Inc.

"A Temple of the Holy Ghost" by Flannery O'Connor: Copyright 1954 by Flannery O'Connor. Reprinted from her volume A GOOD MAN IS HARD TO FIND AND OTHER STORIES by permission of Harcourt Brace Jovanovich, Inc.

"Mr. Parker" by Laurie Colwin: From PASSION AND AFFECT by Laurie Colwin. Copyright © 1973 by Laurie Colwin. Reprinted by permission of Viking Penguin Inc.

"The Duchess and the Smugs" by Pamela Frankau: Pages 3–63 in A WREATH FOR THE ENEMY by Pamela Frankau. Copyright 1952, 1954 by Pamela Frankau. Reprinted by permission of Harper & Row, Publishers, Inc., and International Creative Management.

"The Deal" by Leonard Michaels: From GOING PLACES by Leonard Michaels. Copyright © 1966 by Leonard Michaels. Reprinted by permission of Farrar, Straus & Giroux, Inc.

"Black Boy" by Kay Boyle: Copyright © 1932 by Kay Boyle. Renewed © 1960 by Kay Boyle. Reprinted by permission of A. Watkins, Inc.

"Ball" by Sam Koperwas: Reprinted by permission of *Esquire* Magazine. Copyright © 1975 by Esquire, Inc. Also appeared in *All Our Secrets Are the Same*, © 1976 by Esquire, Inc.

"Barbed Wire" by Robert Canzoneri: Reprinted by permission of International Creative Management. Copyright © 1970 by Robert Canzoneri.

"The Old Chief Mshlanga" by Doris Lessing: From AFRICAN STORIES by Doris Lessing. Copyright © 1951, 1953, 1954, 1957, 1958, 1962, 1963, 1964, 1965 by Doris Lessing. Reprinted by permission of Simon & Schuster, a Division of Gulf & Western Corporation.

"Man and Daughter in the Cold" by John Updike: Copyright © 1968 by John Updike. Reprinted from MUSEUMS AND WOMEN AND OTHER STORIES by John Updike by permission of Alfred A. Knopf, Inc. Originally appeared in *The New Yorker*.

"Simple Arithmetic" by Virginia Moriconi: Every effort has been made to contact the author. The publishers will be happy to arrange formal acknowledgment and customary payment if the author will write to them.

"The Rocking Horse Winner" by D. H. Lawrence: From THE COMPLETE SHORT STORIES, vol. III, by D. H. Lawrence. Copyright 1934 by Frieda Lawrence, © renewed 1962 by Angelo Ravagli and C. M. Weekley, Executors of the Estate of Frieda Lawrence Ravagli. Reprinted by permission of Viking Penguin Inc.

"The Ghost of Martin Luther King" by Hal Bennett: copyright © 1973 by George H. Bennett, originally appeared in *Playboy*, from the book INSANITY RUNS IN OUR FAMILY by Hal Bennett. Reprinted by permission of Doubleday & Company, Inc.

Contents

Introduction

"Adolescence" is an ambiguous word: to the social scientist, who observes it, it's a stage in human development; to the adolescent, who lives it, it's a beleaguered state; to the parent or citizen who must deal with it, it's a set of problems with no clear solution. What to do about rising juvenile crime and illiteracy? The man in the street (or in the bar), critical of contemporary permissiveness, calls for a get-tough policy; educators and social psychologists theorize, while newspapers and TV sensationalize. Our social problems, by now epidemic, seem intractable.

Although stories don't solve problems, they *can* deepen our understanding, alter our perspectives, and, so, indirectly lead us toward a more honest contemplation of our common predicament. The seventeen stories in *Stepping Stones* are a composite portrait of the richly varied experience of adolescence, especially its interaction with the larger, more powerful adult society. They provide an overview of failure, of cross-purpose, of pain, and of growth.

Seven stories present what is called an initiation theme—an adolescent, through contact with the unfamiliar, comes to some new awareness of self or of parent or, simply, of life. In James Gould Cozzens's "Total Stranger" the adolescent is initiated into a fresh awareness of his seemingly stuffy father through their chance encounter with the father's former woman friend; the revelation that the father was once considered "fun," quite apart from its shock value, provides a general truth: personality, far from being static, is subject over the years to profound change. In Doris Lessing's "The Old Chief Mshlanga" the heroine's own outsiderness leads her to identify with the ethnic underdog—with the African natives' forced alienation from their own land, imposed on them by the official arrogance of the whites, and personified for the girl principally by her own father. In Pamela Frankau's "The Duchess and the Smugs" Penelope's dilemma tests her courage to live beyond the merely respectable and conventional; her initiation is into a world that sometimes demands spontaneous, difficult moral choices. In Laurie Colwin's "Mr. Parker" Jane is initiated into an imperfect awareness that as she grows older, the world changes in relation to her. In Thomas Dabney Mabry's "The Indian Feather" two themes are developed: first, the boy's initiation into a world of adult responsibility and, second, the differing preoccupations of adulthood and adolescence, illuminated most forcefully in the story's final scene. In Robert Canzoneri's "Barbed Wire" the young protagonist emerges with imperfect knowledge of his father's death, but consequently with a deeper sense of the elusiveness of knowledge and of people's need to invent what they don't know. In Hal Bennett's "The Ghost of Martin Luther King" the dignity and humanity of David's ghostly visitor expose the deficiencies of his real-life models: the father's pathetic cowardice and the uncle's frightening brutality.

Three of the above stories (Cozzens, Lessing, Colwin) and ten others in the collection deal with tensions and conflicts between adolescents and adults, and inevitably with those breakdowns of sympathy or understanding called the generation gap. Because these are stories of neglect or abrasiveness, they register an attitude, a moral position, but that position is *implied* rather than stated. Of these thirteen stories it is significant that only in Leonard Michaels's story is an adult the "victim"; in the other twelve it is selfishness, insensitivity, or quirkiness on the part of the adult that victimizes the teenager. "Samuel" shrewdly assesses grown-up unease and ambivalence when confronted with raucous teenage behavior, with one particularly edgy adult inadvertently precipitating the tragedy. "Simple Arithmetic" by Virginia Moriconi and "Manhood" by John Wain are both funny and scathing commentaries on the egoism of parents; Stephen's parents just can't be bothered (except financially), and Rob's father bothers *too much* as he tries grotesquely to make Rob into everything that he himself wasn't. Parental manipulativeness is also at issue in Sam Koperwas's "Ball," in which the increasingly fantastical action produces a realistic theme: the father ironically succeeds in dehumanizing his sensitive son—even to the point of indifference to his own death. Similarly, D. H. Lawrence's "The Rocking-Horse Winner" is a parable or fable in which Paul's feverish rocking symbolizes the family's agitated need for money. In Flannery O'Connor's "A Temple of the Holy Ghost" the generation gap turns farcical: the grown-ups are unable to control the kids' silliness and "profane" thoughts; the story's comic tension derives from the raw energy of the young colliding with the genteel forms of rural southern life. "A Lot You Got to Holler" by Nelson Algren suggests that although parents point the finger, children are the bigger victims: the adolescent-narrator's father hasn't really earned the right to admonish the boy, and modern psychology would support the story's basic insight that the quest for money is often symbolic of a search for love. Kay Boyle's "Black Boy," though half a century old, does not seem dated in its generational split between the openness of youth and the bigoted paranoia of old age. In Michaels's "The Deal," the story in which the victim of generational conflict is the adult, what makes the story persuasive is that this adult is not a patsy, not a classic victim "type," but a resourceful woman defeated by a cultural condition beyond her control—the ignorant macho pride that regrettably but understandably sustains ghettoized teenagers.

Conflict between the generations is extremely common in life and literature, but "Total Stranger," "The Indian Feather," and "Barbed Wire" are morally neutral, are concerned with interaction, not opposition. This is also true of John Updike's "Man and Daughter in the Cold," which is an atypical story in that it is the *adult* who gains a crucial insight through interaction with an adolescent; the daughter's superiority on the skiing slopes temporarily obliterates the father's built-in supremacy, establishes a *human* equality, and provides him (and the reader) with a revelation: that love exists most perfectly among equals, and not when one is "playing" the parent and the other is then forced into playing the child.

Stepping Stones presents a panoramic view of adolescents groping and sometimes stumbling in the perilous land of the adult.

ROBERT S. GOLD

Manhood

BY JOHN WAIN

Swiftly free-wheeling, their breath coming easily, the man and the boy steered their bicycles down the short dip which led them from woodland into open country. Then they looked ahead and saw that the road began to climb.

"Now, Rob," said Mr. Willison, settling his plump haunches firmly on the saddle, "just up that rise and we'll get off and have a good rest."

"Can't we rest now?" the boy asked. "My legs feel all funny. As if they're turning to water."

"Rest at the top," said Mr. Willison firmly. "Remember what I told you? The first thing any athlete has to learn is to break the fatigue barrier."

"I've broken it already. I was feeling tired when we were going along the main road and I—"

"When fatigue sets in, the thing to do is to keep going until it wears off. Then you get your second wind and your second endurance."

"I've already done that."

"Up we go," said Mr. Willison, "and at the top we'll have a good rest." He panted slightly and stood on his pedals, causing his machine to sway from side to side in a labored manner. Rob, falling silent, pushed doggedly at his pedals. Slowly, the pair wavered up the straight road to the top. Once there, Mr. Willison dismounted with exaggerated steadiness, laid his bicycle carefully on its side, and spread his jacket on the ground before sinking down to rest. Rob slid hastily from the saddle and flung himself full-length on the grass.

"Don't lie there," said his father. "You'll catch cold."

"I'm all right. I'm warm."

"Come and sit on this. When you're over-heated, that's just when you're prone to—"

"I'm all *right*, Dad. I want to lie here. My back aches."

"Your back needs strengthening, that's why it aches. It's a pity we don't live near a river where you could get some rowing."

The boy did not answer, and Mr. Willison, aware that he was beginning to sound like a nagging, over-anxious parent, allowed himself to be defeated and did not press the suggestion about Rob's coming to sit on his jacket. Instead, he waited a moment and then glanced at his watch.

"Twenty to twelve. We must get going in a minute."

"*What?* I thought we were going to have a rest."

"Well, we're having one, aren't we?" said Mr. Willison reasonably. "I've got my breath back, so surely you must have."

"My back still aches. I want to lie here a bit."

"Sorry," said Mr. Willison, getting up and moving over to his bicycle. "We've got at least twelve miles to do and lunch is at one."

"Dad, why did we have to come so far if we've got to get back for one o'clock? I know, let's find a telephone box and ring up Mum and tell her we—"

"Nothing doing. There's no reason why two fit men shouldn't cycle twelve miles in an hour and ten minutes."

"But we've already done about a million miles."

"We've done about fourteen, by my estimation," said Mr. Willison stiffly. "What's the good of going for a bike ride if you don't cover a bit of distance?"

He picked up his bicycle and stood waiting. Rob, with his hand over his eyes, lay motionless on the grass. His legs looked thin and white among the rich grass.

"Come on, Rob."

The boy showed no sign of having heard. Mr. Willison got on to his bicycle and began to ride slowly away. "Rob," he called over his shoulder, "I'm going."

Rob lay like a sullen corpse by the roadside. He looked horribly like the victim of an accident, unmarked but dead from internal injuries. Mr. Willison cycled fifty yards, then a hundred, then turned in a short, irritable circle and came back to where his son lay.

"Rob, is there something the matter or are you just being awkward?"

The boy removed his hand and looked up into his father's face. His eyes were surprisingly mild: there was no fire of rebellion in them.

"I'm tired and my back aches. I can't go on yet."

"Look, Rob," said Mr. Willison gently, "I wasn't going to tell you this, because I meant it to be a surprise, but when you get home you'll find a present waiting for you."

"What kind of present?"

"Something very special I've bought for you. The

man's coming this morning to fix it up. That's one reason why I suggested a bike ride this morning. He'll have done it by now."

"What is it?"

"Aha. It's a surprise. Come on, get on your bike and let's go home and see."

Rob sat up, then slowly clambered to his feet. "Isn't there a short cut home?"

"I'm afraid not. It's only twelve miles."

Rob said nothing.

"And a lot of that's downhill," Mr. Willison added brightly. His own legs were tired and his muscles fluttered unpleasantly. In addition, he suddenly realized he was very thirsty. Rob, still without speaking, picked up his bicycle, and they pedalled away.

"Where is he?" Mrs. Willison asked, coming into the garage.

"Gone up to his room," said Mr. Willison. He doubled his fist and gave the punch-ball a thudding blow. "Seems to have fixed it pretty firmly. You gave him the instructions, I suppose."

"What's he doing up in his room? It's lunch-time."

"He said he wanted to rest a bit."

"I hope you're satisfied," said Mrs. Willison. "A lad of thirteen, nearly fourteen years of age, just when he should have a really big appetite, and when the lunch is put on the table he's *resting*—"

"Now look, I know what I'm—"

"Lying down in his room, resting, too tired to eat because you've dragged him up hill and down dale on one of your—"

"We did nothing that couldn't be reasonably expected of a boy of his age."

"How do you know?" Mrs. Willison demanded. "You never did anything of that kind when you were a boy. How do you know what can be reasonably—"

"Now look," said Mr. Willison again. "When I was a boy, it was study, study, study all the time, with the fear of unemployment and insecurity in everybody's mind. I was never even given a bicycle. I never boxed, I never rowed, I never did anything to develop my physique. It was just work, work, work, pass this exam, get that certificate. Well, I did it and now I'm qualified and in a secure job. But you know as well as I do that they let me down. Nobody encouraged me to build myself up."

"Well, what does it matter? You're all right—"

"Grace!" Mr. Willison interrupted sharply. "I am not all right and you know it. I am under average height, my chest is flat and I'm—"

"What nonsense. You're taller than I am and I'm—"

"No son of mine is going to grow up with the same wretched physical heritage that I—"

"No, he'll just have heart disease through over-taxing his strength, because you haven't got the common sense to—"

"His heart is one hundred per cent all right. Not three weeks have gone by since the doctor looked at him."

"Well, why does he get so over-tired if he's all right? Why is he lying down now instead of coming to the table, a boy of his age?"

A slender shadow blocked part of the dazzling sun in the doorway. Looking up simultaneously, the Willisons greeted their son.

"Lunch ready, Mum? I'm hungry."

"Ready when you are," Grace Willison beamed. "Just wash your hands and come to the table."

"Look, Rob," said Mr. Willison. "If you hit it with your left hand and then catch it on the rebound with your right, it's excellent ring training." He dealt the punch-ball two amateurish blows. "That's what they call a right cross," he said.

"I think it's fine. I'll have some fun with it," said Rob. He watched mildly as his father peeled off the padded mittens.

"Here, slip these on," said Mr. Willison. "They're just training gloves. They harden your fists. Of course, we can get a pair of proper gloves later. But these are specially for use with the ball."

"Lunch," called Mrs. Willison from the house.

"Take a punch at it," Mr. Willison urged.

"Let's go and eat."

"Go on. One punch before you go in. I haven't seen you hit it yet."

Rob took the gloves, put on the right-hand one, and gave the punch-ball one conscientious blow, aiming at the exact center. "Now let's go in," he said.

"Lunch!"

"All right. We're coming . . ."

"Five feet eight, Rob," said Mr. Willison, folding up the wooden ruler. "You're taller than I am. This is a great landmark."

"Only *just* taller."

"But you're growing all the time. Now all you have to do is to start growing outwards as well as upwards. We'll have you in the middle of that scrum. The heaviest forward in the pack."

Rob picked up his shirt and began uncertainly poking his arm into the sleeves.

"When do they pick the team?" Mr. Willison asked. "I should have thought they'd have done it by now."

"They have done it," said Rob. He bent down to pick up his socks from under a chair.

"They have? And you—"

"I wasn't selected," said the boy, looking intently at the socks as if trying to detect minute differences in color and weave.

Mr. Willison opened his mouth, closed it again, and stood for a moment looking out of the window. Then he gently laid his hand on his son's shoulder. "Bad luck," he said quietly.

"I tried hard," said Rob quickly.

"I'm sure you did."

"I played my hardest in the trial games."

"It's just bad luck," said Mr. Willison. "It could happen to anybody."

There was silence as they both continued with their dressing. A faint smell of frying rose into the air, and they could hear Mrs. Willison laying the table for breakfast.

"That's it, then, for this season," said Mr. Willison, as if to himself.

"I forgot to tell you, though," said Rob. "I was selected for the boxing team."

"You *were?* I didn't know the school had one."

"It's new. Just formed. They had some trials for it at the end of last term. I found my punching was better than most people's because I'd been getting plenty of practice with the ball."

Mr. Willison put out a hand and felt Rob's biceps.

"Not bad, not bad at all," he said critically. "But if you're going to be a boxer and represent the school, you'll need more power up there. I tell you what. We'll train together."

"That'll be fun," said Rob. "I'm training at school too."

"What weight do they put you in?"

"It isn't weight, it's age. Under fifteen. Then when you get over fifteen you get classified into weights."

"Well," said Mr. Willison, tying his tie, "you'll be in a good position for the under-fifteens. You've got six months to play with. And there's no reason why you shouldn't steadily put muscle on all the time. I suppose you'll be entered as a team, for tournaments and things?"

"Yes. There's a big one at the end of next term. I'll be in that."

Confident, joking, they went down to breakfast. "Two eggs for Rob, Mum," said Mr. Willison. "He's in training. He's going to be a heavyweight."

"A heavyweight what?" Mrs. Willison asked, teapot in hand.

"Boxer," Rob smiled.

Grace Willison put down the teapot, her lips compressed, and looked from one to the other. *"Boxing?"* she repeated.

"Boxing," Mr. Willison replied calmly.

"Over my dead body," said Mrs. Willison. "That's one sport I'm definite that he's never going in for."

"Too late. They've picked him for the under-fifteens. He's had trials and everything."

"Is this true, Rob?" she demanded.

"Yes," said the boy, eating rapidly.

"Well, you can just tell them you're dropping it. Baroness Summerskill—"

"To hell with Baroness Summerskill!" her husband shouted. "The first time he gets a chance to do something, the first time he gets picked for a team and given a chance to show what he's made of, and you have to bring up Baroness Summerskill."

"But it injures their brains! All those blows on the front of the skull. I've read about it—"

"Injures their brains!" Mr. Willison snorted. "Has it injured Ingemar Johansson's brain? Why, he's one of the acutest business men in the world!"

"Rob," said Mrs. Willison steadily, "when you get to school, go and see the sports master and tell him you're giving up boxing."

"There isn't a sports master. All the masters do bits of it at different times."

"There must be one who's in charge of the boxing. All you have to do is to tell him—"

"Are you ready, Rob?" said Mr. Willison. "You'll be late for school if you don't go."

"I'm in plenty of time, Dad. I haven't finished my breakfast."

"Never mind, push along, old son. You've had your egg and bacon, that's what matters. I want to talk to your mother."

Cramming a piece of dry toast into his mouth, the boy picked up his satchel and wandered from the room. Husband and wife sat back, glaring hot-eyed at each other.

The quarrel began, and continued for many days. In the end it was decided that Rob should continue boxing until he had represented the school at the tournament in March of the following year, and should then give it up.

"Ninety-six, ninety-seven, ninety-eight, ninety-nine, a hundred," Mr. Willison counted. "Right, that's it. Now go and take your shower and get into bed."

"I don't feel tired, honestly," Rob protested.

"Who's manager here, you or me?" Mr. Willison asked bluffly. "I'm in charge of training and you can't say my methods don't work. Fifteen solid weeks and you start questioning my decisions on the very night of the fight?"

"It just seems silly to go to bed when I'm not—"

"My dear Rob, please trust me. No boxer ever went into a big fight without spending an hour or two in bed, resting, just before going to his dressing-room."

"All right. But I bet none of the others are bothering to do all this."

"That's exactly why you're going to be better than the others. Now go and get your shower before you catch cold. Leave the skipping-rope, I'll put it away."

After Rob had gone, Mr. Willison folded the skipping-rope into a neat ball and packed it away in the case that contained the •boy's gloves, silk dressing gown, lace-up boxing boots, and trunks with the school badge sewn into the correct position on the right leg. There would be no harm in a little skipping, to limber up and conquer his nervousness while waiting to go on. Humming, he snapped down the catches of the small leather case and went into the house.

Mrs. Willison did not lift her eyes from the television set as he entered. "All ready now, Mother," said Mr. Willison. "He's going to rest in bed now, and

go along at about six o'clock. I'll go with him and
wait till the doors open to be sure of a ringside seat."
He sat down on the sofa beside his wife, and tried to
put his arm round her. "Come on, love," he said
coaxingly. "Don't spoil my big night."

She turned to him and he was startled to see her
eyes brimming with angry tears. "What about my big
night?" she asked, her voice harsh. "Fourteen years
ago, remember? When he came into the world."

"Well, what about it?" Mr. Willison parried, uneasily aware that the television set was quacking and
signaling on the fringe of his attention, turning the
scene from clumsy tragedy into a clumsier farce.

"Why didn't you tell me then?" she sobbed. "Why
did you let me have a son if all you were interested
in was having him punched to death by a lot of rough
bullet-headed louts who—"

"Take a grip on yourself, Grace. A punch on the
nose won't hurt him."

"You're an unnatural father," she keened. "I don't
know how you can bear to send him into that ring
to be beaten and thumped—Oh, why can't you stop
him now? Keep him at home? There's no *law* that
compels us to—"

"That's where you're wrong, Grace," said Mr. Willison sternly. "There is a law. The unalterable law
of nature that says that the young males of the species
indulge in manly trials of strength. Think of all the
other lads who are going into the ring tonight. Do
you think their mothers are sitting about crying and
kicking up a fuss? No—they're proud to have strong,
masculine sons who can stand up in the ring and
take a few punches."

"Go away, please," said Mrs. Willison, sinking back

with closed eyes. "Just go right away and don't come near me until it's all over."

"Grace!"

"Please. Please leave me alone. I can't bear to look at you and I can't bear to hear you."

"You're hysterical," said Mr. Willison bitterly. Rising, he went out into the hall and called up the stairs. "Are you in bed, Rob?"

There was a slight pause and then Rob's voice called faintly, "Could you come up, Dad?"

"Come up? Why? Is something the matter?"

"Could you come up?"

Mr. Willison ran up the stairs. "What is it?" he panted. "D'you want something?"

"I think I've got appendicitis," said Rob. He lay squinting among the pillows, his face suddenly narrow and crafty.

"I don't believe you," said Mr. Willison shortly. "I've supervised your training for fifteen weeks and I know you're as fit as a fiddle. You can't possibly have anything wrong with you."

"I've got a terrible pain in my side," said Rob. "Low down on the right-hand side. That's where appendicitis comes, isn't it?"

Mr. Willison sat down on the bed. "Listen, Rob," he said. "Don't do this to me. All I'm asking you to do is to go into the ring and have one bout. You've been picked for the school team and everyone's depending on you."

"I'll die if you don't get the doctor." Rob suddenly hissed. "Mum!" he shouted.

Mrs. Willison came bounding up the stairs. "What is it, my pet?"

"My stomach hurts. Low down on the right-hand side."

"Appendicitis!" She whirled to face Mr. Willison. "That's what comes of your foolishness!"

"I don't believe it," said Mr. Willison. He went out of the bedroom and down the stairs. The television was still jabbering in the living-room, and for fifteen minutes Mr. Willison forced himself to sit staring at the strident puppets, glistening in metallic light, as they enacted their Lilliputian rituals. Then he went up to the bedroom again. Mrs. Willison was bathing Rob's forehead.

"His temperature's normal," she said.

"Of course his temperature's normal," said Mr. Willison. "He doesn't want to fight, that's all."

"Fetch the doctor," said a voice from under the cold flannel that swathed Rob's face.

"We will, pet, if you don't get better very soon," said Mrs. Willison, darting a murderous glance at her husband.

Mr. Willison slowly went downstairs. For a moment he stood looking at the telephone, then picked it up and dialled the number of the grammar school. No one answered. He replaced the receiver, went to the foot of the stairs and called, "What's the name of the master in charge of this tournament?"

"I don't know," Rob called weakly.

"You told me you'd been training with Mr. Granger," Mr. Willison called. "Would he know anything about it?"

Rob did not answer, so Mr. Willison looked up all the Grangers in the telephone book. There were four in the town, but only one was M.A. "That's him," said

Mr. Willison. With lead in his heart and ice in his fingers, he dialled the number.

Mrs. Granger fetched Mr. Granger. Yes, he taught at the school. He was the right man. What could he do for Mr. Willison?

"It's about tonight's boxing tournament."

"Sorry, what? The line's bad."

"Tonight's boxing tournament."

"Have you got the right person?"

"You teach my son, Rob—we've just agreed on that. Well, it's about the boxing tournament he's supposed to be taking part in tonight."

"Where?"

"Where? At the school, of course. He's representing the under-fifteens."

There was a pause. "I'm not quite sure what mistake you're making, Mr. Willison, but I think you've got hold of the wrong end of at least one stick." A hearty, defensive laugh. "If Rob belongs to a boxing-club it's certainly news to me, but in any case it can't be anything to do with the school. We don't go in for boxing."

"Don't go in for it?"

"We don't offer it. It's not in our curriculum."

"Oh," said Mr. Willison. "Oh. Thank you. I must have—well, thank you."

"Not at all. I'm glad to answer any queries. Everything's all right, I trust?"

"Oh, yes," said Mr. Willison, "yes, thanks. Everything's all right."

He put down the telephone, hesitated, then turned and began slowly to climb the stairs.

The Duchess and the Smugs

BY PAMELA FRANKAU

There had been two crises already that day before the cook's husband called to assassinate the cook. The stove caught fire in my presence; the postman had fallen off his bicycle at the gate and been bitten by Charlemagne, our sheep dog, whose policy it was to attack people only when they were down.

Whenever there were two crises my stepmother Jeanne said, "*Jamais deux sans trois.*" This morning she and Francis (my father) had debated whether the two things happening to the postman could be counted as two separate crises and might therefore be said to have cleared matters up. I thought that they were wasting their time. In our household things went on and on and on happening. It was a hotel, which made the doom worse: it would have been remarkable to have two days without a crisis and even if we did, I doubted whether the rule would apply in reverse, so that we could augur a third. I was very fond of the word augur.

I was not very fond of the cook. But when I was sitting on the terrace in the shade working on my Anthology of Hates, and a man with a bristled chin told me in *patois* that he had come to kill her, I thought it just as well for her, though obviously disappointing for her husband, that she was off for the afternoon. He carried a knife that did not look particularly sharp; he smelt of licorice, which meant that he had been drinking Pernod. He stamped up and down, making speeches about his wife and Laurent the waiter, whom he called a *salaud* and many other words new to me and quite difficult to understand.

I said at last, "Look, you can't do it now, because she has gone over to St. Raphael in the bus. But if you wait I will fetch my father." I took the Anthology with me in case he started cutting it up.

I went down the red rock steps that sloped from the garden to the pool. The garden looked the way it always looked, almost as brightly colored as the post cards of it that you could buy at the desk. There was purple bougainvillaea splashing down the white walls of the hotel; there were hydrangeas of the exact shade of pink blotting paper; there were huge silver-gray cacti and green umbrella pines against a sky that was darker blue than the sky in England.

I could not love this garden. Always it seemed to me artificial, spiky with color, not quite true. My idea of a garden was a green lawn and a little apple orchard behind a gray stone house in the Cotswolds. I saw that garden only once a year, in September. I could conjure it by repeating inside my head—

> And autumn leaves of blood and gold
> That strew a Gloucester lane.

Then the homesickness for the place that was not my home would make a sharp pain under my ribs. I was ashamed to feel so; I could not talk about it; not even to Francis, with whom I could talk about most things.

I came to the top of the steps and saw them lying around the pool, Francis and Jeanne and the two novelists who had come from Antibes for lunch. They were all flat on the yellow mattresses, talking.

I said, "Excuse me for interrupting you, but the cook's husband has come to assassinate the cook."

Francis got up quickly. He looked like Mephistopheles. There were gray streaks in his black hair; all the lines of his face went upward and the pointed mustache followed the lines. His body was dark brown and hairy, except that the scars on his back and legs, where he was burned when the airplane was shot down, did not tan with the sun.

"It's a hot afternoon for an assassination," said the male novelist as they ran up the steps together.

"Perhaps," said Francis, "he can be persuaded to wait until the evening."

"He will have to," I said, "because the cook is in St. Raphael. I told him so."

"Penelope," said my stepmother, sitting up on the yellow mattress, "you had better stay with us."

"But I am working on my book."

"All right, *chérie;* work on it here."

The lady novelist, who had a sparkling, triangular face like a cat, said, "I wish you would read some of it to us. It will take our minds off the current blood-curdling events."

I begged her to excuse me, adding that I did not anticipate any bloodcurdling events because of the battered look of the knife.

Jeanne said that the cook would have to go in any

case, but that her love for Laurent was of a purely spiritual character.

I said, "Laurent is a smoothy, and I do not see how anybody could be in love with him."

"A certain smoothness is not out of place in a head-waiter," said the lady novelist.

I did not tell her my real reason for disliking Laurent; he made jokes. I hated jokes more than anything. They came first in the Anthology: they occupied whole pages: I had dozens and dozens: it was a loose-leaf book, so that new variations of hates already listed could be inserted at will.

Retiring from the conversation, I went to sit on the flat rock at the far end of the pool. Francis and the male novelist returned very soon. Francis came over to me. I shut the loose-leaf book.

"The cook's husband," he said, "has decided against it."

"I thought he would. I imagine that if you are really going to murder somebody you do not impart the intention to others."

"Don't you want to swim?" said Francis.

"No, thank you. I'm working."

"You couldn't be sociable for half an hour?"

"I would rather not."

"I'll write you down for RCI," he threatened.

RCI was Repulsive Children Incorporated, an imaginary foundation which Francis had invented a year before. It came about because a family consisting mainly of unusually spoiled children stayed at the hotel for two days, and were asked by Francis to leave on the third, although the rooms were booked for a month. According to Francis, RCI did a tremendous business and there were qualifying examinations

wherein the children were tested for noise, bad manners, whining, and brutal conduct. I tried to pretend
that I thought this funny.

"Will you please let me work for a quarter of an
hour?" I asked him. "After all, I was disturbed by the
assassin."

"All right. Fifteen minutes," he said. "After which
you qualify."

In fact I was not telling him the truth. I had a
rendezvous at this hour every day. At four o'clock
precisely I was sure of seeing the people from the next
villa. I had watched them for ten days and I knew how
Dante felt when he waited for Beatrice to pass him
on the Ponte Vecchio. Could one, I asked myself, be
in love with four people at once? The answer seemed
to be Yes. These people had become a secret passion.

The villa was called La Lézardière; a large, stately
pink shape with green shutters; there was a gravel
terrace, planted with orange trees and descending in
tiers, to a pool that did not sprawl in a circle of red
rocks as our did, but was a smooth gray concrete. At
the tip of this pool there was a real diving board. A
long gleaming speedboat lay at anchor in the deep
water. The stage was set and I waited for the actors.

They had the quality of Vikings; the father and
mother were tall, handsome, white-skinned, and fair-
haired. The boy and girl followed the pattern. They
looked as I should have preferred to look. (I was as
dark as Francis, and, according to the never-ceasing
stream of personal remarks that seemed to be my lot
at this time, I was much too thin. And not pretty. If
my eyes were not so large I knew that I should be
quite ugly. In Francis' opinion, my face had character.

"But this, as Miss Edith Cavell said of patriotism," I told him, "is not enough.")

Oh, to look like the Bradleys; to be the Bradleys, I thought, waiting for the Bradleys. They were fair, august, and enchanted; they wore the halo of being essentially English. They were Dad and Mum and Don and Eva. I spied on them like a huntress, strained my ears for their words, cherished their timetable. It was regular as the clock. They swam before beakfast and again at ten, staying beside the pool all the morning. At a quarter to one the bell would ring from the villa for their lunch. Oh, the beautiful punctuality of those meals! Sometimes we did not eat luncheon until three and although Jeanne told me to go and help myself from the kitchen, this was not the same thing at all.

In the afternoon the Bradleys rested on their terrace in the shade. At four they came back to the pool. They went fishing or waterskiing. They were always doing something. They would go for drives in a magnificent gray car with a white hood that folded back. Sometimes they played a catching game beside the pool; or they did exercises in a row, with the father leading them. They had cameras and butterfly nets and field-glasses. They never seemed to lie around and talk, the loathed recreation in which I was expected to join.

I took Don and Eva to be twins; and perhaps a year younger than I. I was just fourteen. To be a twin would, I thought, be a most satisfying destiny. I would even have changed places with the youngest member of the Bradley family, a baby in a white perambulator with a white starched nurse in charge of it. If I could be the baby, I should at least be sure of growing up and becoming a Bradley, in a white shirt and gray shorts.

Their magic linked with the magic of my yearly fortnight in England, when, besides having the gray skies and the green garden, I had acquaintance with other English children not in the least like me: solid, pink-cheeked sorts with ponies; they came over to tea at my aunt's house and it was always more fun in anticipation than in fact, because I seemed to make them shy. And I could never tell them that I yearned for them.

So, in a way, I was content to watch the Bradleys at a distance. I felt that it was hopeless to want to be friends with them; to do the things that they did. I was not only different on the outside, but different on the inside, which was worse. On the front page of the Anthology I had written: "I was born to trouble as the sparks fly upward," one of the more consoling quotations because it made the matter seem inevitable.

Now it was four o'clock. My reverie of the golden Bradleys became the fact of the golden Bradleys, strolling down to the water. Dad and Don were carrying the water-skis. I should have only a brief sight of them before they took the speedboat out into the bay. They would skim and turn far off, tantalizing small shapes on the shiny silky sea. Up on the third tier of the terrace, between the orange trees, the neat white nurse was pushing the perambulator. But she was only faintly touched with the romance that haloed the others. I mourned.

Then a most fortunate thing happened. There was a drift of strong current around the rocks and as the speedboat moved out toward the bay, one of the water-skis slipped off astern, and was carried into the pool under the point where I sat. Don dived in after it; I ran down the slope of rock on their side, to shove it off from the edge of the pool.

"Thanks most awfully," he said. He held on to the fringed seaweed and hooked the water-ski under his free arm. Now that he was so close to me I could see that he had freckles; it was a friendly smile and he spoke in the chuffy, English boy's voice that I liked.

"It's rather fun, water-skiing."

"It looks fun. I have never done it."

"Would you like to come out with us?" he jerked his head towards the boat: "Dad's a frightfully good teacher."

I groaned within me, like the king in the Old Testament. Here were the gates of Paradise opening and I must let them shut again, or be written down for RCI.

"Painful as it is to refuse," I said, "my father has acquired visitors and I have sworn to be sociable. The penalty is ostracism." (Ostracism was another word that appealed to me.)

Don, swinging on the seaweed, gave a gurgle of laughter.

"What's funny?" I asked.

"I'm terribly sorry. Wasn't that meant to be funny?"

"Wasn't what meant to be funny?"

"The way you talked."

"No, it's just the way I talk," I said, drooping with sadness.

"I like it awfully," said Don. This was warming to my heart. By now the speedboat was alongside the rock point. I could see the Viking heads; the delectable faces in detail. Mr. Bradley called: "Coming aboard?"

"She can't," said Don. "Her father has visitors; she'll be ostracized." He was still giggling and his voice shook.

"Oh dear, that's too bad," said Mrs. Bradley. "Why don't you ask your father if you can come tomorrow?"

"I will, most certainly," I said, though I knew that I need never ask permission of Jeanne or Francis for anything that I wanted to do.

I felt as though I had been addressed by a goddess. Don gurgled again. He flashed through the water and they pulled him into the boat.

I had to wait for a few minutes alone, hugging my happiness, preparing a kind of vizor to pull down over it when I went back to the group on the yellow mattresses.

"Making friends with the Smugs?" Francis greeted me.

"What an enchanting name," said the lady novelist.

"It isn't their name; it's what they are," said Francis.

I heard my own voice asking thinly: "Why do you call them that?" He shocked me so much that my heart began to beat heavily and I shivered. I tried to conceal this by sitting crouched and hugging my knees. I saw him watching me.

"Well, aren't they?" he said gently. I had given myself away. He had guessed that they meant something to me.

"I don't know. I don't think so. I want to know why you think so."

"Partly from observation," said Francis. "Their gift for organized leisure; their continual instructions to their children; the expressions on their faces. And the one brief conversation that I've conducted with Bradley—he congratulated me on being able to engage in

a commercial enterprise on French soil. According to
Bradley, you can never trust the French." He imitated
the chuffy English voice.

"Isn't 'commercial enterprise' rather an optimistic
description of Chez François?" asked the lady novelist,
and the male novelist laughed. Francis was still looking at me.

"Why do you like them, Penelope?"

I replied with chilled dignity: "I did not say that I
liked them. They invited me to go water-skiing with
them tomorrow."

Jeanne said quickly: "That will be fun. You know,
Francis, you are becoming too intolerant of your own
countrymen: it is enough in these days for you to meet
an Englishman to make you dislike him." This was
comforting; I could think this and feel better. Nothing, I thought, could make me feel worse than for
Francis to attack the Bradleys. It was another proof
that my loves, like my hates, must remain secret, and
this was loneliness.

II

I awoke next morning full of a wild surmise. I went
down early to the pool and watched Francis taking
off for Marseilles in his small, ramshackle seaplane. He
flew in a circle over the garden as he always did, and
when the seaplane's long boots pointed for the west, I
saw Don and Eva Bradley standing still on the gravel
terrace to watch it. They were coming down to the
pool alone. Offering myself to them, I went out to the
flat rock. They waved and beckoned and shouted.

"Is that your father flying the seaplane?"

"Yes."

"Does he take you up in it?"

"Sometimes."

"Come and swim with us," Don called.

I ran down the rock slope on their side. I was shy now that we stood together. I saw that Eva was a little taller than Don; that she also was freckled; and that they had oiled their skins against sunburn as the grownups did. Don wore white trunks and Eva a white swimming suit. They laughed when I shook hands with them, and Don made me an elaborate bow after the handshake. Then they laughed again.

"Are you French or English?"

That saddened me. I said, "I am English, but I live here because my stepmother is a Frenchwoman and my father likes the Riviera."

"We know that," said Don quickly. "He was shot down and taken prisoner by the Germans and escaped and fought with the Resistance, didn't he?"

"Yes. That is how he met Jeanne."

"And he's Francis Wells, the poet?"

"Yes."

"And the hotel is quite mad, isn't it?"

"Indubitably," I said. It was another of my favorite words. Eva doubled up with laughter. "Oh, that's wonderful. I'm *always* going to say indubitably."

"Is it true," Don said, "that guests only get served if your father likes the looks of them, and that he charges nothing sometimes, and that all the rooms stay empty for weeks if he wants them to?"

"It is true. It does not seem to me the most intelligent way of running an hotel, but that is none of my business."

"Is he very rich?" asked Eva.

Don said quickly: "Don't, Eva, that's not polite."

"He isn't rich or poor," I said. I could not explain our finances to the Bradleys any more than I could explain them to myself. Sometimes we had money. When we had not, we were never poor in the way that other people were poor. We were "broke," which, as far as I could see, meant being in debt but living as usual and talking about money.

"Do you go to school in England?"

"No," I said, handing over my chief shame. "I am a day boarder at a convent school near Grasse. It is called Notre Dames des Oliviers."

"Do you like it?"

"I find it unobjectionable," I said. It would have been disloyal to Francis and Jeanne to tell these people how little I liked it.

"Do they teach the same things as English schools?"

"Roughly."

"I expect you're awfully clever," said Eva, "and tops at everything."

How did she know that? Strenuously, I denied it. Heading the class in literature, composition, and English poetry was just one more way of calling attention to myself. It was part of the doom of being noticeable, of not being like Other People. At Les Oliviers, Other People were French girls, strictly brought up, formally religious, cut to a foreign pattern. I did not want to be they, as I wanted to be the Bradleys: I merely envied their uniformity.

God forbid that I should tell the Bradleys about winning a special prize for a sonnet; about being chosen to recite Racine to hordes of parents; about any of it. I defended myself by asking questions in my turn. Eva went to an English boarding school in Sussex; Don would go to his first term at public school this autumn. I had guessed their ages correctly. They were just thirteen. "Home" was Devonshire.

"I would greatly love to live in England," I said.

"I'd far rather live in an hotel on the French Riviera. Lucky Penelope."

"I am not lucky Penelope; I am subject to dooms."

"How heavenly. What sort of dooms?"

"For example, getting an electric shock in science class, and finding a whole nest of mice in my desk," I said. "And being the only person present when a lunatic arrived believing the school to be Paradise."

"Go on. Go on," they said. "It's wonderful. Those aren't dooms, they are adventures."

"Nothing that happens all the time is an adventure," I said. "The hotel is also doomed."

They turned their heads to look up at it; from here, through the pines and the cactus, we could see the red crinkled tiles of its roof, the bougainvillaea, the top of the painted blue sign that announced *"Chez François."*

"It can't be doomed," Don said. "Don't famous people come here?"

"Oh yes. But famous people are more subject to dooms than ordinary people."

"How?"

"In every way you can imagine. Important telegrams containing money do not arrive. Their wives leave them; they are recalled on matters of state."

"Does Winston Churchill come?"

"Yes."

"And Lord Beaverbrook and Elsa Maxwell and the Duke of Windsor and Somerset Maugham?"

"Yes. Frequently. All their signed photographs are kept in the bar. Would you care to see them?"

Here I encountered the first piece of Bradley dogma.
Don and Eva, who were splashing water on each
other's hair ("Dad is most particular about our not
getting sunstroke"), looked doubtful.

"We *would* love to."

"I'm sure it's all right, Eva; because she lives there."

"I don't know. I think we ought to ask first. It is a
bar, after all."

Ashamed, I hid from them the fact that I often
served in the bar when Laurent was off duty.

"Oh, do let's chance it," said Don.

"I don't believe we ought to."

Mr. and Mrs. Bradley had gone over to Nice and
would not return until the afternoon, so a deadlock
threatened. The white starched nurse appeared at
eleven o'clock with a Thermos-flask of cold milk and
a plate of buns. I gave birth to a brilliant idea; I told
her that my stepmother had invited Don and Eva to
lunch with us.

It was a little difficult to convince them after the
nurse had gone, that Jeanne would be pleased to have
them to lunch without an invitation. When I led them
up through our garden, they treated it as an adventure,
like tiger shooting.

Jeanne welcomed them, as I had foretold, and the
lunch was highly successful, although it contained several things, such as *moules,* which the Bradleys were
not allowed to eat. We had the terrace to ourselves.
Several cars drove up and their owners were told
politely that lunch could not be served to them. This
delighted Don and Eva. They were even more delighted when Jeanne told them of Francis' ambition,
which was to have a notice: "Keep Out; This Means
You," printed in seventeen languages. One mystery

about the Bradleys was that they seemed to like jokes. They thought that I made jokes. When they laughed at my phrases they did not laugh as the grownups did, but in the manner of an appreciative audience receiving a comedian. Eva would hold her stomach and cry: "Oh *stop!* It hurts to giggle like this; it really hurts."

I took them on a tour of the hotel. The salon was furnished with some good Empire pieces. The bedrooms were not like hotel bedrooms, but more like rooms in clean French farmhouses, with pale walls and dark wood and chintz. All the rooms had balconies where the guests could eat their breakfast. There were no guests.

"And Dad says people *clamor* to stay here in the season," Don said, straddled in the last doorway.

"Yes, they do. Probably some will be allowed in at the end of the week," I explained, "but the Duchess is arriving from Venice at any moment and Francis always waits for her to choose which room she wants, before he lets any. She is changeable."

Eva said, "I can't get over your calling your father Francis. Who is the Duchess?"

"The Duchessa di Terracini. She is half Italian and half American."

"Is she very beautiful?"

"Very far from it. She is seventy and she looks like a figure out of a waxworks. She was celebrated for her lovers but now she only loves roulette." I did not wish to be uncharitable about the Duchess, whose visit was to be dreaded, and these were the nicest things that I could make myself say. The only thing in her favor was that she had been a friend of my mother, who was American and utterly beautiful and whom I did not remember.

"Lovers?" Eva said, looking half pleased and half horrified. Don flushed and looked at his feet. I had learned from talks at school that reactions to a mention of the facts of life could be like this. I knew also that Francis despised the expression, "the facts of life," because, he said, it sounded as though all the other things that happened in life were figments of the imagination.

"A great many people loved the Duchess desperately," I said. "She was engaged to an Austrian Emperor; he gave her emeralds, but somebody shot him."

"Oh well, then, she's practically history, isn't she?" Eva said, looking relieved.

III

I might have known that the end of the day would bring doom. It came hard upon the exquisite pleasure of my time in the speedboat with the Bradleys. This was even better than I had planned it in anticipation, a rare gift. I thought that the occasion must be under the patronage of a benign saint or what the Duchess would call a favorable aura; the only worry was Mrs. Bradley's worry about my having no dry clothes to put on after swimming; but with typical Bradley organization there were an extra white shirt and gray shorts in the boat. Dressed thus I felt like a third twin.

The sea changed color; the sea began to be white and the rocks a darker red.

"Would you like to come back and have supper with us, Penelope?"

I replied, "I can imagine nothing that I would like more."

"She *does* say wonderful things, doesn't she?" said

Eva. I was drunk by now on Bradley admiration and almost reconciled to personal remarks.

"Penelope speaks very nice English," said Mrs. Bradley.

"Will you ask your stepmother then?" she added as we tied up the boat. I was about to say this was unnecessary when Don gave my ribs a portentous nudge; he said quickly, "Eva and I will walk you up there." It was obvious that the hotel exercised as much fascination for them as they for me.

When the three of us set off across the rocks Mr. Bradley called, "Seven o'clock sharp, now!" and Eva made a grimace. She said, "Wouldn't it be nice not to have to be punctual for anything?"

"I never have to be," I said, "except at school, and I think that I prefer it to having no timetable at all."

"Oh, my goodness! Why?"

"I like days to have a shape," I said.

"Can you just stay out to supper when you want to? Always? Without telling them?"

"Oh, yes."

"What would happen if you stayed away a whole night?"

I said that I had never tried. And now we went into the bar because Don said that he wanted to see the photographs again. Laurent was there; straw-colored and supercilious in his white coat. He began to make his jokes: *"Mesdames, monsieur, bon soir.* What may I serve you? A Pernod? A champagne cocktail?" He flashed along the shelves, reading out the name of each drink, muttering under his breath, *"Mais non; c'est terrible;* we have nothing that pleases our distinguished visitors." I saw that the Bradleys were enchanted with him.

We walked all round the gallery of photographs and were lingering beside Winston Churchill when the worst thing happened. I heard it coming. One could always hear the Duchess coming. She made peals of laughter that sounded like opera; the words came fast and high between the peals.

And here she was, escorted by Francis. She cried, "Ah my love, my love," and I was swept into a complicated, painful embrace, scratched by her jewelry, crushed against her stays, and choked with her scent before I got a chance to see her in perspective. When I did, I saw that there were changes since last year and that these were for the worse. Her hair, which had been dyed black, was now dyed bright red. Her powder was whiter and thicker than ever; her eyelids were dark blue; she had new false eyelashes of greater length that made her look like a Jersey cow.

She wore a dress of dark blue chiffon, sewn all over with sequin stars, and long red gloves with her rings on the outside; she tilted back on her heels, small and bony, gesticulating with the gloves.

"Beautiful—beautiful—beautiful!" was one of her slogans. She said it now; she could not conceivably mean me; she just meant everything. The Bradleys had become awed and limp all over. When I introduced them they shook hands jerkily, snatching their hands away at once. Francis took from Laurent the bottle of champagne that had been on ice awaiting the Duchess; he carried it to her favorite table, the corner table beside the window. She placed upon the table a sequin bag of size, a long chiffon scarf, and a small jeweled box that held *bonbons au miel,* my least favorite sweets, reminding me of scented glue.

Francis uncorked the champagne.

"But glasses for all of us," the Duchess said. "A glass for each." The Bradleys said, "No thank you very much," so quickly that they made it sound like one syllable and I imitated them.

"But how good for you," cried the Duchess. "The vitalizing, the magnificent, the harmless grape. All children should take a little to combat the lassitude and depressions of growth. My mother used to give me a glass every morning after my fencing lesson. *Et toi*, Penelope? More than once last year you have taken your *petit verre* with me."

"Oh, didn't you know? Penelope is on the water wagon," said Francis, and the Duchess again laughed like opera. She cried, *"Santé, santé!"* raising her glass to each of us. Francis helped himself to a Pernod and perched on the bar, swinging his legs. The Bradleys and I stood in a straight, uncomfortable row.

"Of youth," said the Duchess, "I recall three things. The sensation of time seeming endless, as though one were swimming against a current; the insipid insincerity of one's teachers; and bad dreams, chiefly about giants."

Sometimes she expected an answer to statements of this character; at other times she went on talking: I had known her to continue without a break for fifteen minutes.

"I used to dream about giants," said Eva.

"How old are you, Miss?"

"Thirteen."

"At fifteen the dreams become passionate," said the Duchess, sounding lugubrious about it.

"What do you dream about now?" asked Don, who had not removed his eyes from her since she came.

"Packing, missing airplanes; losing my clothes," said the Duchess. "Worry—worry—worry; but one is never bored in a dream, which is more than can be said for real life. Give me your hand," she snapped at Eva. She pored over it a moment, and then said briskly, "You are going to marry very young and have three children; an honest life; always be careful in automobiles." Don's hand was already stretched out and waiting. She gave him two wives, a successful business career, and an accident "involving a horse between the ages of twenty and twenty-three."

"That is tolerably old for a horse," Francis interrupted.

"Sh-h," said the Duchess, "perhaps while steeplechasing; it is not serious." She blew me a little kiss: "Penelope I already know. She is as clear to me as a book written by an angel. Let me see if there is any change," she commanded, a medical note in her voice: "Beautiful—beautiful—beautiful! Genius and fame and passion are all here."

"Any dough?" asked Francis.

"I beg your pardon," said the Duchess, who knew perfectly well what dough meant, but who always refused to recognize American slang.

"I refer to cash," said Francis looking his most Mephistophelean; "My ambition for Penelope is that she acquire a rich husband, so that she may subsidize Papa in his tottering old age."

"Like so many creative artists, you have the soul of a fishmonger," said the Duchess. She was still holding my hand; she planted a champagne-wet kiss on the palm before she let it go. "I have ordered our dinner, Penelope. It is to be the *écrevisses au gratin* that you like with small *goûters* of caviar to begin with and *fraises des bois* in kirsch afterward."

I had been anticipating this hurdle; she always insisted that I dine with her on her first evening, before she went to the Casino at nine o'clock.

"I am very sorry, Duchessa; you must excuse me. I am having supper with Don and Eva." I saw Francis raise one eyebrow at me. "I really didn't know you were coming tonight," I pleaded.

"No, that is true," said the Duchess, "but I am very disappointed. I have come to regard it as a regular tryst." She put her head on one side. "Why do you not all three stay and dine with me? We will make it a *partie carrée*. It could be managed, Francis? Beautiful —beautiful—beautiful! There. That is settled."

"I'm most awfully sorry; we'd love to," Eva said. "But we couldn't possibly. Supper's at seven and Mum's expecting us."

"Thank you very much, though," said Don, who was still staring at her. "Could we do it another time?"

"But of course! Tomorrow; what could be better? Except tonight," said the Duchess. "I was looking to Penelope to bring me good luck. Do you remember last year, how I took you to dine at the Carlton and won a fortune afterward?"

"And lost it on the following afternoon," said Francis. The Duchess said an incomprehensible Italian word that sounded like a snake hissing. She took a little ivory hand out of her bag and pointed it at him.

"I thought one never could win at roulette," said Don. "According to my father, the game is rigged in favor of the Casino."

"Ask your father why there are no taxes in Monaco," said the Duchess. "In a game of this mathematic there is no need for the Casino to cheat. The majority loses naturally, not artificially. And tell him further that all European Casinos are of the highest order of probity, with the possible exception of Estoril and Budapest. Do you know the game?"

When the Bradleys said that they did not, she took from her bag one of the cards that had upon it a replica of the wheel and the cloth. She embarked upon a roulette lesson. The Bradleys were fascinated and of course we were late for supper. Francis delayed me further, holding me back to speak to me on the terrace: "Do you have to have supper with the Smugs?"

"Please don't call them that. Yes, I do."

"It would be reasonable, I should think, to send a message saying that an old friend of the family had arrived unexpectedly."

Of course it would have been reasonable; Mrs. Bradley had expected me to ask permission. But nothing would have made me stay.

"I'm extremely sorry, Francis; I can't do it."

"You should know how much it means to her. She has ordered your favorite dinner. All right," he said, "I see that it is useless to appeal to your better nature. Tonight you qualify for RCI." He went back to the bar, calling, "The verdict can always be withdrawn if the candidate shows compensating behavior."

"Didn't you want to stay and dine with the Duchess?" asked Don, as we raced through the twilit garden.

"I did not. She embarrasses me greatly."

"I thought she was terrific. I do hope Mum and Dad will let us have dinner with her tomorrow."

"But *don't* say it's *écrevisses*, Don, whatever you do.

There's always a row about shell fish," Eva reminded him.

"I wouldn't be such an ass," Don said. "And the only thing that would give it away would be if you were ill afterward."

"Why should it be me?"

"Because it usually is," said Don.

I awoke with a sense of doom. I lay under my mosquito curtain, playing the scenes of last evening through in my mind. A slight chill upon the Viking parents, due to our being late; smiles pressed down over crossness, because of the visitor. Don and Eva pouring forth a miscellany of information about the Duchess and the signed photographs; myself making mental notes, a devoted sociologist studying a favorite tribe: grace before supper; no garlic in anything; copies of *Punch* and the English newspapers; silver napkin rings; apple pie. The secret that I found in the Cotswold house was here, I told myself; the house in Devonshire took shape; on the walls there were photographs of it; a stream ran through the garden; they rode their ponies on Dartmoor; they had two wire-haired terriers called Snip and Snap. I collected more evidence of Bradley organization: an expedition tomorrow to the Saracen village near Brignoles; a Current-Affairs Quiz that was given to the family by their father once a month.

No, I said to myself, brooding under my mosquito net, nothing went wrong until after the apple pie. That was when Eva had said, "The Duchess told all our fortunes." The lines spoken were still in my head:

Don saying, "Penelope's was an absolute fizzer; the Duchess says she will have genius, fame, and passion." Mr. Bradley's Viking profile becoming stony; Mrs. Bradley's smooth white forehead puckering a little as she asked me gently, "Who is this wonderful lady?"

Myself replying, "The Duchessa de Terracini," and Mrs. Bradley remarking that this was a beautiful name. But Mr. Bradley's stony face growing stonier and his officer-to-men voice saying, "Have we all finished?"; then rising so that we rose too and pushed in our chairs and bowed our heads while he said grace.

After that there was a spirited game of Monopoly. "But the atmosphere," I said to myself, "went on being peculiar." I had waited for Don and Eva to comment on it when they walked me home, but they were in a rollicking mood and appeared to have noticed nothing.

"Indubitably there is a doom," I thought while I put on my swimming suit, "and since I shall not see them until this evening because of the Saracen village, I shall not know what it is."

As I crossed the terrace, the Duchess popped her head out of the corner window above me; she leaned like a little gargoyle above the bougainvillaea; she wore a lace veil fastened under her chin with a large diamond.

"Good morning, Duchessa. Did you win?"

"I lost consistently, and your friends cannot come to dine tonight, as you may know; so disappointing, though the note itself is courteous." She dropped it into my hands. It was written by Mrs. Bradley; fat, curly handwriting on paper headed

CROSSWAYS
CHAGFORD
DEVON

It thanked the Duchess and regretted that owing to the expedition Don and Eva would not be able to accept her kind invitation to supper.

I knew that the Bradleys would be back by six.

IV

I spent most of the day alone working on the Anthology. I had found quite a new Hate, which was headed "Characters." People called the Duchess a character and this was said to others who came here. I made a brief description of each and included some of their sayings and habits.

There was the usual paragraph about the Duchess in the *Continental Daily Mail;* it referred to her gambling and her emeralds and her *joie-de-vivre.* *Joie-de-vivre* seemed to be a worthy subject for Hate and I entered it on a separate page, as a subsection of Jokes.

At half-past-four, to my surprise, I looked up from my rock writing desk and saw the Bradleys' car sweeping in from the road. Presently Eva came running down the tiers of terrace alone. When she saw me she waved, put her finger to her lips, and signaled to me to stay where I was. She came scrambling up.

"I'm so glad to see you. There's a row. I can't stay long. Don has been sent to bed."

"Oh, dear. I was conscious of an unfavorable aura," I said. "What happened?"

Eva looked miserable. "It isn't anything against you, of course. They like you terribly. Mum says you have beautiful manners. When Don and I said we wanted you to come and stop a few days with us at Crossways in September, it went down quite *well.* Would you like to?" she asked, gazing at me, "or would it be awfully boring?"

I was momentarily deflected from the doom and the row. "I cannot imagine anything that would give me greater pleasure," I said. She wriggled her eyebrows, as usual, at my phrases.

"That isn't just being polite?"

"I swear by yonder horned moon it isn't."

"But of course it may not happen now," she said in melancholy, "although it wasn't *your* fault. After all you didn't make us meet the Duchess on purpose."

"Was the row about the Duchess?"

"Mm—m."

"Because of her telling your fortunes and teaching you to play roulette? I did have my doubts, I admit."

"Apparently they were quite cross about that, but of course they couldn't say so in front of you. Daddy had *heard* of the Duchess, anyway. And they cracked down on the dinner party and sent a note. And Don kept on asking why until he made Daddy furious; and there seems to have been something in the *Continental Mail,* which we are not allowed to read."

"Here it is," I said helpfully. She glanced upward over her shoulder. I said, "Have no fear. We are invisible from the villa at this angle."

She raised her head from the paper and her eyes shone; she said, "Isn't it wonderful?" I had thought it a pedestrian little paragraph, but I hid my views.

"Mummy said that the Duchess wasn't at all the sort of person she liked us to mix with, and that no lady would sit in a bar drinking champagne when there were children present, and that we shouldn't have gone into the bar again anyway. And Don lost his temper and was quite rude. So that we came home

early instead of having tea out; and Dad said that Don
had spoiled the day and asked him to apologize. And
Don said a word that we aren't allowed to use and
now he's gone to bed. Which is awful for him because he's too big to be sent to bed. And I'll have to
go back. I'm terribly sorry."

"So am I," I said. "Please tell your mother that I deplore the Duchess deeply, and that I always have."

As soon as I had spoken, I became leaden inside
myself with remorse. It was true that I deplored the
Duchess because she was possessive, overpowering, and
embarrassing, but I did not disapprove of her in the
way that the Bradleys did. I was making a desperate
effort to salvage the thing that mattered most to me.

In other words, I was assuming a virtue though I
had it not, and while Shakespeare seemed to approve
of this practice, I was certain that it was wrong. (And
I went on with it. I added that Francis would not
have dreamed of bringing the Duchess into the bar if
he had known that we were there. This was an outrageous lie. Francis would have brought the Duchess
into the bar if the Archbishop of Canterbury were
there—admittedly an unlikely contingency.)

When Eva said that this might improve matters and
might also make it easier for Don to apologize, because
he had stuck up for the Duchess I felt lower than the
worms.

Which is why I quarreled with Francis. And knew
that was why. I had discovered that if one were feeling guilty one's instinct was to put the blame on
somebody else as soon as possible.

Francis called to me from the bar door as I came
up onto the terrace. I had been freed from RCI on
the grounds of having replaced Laurent before lunch

at short notice. He grinned at me. "Be an angel and take these cigarettes to Violetta's room, will you, please? I swear that woman smokes two at a time."

"I am sorry," I said. "I have no wish to run errands for the Duchess just now."

Francis, as usual, was reasonable. "How has she offended you?" he asked.

I told him about the Bradleys, about the possible invitation to Devonshire; I said that, thanks to the Duchess cutting such a petty figure in the bar, not to mention the *Continental Mail,* my future was being seriously jeopardized. I saw Francis' eyebrows twitching.

He said, "Penelope, you are a thundering ass. These people are tedious *petits bourgeois,* and there is no reason to put on their act just because you happen to like their children. And I see no cause to protect anybody, whether aged seven or seventy, from the sight of Violetta drinking champagne."

"Mrs. Bradley said that no lady would behave in such a way."

"Tell Mrs. Bradley with my love and a kiss that if she were a tenth as much of a lady as Violetta she would have cause for pride. And I am not at all sure," he said, "that I like the idea of your staying with them in Devonshire."

This was, as the French said, the *comble.*

"Do you mean that you wouldn't let me go?" I asked, feeling as though I had been struck by lightning.

"I did not say that. I said I wasn't sure that I liked the idea."

"My God, why not?"

"Do not imagine when you say, 'My God,'" said

Francis, "that you add strength to your protest. You merely add violence."

He could always make me feel a fool when he wanted to. And I could see that he was angry; less with me than with the Bradleys. He said, "I don't think much of the Smugs, darling, as you know. And I think less after this. Violetta is a very remarkable old girl, and if they knew what she went through in Rome when the Germans were there, some of that heroism might penetrate even their thick heads. Run along with those cigarettes now, will you please?"

I was trembling with rage; the worst kind of rage, hating me as well as everything else. I took the cigarettes with what I hoped was a dignified gesture, and went.

The Duchess was lying on the chaise longue under her window; she was swathed like a mummy in yards of cyclamen chiffon trimmed with marabou. She appeared to be reading three books at once; a novel by Ignazio Silone, Brewer's *Dictionary of Phrase and Fable,* and a *Handbook of Carpentry for Beginners.*

The room, the best of the rooms, having two balconies, had become unrecognizable. It worried me with its rampaging disorder. Three wardrobe trunks crowded it: many dresses, scarves, and pairs of small pointed shoes had escaped from the wardrobe trunks. The Duchess always brought with her large unexplained pieces of material; squares of velvet, crepe de chine, and damask, which she spread over the furniture. The writing table had been made to look like a table in a museum; she had put upon it a black crucifix and two iron candlesticks, a group of ivory figures, and a velvet book with metal clasps.

Despite the heat of the afternoon the windows were shut; the room smelled of smoke and scent.

"Beautiful—beautiful—beautiful!" said the Duchess, holding out her hands for the cigarettes. "There are the *bonbons au miel* on the bedside table. Help yourself liberally, and sit down and talk to me."

"No, thank you very much. If you will excuse me, Duchess, I have to do some work now."

"I will not excuse you, darling. Sit down here. Do you know why I will not excuse you?"

I shook my head.

"Because I can see that you are unhappy, frustrated, and restless." She joined her fingertips and stared at me over the top of them. "Some of it I can guess," she said, "and some of it I should dearly like to know. Your mother would have known."

I was silent; she was hypnotic when she spoke of my mother, but I could not make myself ask her questions.

"Genius is not a comfortable possession. What do you want to do most in the world, Penelope?"

The truthful reply would have been, "To be like other people. To live in England; with an ordinary father and mother who do not keep a hotel. To stop having dooms; never to be told that I am a genius, and to have people of my own age to play with so that I need not spend my life listening to grownups."

I said, "I don't know."

The Duchess sighed and beat a tattoo with her little feet inside the marabou; they looked like clockwork feet.

"You are, beyond doubt, crying for the moon. Everybody at your age cries for the moon. But if you will not tell me which moon, I cannot be of assistance. What is the book that you are writing?"

"It is an Anthology of Hates," I said, and was much surprised that I had told her because I had not told anybody.

"Oho," said the Duchess. "Have you enough Hates to make an anthology?"

I nodded.

"Is freedom one of your hates?"

I frowned; I did not want to discuss the book with her at all and I could not understand her question. She was smiling in a maddening way that implied more knowledge of me than I myself had.

"Freedom is the most important thing that there is. You have more freedom than the average child knows. One day you will learn to value this and be grateful for it. I will tell you why." Her voice had taken on the singsong, lecturing note that preceded a fifteen-minute monologue. I stared at the figures on the writing table. She had let her cigarette lie burning in the ash tray, and a small spiral of smoke went up like incense before the crucifix; there was this, there was the hot scented room and the sound of her voice: "It is necessary to imprison children to a certain degree, for their discipline and their protection. In schools, they are largely hidden away from life, like bees in a hive. This means that they learn a measure of pleasant untruth; a scale of simple inadequate values that resemble the true values in life only as much as a plain colored poster of the Riviera resembles the actual coastline.

"When they emerge from the kindly-seeming prisons, they meet the world of true dimensions and true values. These are unexpectedly painful and irregular.

Reality is always irregular and generally painful. To be unprepared for its shocks and to receive the shocks upon a foundation of innocence is the process of growing up. In your case, Penelope, you will be spared many of those pains. Not only do you have now a wealth of freedom which you cannot value because you have not experienced the opposite, but you are also endowing yourself with a future freedom; freedom from the fear and shock and shyness which make the transition from youth to maturity more uncomfortable than any other period of existence. Francis is bringing you up through the looking-glass, back-to-front. You are learning what the adult learns, and walking through these lessons toward the light-heartedness that is usually to be found in childhood but lost later. I wonder how long it will take you to find that out." She sat up on her elbows and stared at me again. "Do you know what I think will happen to your Anthology of Hates when you do find it out? You will read it through and find that these are not Hates any more."

By this last remark she had annoyed me profoundly, and now she clapped her hands and cried, "If young people were only allowed to gamble! It takes the mind off every anxiety. If I could take you to the Casino with me tonight, Penelope! Wouldn't that be splendid? Disguised as a young lady of fashion!" She sprang off the chaise longue, snatched the square of velvet from the bed and flung it over my shoulders. Its weight almost bore me to the ground, it was heavy as a tent and it smelled musty. "Look at yourself in the mirror!" cried the Duchess. "Beautiful—beautiful —beautiful! A Principessa!" She scuttled past me. "We will place this silver girdle here." She lashed it so tightly that it hurt my stomach; I was stifled; it felt like being dressed in a carpet. "Take this fan and these gloves." They were long white kid gloves, as hard as biscuits; she forced my fingers in and cajoled the gloves up my arms as far as the shoulders.

"The little amethyst circlet for your head."

She caught some single hairs as she adjusted it and put one finger in my eye. Sweat was trickling all over me.

"Now you have a very distinct resemblance to your mother," said the Duchess, standing before me and regarding me with her head on one side.

"This is the forecast of your womanhood. Will you please go downstairs at once and show yourself to Jeanne?"

I said that I would rather not. She was peevishly disappointed. I struggled out of the ridiculous costume; hot, dispirited, no fonder of myself than before, I got away.

V

My bedroom was on the ground floor, with a window that opened onto the far end of the terrace. It was late, but I was still awake and heard Francis and Jeanne talking outside. I did not mean to listen, but their voices were clear and when I heard the name "Bradley" I could not help listening.

"I agree with you," Jeanne said, "that it is all an outrageous fuss. But these Bradleys mean a great deal to Penelope."

"Wish I knew why," said Francis. "They represent the worst and dullest aspect of English 'county'; a breed that may soon become extinct and no loss, either."

"They are the kind of friends that she has never had; English children of her own age."

Their footsteps ceased directly outside my window. I heard Francis sigh. *"Ought* we to send her to school in England, do you think?"

"Perhaps next year."

"That will be too late, beloved."

I had heard him call Jeanne "beloved" before, but tonight the word touched my heart, perhaps because I was already unhappy; it made me want to cry. "She will be fifteen," Francis said. "First she'll kill herself trying to fit into the pattern and if she succeeds in the task, we shall never see her again. God knows what we'll get but it won't be Penelope."

"She will change in any case, whether she stays or goes, darling; they always do."

"Perhaps I've done a poor job with her from the beginning," Francis said: he spoke my mother's name. And then I was so sure I must listen no more, that I covered my ears with my hands. When I took them away Jeanne was saying, "You are always sad when your back is hurting you. Come to bed. Tomorrow I'll invite the Bradley children for lunch again; on Thursday when Violetta's in Monte Carlo."

"Why should we suck up to the Smugs?" Francis grumbled, and Jeanne replied, "Only because of Penelope, *tu le sais,*" and they walked away down the terrace.

I wept because they destroyed my defenses; my conscience still troubled me for the speeches of humbug that I had made to Eva, for quarreling with Francis, and for being uncivil to the Duchess. It was a weary load. If the Bradleys accepted the invitation to lunch, it would seem that God was not intending to punish me for it, but exactly the reverse, and that was a bewildering state of affairs.

By morning, however, God's plan became clear. Jeanne brought me my breakfast on the terrace. She sat with me while I ate it. I thought, as I had thought before, that she looked very young; more an elder sister than a stepmother, with her short, flying dark hair, the blue eyes in the brown face, the long slim brown legs. She smoked a *caporal* cigarette.

I could hardly wait for her to tell me whether she had healed the breach with the Bradleys. But I dared not ask. Their talk on the terrace had been too intimate for me to admit that I had heard it. She said, "Penelope, the situation with your friends at La Lézardière has become a little complex."

My heart beat downward heavily and I did not want to eat any more.

"I thought that it would give you pleasure if I asked them to lunch and would perhaps clear up any misunderstanding. But I have been talking to Mrs. Bradley and apparently she would prefer them not to visit the hotel."

I did not know whether I was blushing for the hotel, for my own disappointment, or for the Bradleys; I was only aware of the blush, flaming all over my skin, most uncomfortably.

"Mrs. Bradley was friendly and polite, you must not think otherwise. She wants you to swim with them as much as you like; she said that she hoped you would go out in the speedboat again. But her exact phrase was, 'We feel that the hotel surroundings are just a little too grown-up for Don and Eva.' "

I was silent.

"So, I thought that I would tell you. And ask you not to be unhappy about it. People are entitled to their views, you know, even when one does not oneself agree with them."

"Thank you, Jeanne: I am not at all unhappy," I said, wishing that my voice would not shake. "And if the Bradleys will not come to me, I am damned if I am going to them." And I rose from the table. She came after me, but when she saw that I was near to tears she gave me a pat on the back and left me alone.

This was the point at which I discovered that hate did not cast out love, but that it was, on the contrary, possible to hate and love at the same time. I could not turn off my infatuation for the Bradleys, much as I longed to do so. They were still the desirable Vikings. The stately pink villa above the orange trees, the gray rocks where the diving board jutted and the speedboat lay at anchor, remained the site of romance, the target of forlorn hopes. It hurt me to shake my head and retire from the flat rock when Don and Eva beckoned me. They seemed to understand quickly enough, more quickly than their parents did. Mr. Bradley still called, "Coming aboard?" and Mrs. Bradley waved to me elaborately on every possible occasion. The children turned their heads away. For two days I saw them all like figures set behind a glass screen; only the echo of their voices reached me; I gave up haunting the beach and worked in a corner of the garden; the regularity of their timetable made it easy to avoid the sight of them. I told myself that they were loathsome, that they were the Smugs, that Don and Eva were both candidates for RCI. I even considered including them in the Anthology of Hates, but I found it too difficult. Now they had indeed become the moon that the Duchess told me I cried for. I cherished dreams of saving Don's life or Eva's at great risk to myself, and being humbly thanked and praised by their parents. Then I hoped that they would all die in a fire, or better still that I would die and they would come to my funeral.

In these two days I found myself looking at my home differently; seeing it in Bradley perspective. I had been plagued by the crises and irregularities but never ashamed of them. Was I ashamed now? I could not be sure; the feeling was one of extra detachment and perception; I was more than ever aware of the garden's bright colors, of the garlic smells from the kitchen, of the dusky coolness in the bar; every time that I walked through the salon I looked at it with startled visitors' eyes; Bradleys' eyes:

"It's pretty, of course; it's like a little room in a museum, but it isn't the sort of place where one wants to *sit*." The terrace with the blue and white umbrellas above the tables, the stone jars on the balustrade, the lizards flickering along the wall, seemed as temporary as the deck of a ship on a short voyage. I felt as though I were staying here, not living here. And there was no consolation in my own room with my own books because here the saddest thoughts came and they seemed to hang in the room waiting for me, as palpable as the tented mosquito net above the bed.

I found that I was seeing Francis, Jeanne, and the Duchess through a grotesque lens; they were at once complete strangers and people whom I knew intimately. I could place them in a Bradley context, thinking, "That is Francis Wells, the poet, the poet who keeps the mad hotel. He always seems to wear the same red shirt. He looks like Mephistopheles when he laughs. And that is his wife, his *second* wife; younger than he is; very gay always, isn't she? What very *short* shorts. And there goes the Duchessa de Terracini, rather a terrible old lady who gambles at the Casino and drinks champagne; doesn't she look ridiculous in all that make-up and chiffon?" And then I would be talking to them in my own voice and with my own thoughts and feeling like a traitor.

I knew that they were sorry for me; that Francis above all approved my defiant refusal. I was aware of their hands held back from consoling gestures, to spare me too much overt sympathy. Even the Duchess did not speak to me of the Bradleys.

For once I welcomed the crises as diversion. And these two days naturally were not free from crisis; a British ambassador and his wife found themselves *en panne* at our gates. All the entrails of their car fell out upon the road and we were obliged to give them rooms for the night.

This would not of itself have been other than a mechanical crisis, because the ambassador and Francis were old friends. Unfortunately the ambassador and the press baron from Cap d'Ail, who was dining with the Duchess, were old enemies. So a fierce political fight was waged in the bar, with both elderly gentlemen calling each other poltroon, and they would have fought a duel had not the electric current failed and the hotel been plunged in darkness till morning. (My only grief was that Don and Eva had missed it. All roads led to the Bradleys.)

On the third morning, which was Thursday, doom

accelerated. I woke to find Francis standing beside my bed.

"Sorry, darling; trouble," he said. "A telephone call just came through from Aix; Jeanne's mother is very ill and I'm going to drive her over there now. Can you take care of you for today?"

He never asked me such questions: this was like a secret signal saying, "I know you are miserable and I am sorry."

"But of course. Please don't worry."

"There are no guests, thank God. Violetta's going over to Monte Carlo; Laurent will be in charge to-night. You might see that he locks up, if I'm not back."

"I will do that."

"But don't let him lock Violetta out, for Heaven's sake."

"I will see that he does not. Can I help Jeanne or do anything for you?"

"No, my love. We are off now. I'll telephone you later." He ducked under the mosquito curtain to kiss me.

"You must pray rather than worry," the Duchess said to me, standing on the doorstep. For her expedition to Monte Carlo, she wore a coat and skirt of white shantung, a bottle-green frilly blouse, and the usual chiffon scarf. She was topped by a bottle-green tricorn hat with a green veil descending from it. "Death is a part of life," she added, pulling on her white gloves.

I could feel little emotion for my stepgrandmother who lived in seclusion near Aix-en-Provence, but I was sorry for Jeanne.

"The best thing that you could do, Penelope," said the Duchess, grasping her parasol like a spear, "would be to come over with me to Monte Carlo. We will lunch delightfully on the balcony of the Hotel de Paris; then you shall eat ices while I am at the tables; then a little stroll and a little glass and we could dine on the port at Villefranche and drive home under the moon. The moon is at the full tonight and I look forward to it. *Viens, chérie, ça te changera les idées,*" she added, holding out her hand.

I thanked her very much and said that I would rather stay here.

When she was placed inside the high purple Isotta-Fraschini, I thought that she and her old hooky chauffeur looked like a Punch-and-Judy show. The car was box-shaped with a fringed canopy under the roof and they swayed as it moved off. I waved good-by.

The first part of the day seemed endless. I sat in the garden on a stone bench under the largest of the umbrella pines. That way I had my back to La Lézardière. I could hear their voices and that was all. When the bell rang for their lunch, I went down to the pool and swam. I swam for longer than usual; then I climbed to the flat rock and lay in the sun. I was almost asleep when I heard Eva's voice. "Penelope!"

She was halfway up the rock; she said, "Look; we are so miserable we've written you this note. I have to go back and rest now." She was like a vision out of the long past; the freckles, the sunburn, and the wet hair. I watched her scuttle down and she turned to wave to me from the lowest tier of the terrace. I gave her a half-wave and opened the note.

It said:

Dear Penelope,

Please don't be cross with us. Mum and Dad are going out to supper tonight. Don't you think that you could come? They have asked us to ask you.

> Always your friends,
> Don and Eva.

I wrote my reply at the *écritoire* in the salon. I wrote:

Much as I appreciate the invitation, I am unable to accept it. Owing to severe illness in the family my father and stepmother have left for Aix. I feel it necessary to stay here and keep an eye on things.

> Penelope.

To run no risk of meeting them, I went into the bar and asked Laurent if he would be so kind as to leave this note at La Lézardière.

Laurent was in one of his moods; he replied sarcastically that it gave him great pleasure to run errands and do favors for young ladies who had not the energy to perform these for themselves. I echoed the former cooks husband, the assassin, and said, "*Salaud,*" but not until he was gone.

After I had answered the note, I alternated between wishing that I had accepted and wishing that I had given them more truthful reasons for my refusal.

Later, I sought comfort by writing to my aunt in England; I sat there conjuring the fortnight as it would be and putting in the letter long descriptions of the things that I wanted to see and do again. It helped. I had covered twelve pages when the telephone rang.

Francis' voice spoke over a bad line: "Hello, Child of Confusion. Everything all right?"

"Yes, indeed. Nothing is happening at all. What is the news?"

"Better," he said. "But Jeanne will have to stay. I may be very late getting back. See that Laurent gives you the cold lobster. Jeanne sends her love."

Nothing would have induced me to ask Laurent for my dinner, but I was perfectly capable of getting it myself and the reference to cold lobster had made me hungry. No reason why I should not eat my dinner at six o'clock. I was on my way to the kitchen by way of the terrace when I heard a voice calling me:

"Penelope!"

I turned, feeling that horrible all-over blush begin. Mrs. Bradley stood at the doorway from the salon onto the terrace. She looked golden and statuesque in a white dress with a scarlet belt. The sight of her was painful. It seemed as though I had forgotten how lovely she was.

"May I talk to you a moment, my dear?"

"Please do," I said, growing hotter and hotter.

"Shall we sit here?" She took a chair beneath one of the blue and white umbrellas. She motioned to me to take the other chair. I said, "Thank you, but I prefer to stand."

She smiled at me. I could feel in my heart the alarming collision of love and hate and now I could see her in two contexts; as a separate symbol, the enemy; as a beloved haunting of my own mind, the Mrs. Bradley of the first days, whom I had made my private possession. Her arms and hands were beautifully shaped, pale brown now against the white of her dress.

"Can't we be friends, Penelope? I think we can, you know, if we try. Don and Eva are so sad and it all seems such a pity."

I said, "But, Mrs. Bradley, you made it happen."

"No, dear. That is what I want to put right. When I talked to your stepmother, I made it quite clear that we all hoped to see much more of you."

"But," I said, "that Don and Eva couldn't come here. As though it were an awful place."

She put her hand on mine; she gave a soft low laugh. "Penelope, how foolish of you. Of course it isn't an awful place. You have just imagined our thinking that, you silly child."

"Did I imagine what you said about the Duchess?"

Still she smiled and kept her hand on mine. "I expect that what I said about the Duchess was quite a little exaggerated to you by Eva and Don. That was an uncomfortable day for all of us. We don't often quarrel in our family; I don't suppose that you do, either. Quarrels are upsetting to everybody and nobody likes them."

"Certainly," I said, "I don't like them."

"Let's try to end this one, Penelope."

Did she guess how badly I wanted to end it? I could not tell.

"Supposing," she said, "that you let me put my point of view to you, as one grown-up person to another. You are very grown-up for your age, you know."

"I do know, and I deplore it."

She gave another little low laugh. "Well, I shouldn't

go on deploring it if I were you. Think what a dull world it would be if we were all made alike."

I winced inside at the cliché because Francis had taught me to wince at clichés. But I pretended that she had not said it. She went on: "Listen, dear. Just because you are so grown-up and this place is your home, you have a very different life from the life that Don and Eva have. I'm not saying that one sort of life is right and the other wrong. They just happen to be different. Now, my husband and I have to judge what is good for Don and Eva, don't we? You'll agree? Just as your father and stepmother have to judge what is good for you."

"Yes. I agree to that." It sounded reasonable; the persuasion of her manner was beginning to work.

"Well, we think that they aren't quite grown-up enough yet to understand and appreciate all the things that you understand and appreciate. That's all. It's as though you had a stronger digestion and could eat foods that might upset them. Do you see?"

When I was still silent, she added, "I think you should. Your stepmother saw perfectly."

"I suppose I see."

"Do try."

In fact I was trying hard; but the struggle was different from the struggle that she imagined. I felt as though I were being pulled over the line in a tug of war. Inside me there was a voice saying, "No, no. This is wrong. Nothing that she says can make it right. It is not a matter of seeing her point of view; you *can* see it; she has sold it to you. But you mustn't surrender." Oddly, the voice seemed to be the voice of the Duchess. I felt as though the Duchess were inside me, arguing.

I looked into the lovely, smiling face. "Do try," Mrs. Bradley repeated. "And do please come and have supper with the children tonight. Let's start all over again; shall we?"

When she held out both hands to me, she had won. I found myself in her arms and she was kissing my hair. I heard her say, "Poor little girl."

VI

Only the smallest shadow stayed in my heart and I forgot it for long minutes. We talked our heads off. It was like meeting them again after years. I found myself quoting in my head: "And among the grass shall find the golden dice wherewith we played of yore." They still loved me; they still laughed at everything I said. When I ended the description of the ambassador fighting the press baron and the failure of the electric lights, they were sobbing in separate corners of the sofa.

"Go on; go on. What did the Duchess do?"

"I think she enjoyed it mightily. She had an electric torch in her bag and she flashed it over them both like a searchlight."

"You do have the loveliest time," said Eva.

"Where is the Duchess tonight?" asked Don.

"In fact I think I heard her car come back about ten minutes ago." I began to describe the car and the chauffeur.

"*Older* than the Duchess? He can't be. I'd love to see them bouncing away under the fringe. Let's go out and look."

"Too late," I said. "At night he takes the car to the garage in Théoule."

"Hark, though," Don said. "There's a car now." He ran to the window; but I knew that it wasn't the Isotta-Fraschini. It was the putt-putt noise of Laurent's little Peugeot.

"How exactly like Laurent," I said. "As soon as the Duchess gets home, he goes out for the evening. And Francis has left him in charge."

It occurred to me now that I should go back. I reminded myself that Charlemagne was an effective watchdog. But I was not comfortable about it.

"D'you mean you ought to go and put the Duchess to bed? Undo her stays; help her off with her wig?"

"It isn't a wig; it's her own hair, and she requires no help. But I do think I should go back. The telephone may ring."

"Well then, the Duchess will answer it."

"She will not. She claims that she has never answered a telephone in her life. She regards them as an intrusion upon privacy."

"Isn't there anybody else in the hotel?"

"No."

"Oh you *can't* go yet," said Eva.

I sat on a little longer. Then I knew that it was no good. "I shall have remorse if I don't," I said, "and that is the worst thing."

"All right, then. We'll go with you."

"Oh, Don—" said Eva.

"Mum and Dad won't be back yet awhile," said Don, "and we'll only stay ten minutes."

"They'll be furious."

"We won't tell them."

Eva looked at me. I said, "I cannot decide for you. I only know I must go."

"Of course if you want to stay behind," Don said
to Eva.

"Of course I don't. What shall we say to Nanny?"

"We can say we went down to the beach."

We crept out, silent in the spirit of adventure. The
moon had risen, the full moon, promised by the
Duchess, enormous and silver and sad; its light made
a splendid path over the sea; the palms and the
orange trees, the rock shapes on the water, were all
sharp and black.

"Here we go on Tom Tiddler's ground," Eva sang.
We took the short cut, scrambling through the olean-
der hedge instead of going round by the gate. I could
hear Don panting with excitement beside me. Almost,
their mood could persuade me that the hotel was an
enchanted place. We came onto the terrace and darted
into the empty bar; Laurent had turned off the lights;
I turned them up for the Bradleys to look at the
photographs.

"What'll we drink?" said Don facetiously, hopping
onto a stool.

"Champagne," said Eva.

"If the Duchess was still awake, she'd give us some
champagne."

"You wouldn't drink it," said Eva.

"I would."

"You wouldn't."

"I jolly well would."

"She's probably in the salon," I said. "She never
goes to bed early."

I put out the lights again and led them to the
salon by way of the terrace. The salon lights were
lit. We looked through the windows.

"There she is," said Don. "She's lying on the sofa."

They bounded in ahead of me. I heard Don say, "Good evening, Duchessa," and Eva echoed it. There was no reply from the Duchess. With the Bradleys, I stood still staring at her. She was propped on the Empire sofa; her red head had fallen sideways on the stiff satin cushion. Her little pointed shoes and thin ankles stuck out from the hem of her shantung skirt and the skirt, which was of great width, drooped down over the edge of the sofa to the floor. On the table beside her she had placed the green tricorn hat, the green scarf, and her green velvet bag. A bottle of champagne stood in an ice pail; the glass had fallen to the floor; since one of her arms dangled limply, I thought that she must have dropped the glass as she went off to sleep.

"Please wake up, Duchessa; we want some champagne," said Don.

He took a step forward and peered into her face, which was turned away from us."

"She looks sort of horrid," he said; "I think she's ill."

For no reason that I could understand I felt that it was impertinent of him to be leaning there so close to her. When he turned back to us, I saw that his face was pale; the freckles were standing out distinctly on the bridge of his nose.

"She is ill, I'm sure," he said. "She's unconscious." He looked at the bottle of champagne. "She must be—" He stopped. I saw that he thought that the Duchess was intoxicated and that he could not bring himself to say so.

"Let's go," Eva said in a thin scared voice. She grabbed Don's hand. "Come on, Penelope. Quick."

"But of course I'm not coming."

They halted. "You can't stay here," Don said. Eva was shivering. There was no sound nor movement from the figure on the sofa. I said, "Certainly I can stay here. What else can I do? If she is ill, I must look after her."

I saw them straining against their own panic. Suddenly they seemed like puppies, very young indeed.

"But *we* can't stay here," Eva said. "Oh, please, Penelope, come with us."

"No indeed. But you go," I said. "It's what you want to do isn't it?"

"It's what we ought to do," Eva stammered through chattering teeth. Don looked a little more doubtful. "Look here, Penelope, you needn't stay with her. When they—they get like that, they sleep it off."

Now I was angry with him. "Please go at once," I said. "This is my affair. And I know what you mean and it isn't true." I found that I had clapped my hands to shoo them off; they went; I heard the panic rush of their feet on the terrace. I was alone with the Duchess.

Now that they were gone, I had no hesitation in approaching her. I said softly, "Hello, Duchessa. It's only me," and I bent above her as Don had done. I saw what he had seen; the shrunken look of the white face with the false eyelashes. Indeed she looked shrunken all over, like a very old doll.

I lowered my head until my ear touched the green frilled chiffon at her breast. I listened for the beat of her heart. When I could not hear it, I lifted the little pointed hand and felt the wrist. There was no pulse here that I could find.

I despised myself because I began to shiver as Eva Bradley had shivered. My fingers would not stay still; it was difficult to unfasten the clasp of the green velvet bag. I thought that there would be a pocket mirror inside and that I must hold this to her lips. Searching for the mirror I found other treasures; the ivory hand that she had aimed at Francis, a cut-glass smelling-bottle, some colored plaques from the Casino, a chain holding a watch, and a cluster of seals.

The mirror, when I found it, was in a folding morocco case with visiting cards in the pocket on the other side. I said, "Excuse me, please, Duchessa," as I held it in front of her face. I held it there a long time; when I took it away the bright surface was unclouded. I knew that the Duchess was dead.

A profound curiosity took away my fear. I had never seen a person lying dead before. It was so strange to think of someone I knew well, as having stopped. But the more I stared at her, the less she looked as though she had stopped; rather, she had gone. This was not the Duchess lying here; it was a little old doll, a toy thing of which the Duchess had now no need. Where, I wondered, had she gone? What had happened to all the things that she remembered, the fencing lessons, and the child's dreams, and the Emperor? What happened, I wondered, to the memories that you carried around in your head? Did they go on with your soul or would a soul not want them? What did a soul want? Did the Duchess's soul like roulette? Theology had never been my strongest subject and I found myself baffled by the rush of abstract questions flowing through my mind.

Then I became aware of her in relation to me. It was impossible to believe that I would not talk to her

again. I was suddenly deeply sorry that I had not dined
with her on the first evening, that I had not gone
down in the fancy-dress to show myself to Jeanne.
She had asked me to do this; she had asked me to
Monte Carlo with her. *"Viens, chérie, ça te changera
les idées."* Always she had been kind. I had not. I had
never been nice to her because she embarrassed me
and now I should never have another chance to be
nice to her.

Automatically I began to perform small meaningless
services. I covered her face with the green scarf, drawing it round her head so that it made a dignified
veil. I fetched a rug and laid it across her feet; I did
not want to see the little shoes. I carried the untouched champagne back to the bar. I lifted her tricorn hat, her bag and gloves off the table; I took
them up to her room. It was more difficult to be in
her room, with the bed turned down and the night
clothes laid there, than it was to be in the salon with
her body. I put the hat, bag, and gloves down on the
nearest chair and I was running out when I saw the
crucifix on the table. I thought that she might be
pleased to have this near her ("Although," I said to
myself, "she isn't there any more, one still goes on
behaving as if she is"), and I carried it down; I set
it on the table beside her. There seemed to be too
many lights here now. I turned off all but one lamp;
this room because a suitable place for her to lie in
state, the elegant little shell of a room with the Empire furnishings. I pulled a high-backed chair from
the wall, set it at the foot of the sofa, and sat down
to watch with her.

Outside the windows the moonlight lay in the garden. I heard her saying, "The moon is at the full to-

night. I look forward to it." I heard her saying, "Naturally, you cry for the moon." I heard her saying, "Death is a part of life," as she pulled on her white gloves.

At intervals I was afraid again; the fear came and went like intermittent seasickness. I did not know what brought it. She was so small and still and gone that I could not fear her. But I felt as though I were waiting for a dreadful thing to walk upon the terrace, and the only poem that would stay in my head was one that had always frightened me a little, "The Lykewake Dirge":

> This ae nighte, this ae nighte,
> Everye nighte and alle,
> Fire and sleet and candlelyte,
> And Christe receive thy saule.

It made shivers down my back. I would have liked to fetch Charlemagne from his kennel, but I had heard that dogs howled in the presence of the dead and this I did not want.

Sitting there so stiffly I became terribly tired: "But it is a vigil," I said to myself, "and it is all that I can do for her." It was not much. It was no true atonement for having failed her in kindness; it could not remit my having betrayed her to the Bradleys. It seemed hours since I had thought of the Bradleys. Now I wondered whether the parents had returned, and with the question there came incredulity that Don and Eva should not have come back. They had simply run off and left me, because they were afraid. The memory of their scared faces made them small and silly in my mind. Beside it, I uncovered the memory of my talk with Mrs. Bradley: the talk that had left a shadow. I admitted the shadow now: it was the note of patronage at the end of all the spell-binding. She had called me "poor little girl."

"You never called me poor little girl," I said in my thoughts to the Duchess. She had called me fortunate and a genius. She had spoken to me of the world, of freedom and maturity. That was truly gown-up conversation. In comparison the echo of Mrs. Bradley saying, "As one grown-up person to another," sounded fraudulent. Some of the magic had left the Bradleys tonight.

I was so tired. I did not mean to sleep, because this was vigil. But I found my head falling forward and the moonlight kept vanishing and the Duchess' voice was quite loud in my ears. "Of death," she said, "I remember three things; being tired, being quiet, and being gone. That's how it is, Penelope." She seemed to think that I could not hear her. She went on calling, "Penelope! Penelope!"

I sat up with a start. Somebody was in fact calling "Penelope": a man's voice from the terrace. I climbed down stiffly from the chair. "Who's that?" I asked, my voice sounding cracked and dry. Mr. Bradley stood against the moonlight.

"Are you there, child? Yes, you are. Come along out of this at once." He looked large and golden and worried; he seized my hand; then he saw the Duchess on the sofa.

"Lord," he said. "She's still out, is she?" He started again. "Did you cover her up like that?"

"Yes. Please talk quietly," I said. "She is dead."

He dropped my hand, lifted the scarf a little way

from her face, and put it back. I saw him looking at
the crucifix.

"I put it there. I thought that she would like it. I
am watching by her," I said.

He looked pale, ruffled, not the way, I thought, that
grown-up people should look. "I'm terribly sorry,"
he said in a subdued voice. "Terribly sorry. Young
Don came along to our room, said he couldn't sleep
for knowing you were over here with her. Of course
he didn't think—"

"I know what he thought, Mr. Bradley," I said
coldly. "Don and Eva are only babies really. Thank
you for coming, just the same."

He said, in his officer-to-men voice, "Out of here
now. There's a good girl."

"I beg your pardon?"

"You're coming to our house. I'll telephone the
doctor from there." He took my hand again; I pulled
it free.

"I'll stay with her, please. You telephone the doctor."

He looked down at me, amazed, almost smiling. He
dropped his voice again. "No, no, no, Penelope. You
mustn't stay."

I said, "I must."

"No, you mustn't. You can't do her any good."

"It is a vigil."

"That's just morbid and foolish. You're coming
over to our house now."

"I am not."

"Yes, you are," he said, and he picked me up in his
arms. To struggle in the presence of the Duchess
would have been unseemly. I remained tractable, stay-

ing in his arms until he had carried me onto the terrace. He began to put me down and at once I twisted free.

"I'm not coming with you. I'm staying with her. She is my friend and she is not your friend. You were rude about her, and stupid," I said to him.

He grabbed me again and I fought: he imprisoned me with my arms to my sides. For the moment he did not try to lift me. He simply held me there.

"Listen, Penelope, don't be hysterical. I'm doing what's best for you. That's all. You can't possibly sit up all night alone with the poor old lady; it's nearly one o'clock now."

"I shall stay with her till dawn; and she is not a poor old lady, just because she is dead. That is a ridiculous cliché."

I was aware of his face close to mine, the stony, regular features, the blue eyes and clipped mustache in the moonlight. The face seemed to struggle for speech. Then it said, "I don't want insolence any more than I want hysteria. You just pipe down and come along. This is no place for you."

"It is my home," I said.

He shook me gently. "Have some sense, will you? I wouldn't let my kids do what you're doing and I won't let you do it."

"Your children," I said, "wouldn't want to do it anyway; they are, in vulgar parlance, a couple of sissies."

At this he lifted me off my feet again and I struck at his face. I had the absurd idea that the Duchess had come to stand in the doorway and was cheering me on. And at this moment there came the miracle. The noise of the car sweeping in from the road was not the little noise of Laurent's car, but the roaring powerful engine that meant that Francis had come home.

The headlights swung yellow upon the moonlit garden. Still aloft in Mr. Bradley's clutch I said, "That is my father, who will be able to handle the situation with dignity."

He set me down as Francis braked the car and jumped out.

"That you, Bradley?" said Francis. "What, precisely, are you doing?"

Mr. Bradley said, "I am trying to make your daughter behave in a sensible manner. I'm very glad to see you."

Francis came up the steps onto the terrace. He sounded so weary that I knew his back hurt him: "Why should it be your concern to make my daughter behave in any manner whatsoever?"

"Really, Wells, you'll have to know the story. There's been a tragedy here tonight, I'm afraid. Just doing what I could to help."

"I will tell him," I said. I was grateful for Francis' arm holding me; my legs had begun to feel as though they were made of spaghetti.

"You let me do the talking, young woman," said Mr. Bradley.

"If you don't mind, I'd prefer to hear it from Penelope," said Francis.

I told him. I told him slowly, leaving out none of it; there seemed less and less breath in my lungs as I continued. "And Mr. Bradley called it morbid and foolish and removed me by force," I ended.

"Very silly of you, Bradley," said Francis.

"Damn it, look at the state she's in!"

"Part of which might be due to your methods of persuasion, don't you think? All right, Penelope, easy now." I could not stop shivering.

"Leaving her alone like that in a place like this. You ought to be ashamed of yourself," Mr. Bradley boomed.

"Quiet, please," said Francis in his most icy voice.

"Damned if I'll be quiet. It's a disgrace and I don't want any part of it."

"Nobody," I said, "asked you to take any part in it, Mr. Bradley."

"Hush," said Francis. "Mr. Bradley meant to be kind and you must be grateful."

"I am not in the least."

"Fine manners you teach her," said Mr. Bradley.

"Quiet, please," said Francis again. "Penelope has perfect manners, mitigated at the moment by perfect integrity and a certain amount of overstrain." Looking up at him, I could see the neat Mephistophelean profile, the delicate shape of his head. I loved him more than I had ever loved him. Mr. Bradley, large and blowing like a bull, was outside this picture, nothing to do with either of us.

Suddenly he looked as though he realized this. He said: "I don't want my wife or my kids mixed up in it either."

"Mixed up in what, precisely?" Francis asked.

I said, "It is possible that he is referring to the inquest. Or do you mean mixed up with me? Because if you do, no problem should arise. After tonight I have not the slightest wish to be mixed up with them or you."

It would have been more effective had I been able

to stop shivering; I was also feeling rather sick, never a help when attempting to make dignified speeches.

Mr. Bradley faded away in the moonlight.

Francis said gently, "Did you mean it? It is easy to say those things in anger."

"I think I meant it. Was the vigil, in your opinion, the right thing to do?"

"It was. I am very pleased with you."

I said, "But I am not sure that I can continue with it for a moment. I feel funny."

Francis took me into the bar; he poured out a glass of brandy and a glass of water, making me drink them in alternate swallows.

"Of course," he said gloomily, "it may make you sick. In which event the last state will be worse than the first."

But it did not; it made me warm.

"They can't *help* being the Smugs, can they?" I said suddenly, and then for the first time I wanted to cry.

"They're all right," said Francis. "They are merely lacking in imagination."

I managed to say, "Sorry," and no more. I knew that he disliked me to cry. This time he said, watching me, "On some occasions it is better to weep."

I put my head down on the table and sobbed, "If only she could come back; I would be nice."

Francis said, "You gave her great pleasure always."

"Oh, not enough."

"Nobody can give anybody enough."

"Not ever?"

"No, not ever. But one must go on trying."

"And doesn't one ever value people until they are gone?"

"Rarely," said Francis.

I went on weeping; I saw how little I had valued him; how little I had valued anything that was mine. Presently he said, "Do you think that you can cry quite comfortably by yourself for a few minutes because I must telephone the doctor?"

Though I said, "Yes, indeed," I stopped crying immediately. As I sat waiting for him, I was saying good-by, to my first dead, to a love that was ended, and to my dream of being like other people.

The next day I tore the Anthology of Hates into pieces and cast the pieces into the sea. I did not read through the pages first, so certain was I that I had done with hating.

Simple Arithmetic

BY VIRGINIA MORICONI

Geneva, January 15

Dear Father:

Well, I am back in School, as you can see, and the place is just as miserable as ever. My only friend, the one I talked to you about, Ronald Fletcher, is not coming back any more because someone persuaded his mother that she was letting him go to waste, since he was extremely photogenic, so now he is going to become a child actor. I was very surprised to hear this, as the one thing Ronnie liked to do was play basketball. He was very shy.

The flight wasn't too bad. I mean nobody had to be carried off the plane. The only thing was, we were six hours late and they forgot to give us anything to eat, so for fourteen hours we had a chance to get quite hungry but, as you say, for the money you save going tourist class, you should be prepared to make a few little sacrifices.

I did what you told me, and when we got to Idlewild I paid the taxi driver his fare and gave him a fifty-cent tip. He was very dissatisfied. In fact he wouldn't give me my suitcase. In fact I don't know what would have happened if a man hadn't come up just while the argument was going on and when he heard what it was all about he gave the taxi driver a dollar and I took my suitcase and got to the plane on time.

During the trip I thought the whole thing over. I did not come to any conclusion. I know I have been very extravagant and unreasonable about money and you have done the best you can to explain this to me. Still, while I was thinking about it, it seemed to me that there were only three possibilities. I could just have given up and let the taxi driver have the suitcase, but when you realize that if we had to buy everything over again that was in the suitcase we would probably have had to spend at least five hundred dollars, it does not seem very economical. Or I could have gone on arguing with him and missed the plane, but then we would have had to pay something like three hundred dollars for another ticket. Or else I could have given him an extra twenty-five cents which, as you say, is just throwing money around to create an impression. What would you have done?

Anyway I got here, with the suitcase, which was the main thing. They took two weekend privileges away from me because I was late for the opening of School. I tried to explain to M. Frisch that it had nothing to do with me if the weather was so bad that the plane was delayed for six hours, but he said that prudent persons allow for continjensies of this kind and make earlier reservations. I don't care about this because the next two weekends are skiing weekends and I have never seen any point in waking up at six o'clock in the morning just to get frozen stiff and endure terrible pain even if sports are a part of growing up, as you say. Besides, we will save twenty-seven dollars by having me stay in my room.

In closing I want to say that I had a very nice Christmas and I apreciate everything you tried to do for me and I hope I wasn't too much of a bother. (Martha explained to me that you had had to take time off from your honeymoon in order to make Christmas for me and I am very sorry even though I do not think I am to blame if Christmas falls on the twenty-fifth of December, especially since everybody knows that it does. What I mean is, if you had wanted to have a long honeymoon you and Martha could have gotten married earlier, or you could have waited until Christmas was over, or you could just have told me not to come and I would have understood.)

I will try not to spend so much money in the future and I will keep accounts and send them to you. I will also try to remember to do the eye exercises and the exercises for fallen arches that the doctors in New York prescribed. Love, Stephen.

New York, January 19

Dear Stephen:

Thank you very much for the long letter of January fifteenth. I was very glad to know that you had gotten back safely, even though the flight was late. (I do not agree with M. Frisch that prudent persons allow for "continjensies" of this kind, now that air travel is as standard as it is, and the service usually so good, but we must remember that Swiss people are, by and large, the most meticulous in the world and nothing offends them more than other people who are not punctual.)

In the affair of the suitcase, I'm afraid that we were both at fault. I had forgotten that there would be an extra charge for luggage when I suggested that you should tip the driver fifty cents. You, on the other hand, might have inferred from his argument that he was simply asking that the tariff—i.e., the fare, plus overcharge for the suitcase—should be paid in full, and regulated yourself accordingly. In any event you arrived, and I am only sorry that obviously you had no time to learn the name and address of your benefactor so that we might have paid him back for his kindness.

I will look forward to going over your accounting and I am sure you will find that in keeping a clear record of what you spend you will be able to cut your cloth according to the bolt and that, in turn, will help you to develop a real regard for yourself. It is a common failing, as I told you, to spend too much money in order to compensate oneself for a lack of inner security, but you can easily see that a foolish purchase does not insure stability, and if you are chronically insolvent you can hardly hope for peace of mind. Your allowance is more than adequate and when you learn to make both ends meet you will have taken a decisive step ahead. I have great faith in you and I know you will find your anchor to windward in your studies, in your sports, and in your companions.

As to what you say about Christmas, you are not obliged to "apreciate" what we did for you. The important thing was that you should have had a good time, and I think we had some wonderful fun together, the three of us, don't you? Until your mother decides where she wants to live and settle down, this is your *home* and you must always think of it that way. Even though I have remarried, I am still your father, first and last, and Martha is very fond of you too, and very understanding about your problems. You may not be aware of it but in fact she is one of the best friends you have. New ideas and new step-mothers take a little getting used to, of course.

Please write me as regularly as you can, since your letters mean a great deal to me. Please try too, at all times, to keep your marks up to scratch, as college entrance is getting harder and harder in this country, and there are thousands of candidates each year for the good universities. Concentrate particularly on spelling. "Contingency" is difficult, I know, but there is no excuse for only one "p" in appreciate"! And *do* the exercises. Love, Father.

Geneva, January 22

Dear Mummy:

Last Sunday I had to write to Father to thank him for my Christmas vacation and to tell him that I got back all right. This Sunday I thought I would write to you even though you are on a cruze so perhaps you will never get my letter. I must say that if they didn't make us write home once a week I don't believe that I would ever write any letters at all. What I mean is that once you get to a point like this, in a place like this, you see that you are supposed to have your life and your parents are supposed to have their lives, and you have lost the connection.

Anyway I have to tell you that Father was wonderful to me and Martha was very nice too. They had thought it all out, what a child of my age might like to do in his vacation and sometimes it was pretty strenuous, as you can image. At the end the School sent the bill for the first term, where they charge you for the extras which they let you have here and it seems that I had gone way over my allowance and besides I had signed for a whole lot of things I did not deserve. So there was a terrible scene and Father was very angry and Martha cried and said that if Father always made such an effort to consider me as a person I should make an effort to consider him as a person too and wake up to the fact that he was not Rockefeller and that even if he was sacrificing himself so that I could go to one of the most expensive schools in the world it did not mean that I should drag everybody down in the mud by my reckless spending. So now I have to turn over a new leaf and keep accounts of every penny and not buy anything which is out of proportion to our scale of living.

Except for that one time they were very affectionate to me and did everything they could for my happiness. Of course it was awful without you. It was the first time we hadn't been together and I couldn't really believe it was Christmas.

I hope you are having a wonderful time and getting the rest you need and please write me when you can. All my love, Stephen.

Geneva, January 29

Dear Father:

Well it is your turn for a letter this week because I wrote to Mummy last Sunday. (I am sure I can say this to you without hurting your feelings because you always said that the one thing you and Mummy wanted was a civilized divorce so we could all be friends.) Anyway Mummy hasn't answered my letter so probably she doesn't aprove of my spelling any more than you do. I am beginning to wonder if maybe it wouldn't be much simpler and much cheaper too if I didn't go to college after all. I really don't know what this education is for in the first place.

There is a terrible scandal here at School which has been very interesting for the rest of us. One of the girls, who is only sixteen, has gotten pregnant and everyone knows that it is all on account of the science instructer, who is a drip. We are waiting to see if he will marry her, but in the meantime she is terrifically upset and she has been expelled from the School. She is going away on Friday.

I always liked her very much and I had a long talk with her last night. I wanted to tell her that maybe it was not the end of the world, that my stepmother was going to have a baby in May, although she never got married until December, and the sky didn't fall in or anything. I thought it might have comforted her to think that grownups make the same mistakes that children do (if you can call her a child) but then I was afraid that it might be disloyal to drag you and Martha into the conversation, so I just let it go.

I'm fine and things are just the same. Love, Stephen.

New York, February 2

Dear Stephen:

It would be a great relief to think that your mother did not "aprove" of your spelling either, but I'm sure that it's not for that reason that you haven't heard from her. She was never any good as a correspondent, and now it is probably more difficult for her than ever. We did indeed try for what you call a "civilized divorce" for all our sakes, but divorce is not any easy thing for any of the persons involved, as you well know, and if you try to put yourself in your mother's place for a moment, you will see that she is in need of time and solitude to work things out for herself. She will certainly write to you as soon as she has found herself again, and meanwhile you must continue to believe in her affection for you and not let impatience get the better of you.

Again, in case you are really in doubt about it, the purpose of your education is to enable you to stand on your own feet when you are a man and make something of yourself. Inaccuracies in spelling will not *simplify* anything.

I can easily see how you might have made a parallel between your friend who has gotten into trouble, and Martha who is expecting the baby in May, but there is only a superficial similarity in the two cases.

Your friend is, or was, still a child, and would have done better to have accepted the limitations of the world of childhood—as you can clearly see for yourself, now that she is in this predicament. Martha, on the other hand, was hardly a child. She was a mature human being, responsible for her own actions and prepared to be responsible for the baby when it came. Moreover I, unlike the science "instructer" am not a drip, I too am responsible for *my* actions, and so Martha and I are married and I will do my best to live up to her and the baby.

Speaking of which, we have just found a new apartment because this one will be too small for us in May. It is right across the street from your old school and we have a kitchen, a dining alcove, a living room, two bedrooms—one for me and Martha, and one for the new baby—and another room which will be for you. Martha felt that it was very important for you to feel that you had a place of your own when you came home to us, and so it is largely thanks to her that we have taken such a big place. The room will double as a study for me when you are not with us, but we will move all my books and papers and paraphernalia whenever you come, and Martha is planning to hang the Japanese silk screen you liked at the foot of the bed.

Please keep in touch, and *please* don't forget the exercises. Love, Father.

Geneva, February 5

Dear Father:

There is one thing which I would like to say to you which is that if it hadn't been for you I would never have heard of a "civilized divorce," but that is the way you explained it to me. I always thought it was crazy. What I mean is, wouldn't it have been better if you had said, "I don't like your mother any more and I would rather live with Martha," instead of insisting that you and Mummy were always going to be the greatest friends? Because the way things are now Mummy probably thinks that you still like her very much, and it must be hard for Martha to believe that she was chosen, and I'm pretty much confused myself, although it is really none of my business.

You will be sorry to hear that I am not able to do any of the exercises any longer. I cannot do the eye exercises because my roommate got so fassinated by

the stereo gadget that he broke it. (But the School
Nurse says she thinks it may be just as well to let
the whole thing go since in her opinion there was a
good chance that I might have gotten more cross-
eyed than ever, fidgeting with the viewer.) And I
cannot do the exercises for fallen arches, at least for
one foot, because when I was decorating the Assembly
Hall for the dance last Saturday, I fell off the stepladder and broke my ankle. So now I am in the In-
firmy and the School wants to know whether to send
the doctor's bill to you or to Mummy, because they
had to call in a specialist from outside, since the
regular School Doctor only knows how to do a very
limited number of things. So I have cost a lot of
money again and I am very very sorry, but if they
were half-way decent in this School they would pay
to have proper equipment and not let the students
risk their lives on broken stepladders, which is something you could write to the Book-Keeping Department, if you felt like it, because I can't, but you
could, and it might do some good in the end.

The girl who got into so much trouble took too
many sleeping pills and died. I felt terrible about
it, in fact I cried when I heard it. Life is very crewel,
isn't it?

I agree with what you said, that she was a child,
but I think she knew that, from her point of view.
I think she did what she did because she thought of
the science instructor as a grownup, so she imagined
that she was perfectly safe with him. You may think
she was just bad, because she was a child and should
have known better, but I think that it was not entirely her fault since here at School we are all encouraged to take the teachers seriously.

I am very glad you have found a new apartment and I hope you won't move all your books and papers when I come home, because that would only make me feel that I was more of a nuisance than ever. Love, Stephen.

New York, February 8

Dear Stephen:

This will have to be a very short letter because we are to move into the new apartment tomorrow and Martha needs my help with the packing.

We were exceedingly shocked by the tragic death of your friend, and very sorry that you should have had such a sad experience. Life can be "crewel" indeed to the people who do not learn how to live it.

When I was exactly your age I broke my ankle too —I wasn't on a defective stepladder, I was playing hockey—and it hurt like the devil. I still remember it and you have all my sympathy. (I have written to the School Physician to ask how long you will have to be immobilized, and to urge him to get you back into the athletic program as fast as possible. The specialist's bill should be sent to me.)

I have also ordered another stereo viewer because, in spite of the opinion of the School Nurse, the exercises are most important and you are to do them *religiously*. Please be more careful with this one no matter how much it may "fassinate" your roommate.

Martha sends love and wants to know what you would like for your birthday. Let us know how the ankle is mending. Love, Father.

Geneva, February 12

Dear Father:

I was very surprised by your letter. I was surprised that you said you were helping Martha to pack because when you and Mummy were married I do not ever remember you packing or anything like that so I guess Martha is reforming your charactor. I was also surprised by what you said about the girl who died. What I mean is, if anyone had told me a story like that I think I would have just let myself get a little worked up about the science instructer because it seems to me that he was a villan too. Of course you are much more riserved than I am.

I am out of the Infirmary and they have given me a pair of crutches, but I'm afraid it will be a long time before I can do sports again.

I hope the new apartment is nice and I do not want anything for my birthday because it will seem very funny having a birthday in School so I would rather not be reminded of it. Love, Stephen.

New York, February 15

Dear Stephen:

This is not an answer to your letter of February twelfth, but an attempt to have a serious discussion with you, as if we were face to face.

You are almost fifteen years old. Shortly you will be up against the stiffest competition of your life when you apply for college entrance. No examiner is going to find himself favorably impressed by "charactor" or "instructer" or "villan" or "riserved" or similar errors. You will have to face the fact that in this world we succeed on our merits, and if we are unsuccessful, on account of sloppy habits of mind, we suffer for it. You are still too young to understand me entirely, but you are not too young to recognize the importance of effort. People who do not make the grade are desperately unhappy all their lives because they have no place in society. If you do not pass the college entrance examinations simply because you are unable to spell, it will be nobody's fault but your own, and you will be gravely handicapped for the rest of your life.

Every time you are in doubt about a word you are to look it up in the dictionary and *memorize* the spelling. This is the least you can do to help yourself.

We are still at sixes and sevens in the new apartment but when Martha accomplishes all she has planned it should be very nice indeed and I think you will like it. Love, Father.

Geneva, February 19

Dear Father:

I guess we do not understand each other at all. If you immaggine for one minute that just by making a little effort I could imaggine how to spell immaggine without looking it up and finding that actually it is "imagine," then you are all wrong. In other words, if you get a letter from me and there are only two or three mistakes well you just have to take my word for it that I have had to look up practically every single word in the dictionary and that is one reason I hate having to write you these letters because they take so long and in the end they are not at all spontainous, no, just wait a second, here it is, "spontaneous," and believe me only two or three mistakes in a letter from me is one of the seven wonders of the the world. What I'm saying is that I am doing the best I can as you would aggree if you could see my dictionary which is falling apart and when you say I should *memmorize* the spelling I can't because it doesn't make any sence to me and never did. Love, Stephen.

New York, February 23

Dear Stephen:

It is probably just as well that you have gotten everything off your chest. We all need to blow up once in a while. It clears the air.

Please don't ever forget that I am aware that spelling is difficult for you. I know you are making a great effort and I am very proud of you. I just want to be sure that you *keep trying*.

I am enclosing a small check for your birthday because even if you do not want to be reminded of it I wouldn't want to forget it and you must know that we are thinking of you. Love, Father.

Geneva, February 26

Dear Father:

We are not allowed to cash personal checks here in the School, but thank you anyway for the money.

I am not able to write any more because we are going to have the exams and I have to study. Love, Stephen.

New York, March 2

Night Letter

Best of luck, stop, keep me posted exam results—love, Father.

Geneva, March 12

Dear Father:

Well, the exams are over. I got a C in English because aparently I do not know how to spell, which should not come as too much of a surprise to you. In Science, Mathematics, and Latin I got A, and in French and History I got a B plus. This makes me first in the class, which doesn't mean very much since none of the children here have any life of the mind, as you would say. I mean they are all jerks, more or less. What am I supposed to do in the Easter vacation? Do you want me to come to New York, or shall I just say here and get a rest, which I could use? Love, Stephen.

New York, March 16

Dear Stephen:

I am *immensely* pleased with the examination results. Congratulations. Pull up the spelling and our worries are over.

Just yesterday I had a leter from your mother. She has taken a little house in Majorca, which is an island off the Spanish coast, as you probably know, and she suggests that you should come to her for the Easter holidays. Of course you are always welcome here—and you could rest as much as you wanted—but Majorca is very beautiful and would certainly appeal to the artistic side of your nature. I have written to your mother, urging her to write to you immediately, and I enclose her address in case you should want to write yourself. Let me know what you would like to do. Love, Father.

Geneva, March 19

Dear Mummy:

Father says that you have invited me to come to you in Majorca for the Easter vacation. Is that true? I would be very very happy if it were. It has been very hard to be away from you for all this time and if you wanted to see me it would mean a great deal to me. I mean if you are feeling well enough. I could do a lot of things for you so you would not get too tired.

I wonder if you will think that I have changed when you see me. As a matter of fact I have changed a lot because I have become quite bitter. I have become quite bitter on account of this School.

I know that you and Father wanted me to have some expearience of what the world was like outside of America but what you didn't know is that Geneva is not the world at all. I mean, if you were born here then perhaps you would have a real life, but I do not know anyone who was born here so all the people I see are just like myself, we are just waiting not to be lost any more. I think it would have been better to have left me in some place where I belonged even if Americans are getting very loud and money conscious. Because actually most children here are Americans, if you come right down to it, only it seems their parents didn't know what to do with them any longer.

Mummy I have written all this because I'm afraid that I have spent too much money all over again and M. Frisch says that Father will have a crise des nerfs when he sees what I have done, and I thought maybe you would understand that I only bought these things because there didn't seem to be anything else to do, and that you could help me somehow or other. Anyway, according to the School, we will have to pay for all these things.

Concert, Segovia (Worth it)	16.00	(Swiss Francs)
School Dance	5.00	
English Drama (What do they mean?)	10.00	
Controle de l'habitant (?)	9.10	
Co-op purchases	65.90	
Ballet Russes (Disappointing)	47.00	
Librairie Prior	59.30	
Concert piano (For practising)	61.00	
Teinturie (They ruined everything)	56.50	
Toilet and Medicine	35.00	
Escalade Ball	7.00	
Pocket Money	160.00	
77 Yoghurts (Doctor's advice)	42.40	
Book account	295.70	
Total:	896.90	(Swiss Francs)

Now you see the trouble is that Father told me I was to spend about fifty dollars a month, because that was my allowance, and that I was not to spend anything more. Anyway, fifty dollars a month would be about two hundred and ten Swiss Francs, and then I had fifteen dollars for Christmas from Granny, and when I got back to School I found four Francs in the pocket of my leather jacket and then I had seventy-nine cents left over from New York, but that doesn't help much, and then Father sent me twenty-five dollars for my birthday but I couldn't cash the check because they do not allow that here in School, so what shall I do?

It is a serious situation as you can see, and it is going to get a lot more serious when Father sees the bill. But whatever you do, I imploar you not to write to Father because the trouble seems to be that I never had a balance foreward and I am afraid that it is impossible to keep accounts without a balance foreward, and even more afraid that by this time the accounts have gone a little bizerk.

Do you want me to take a plane when I come to Majorca? Who shall I say is going to pay for the ticket?

Please do write me as soon as you can, because the holidays begin on March 30 and if you don't tell me what to do I will be way out on a lim. Lots and lots of love, Stephen.

Geneva, March 26

Dear Father:

I wrote to Mummy a week ago to say that I would like very much to spend my Easter vacation in Majorca. So far she has not answered my letter, but I guess she will pretty soon. I hope she will because the holidays begin on Thursday.

I am afraid you are going to be upset about the bill all over again, but in the Spring term I will start anew and keep you in touch with what is going on. Love, Stephen.

P.S. If Mummy doesn't write what shall I do?

The Ghost of Martin Luther King

BY HAL BENNETT

The ghost of Martin Luther King walks these country roads at night. I have seen him moving almost furtively through the hickory grove where trees arch over the road like a cathedral; and he walks with all the solemnity of the dead down the roads of Burnside, as though he is searching for something that he cannot yet find. I have told my mother about the ghost; but she is a large, light-skinned woman more tied to reality than my father; and I can see that something in her is afraid to believe that the dead can return. My father—who is thin, timid and black—is ready to believe; but something in him also resists the idea of ghosts.

My only ally is Roberta Green. Roberta is sixteen, a year younger than myself. So scrawny and black, she is almost ready to believe anything that will reconcile her to the fact that all things black are not beautiful. It is as if nature had played its worst joke on her—she is tall and angular, and the most beautiful thing about her is her eyes, if she would ever look up from the ground. When I told her about the ghost of Martin Luther King, she was eager to believe. But that is because she is lonely all the time, and a ghost is better than no companion at all.

"Will you go with me to see him?" I said.

She looked even harder at the ground. "Does he come late?"

"Very late."

"David, I can't go with you. Mama wouldn't let me."

My father's excuse also had to do with the fact that Martin Luther King walks late at night. My father works at the shoe factory in Dillwyn, and he has to get up at five o'clock in order to be to work by six. So he has not been able to stay up to see the ghost. Following his advice, I have told no one else in Burnside about the sight I have seen, although I did ask Uncle George if he believed in ghosts. Uncle George is my father's brother. "Ghosts?" he said, and he laughed in that robust way he has. "I suppose I do believe in them," he said. But he sounded very skeptical indeed.

As for my mother, there was a time when she might have believed in ghosts. But she was operated on for cancer more than five years ago at the white hospital in Farmville; and the fact that she is still alive has converted her to the rationale of white men. The rest of us are not so ready to believe that white people have stopped being diabolical after three centuries of being devils. My father is always complaining about their arrogance and the injustices he suffers every day in Dillwyn, where he works alongside white people who have been forced from the fields to the factory. Farming is no longer a profitable way of life for the small farmer, white or black, in Virginia; and it is the hard fist of economic necessity more than anything else that has laid low the walls of segregation. The motels and restaurants at Alcanthia Court House need the dollars that black folk earn in Dillwyn. Now they cater regularly to black clientele, although there was a time when their doors were closed to all but whites. My mother sees this as a sign of progress and of a new benevolence on the part of white people. The doctors at Farmville cut off her left breast and reamed out her insides to stifle the cancer; and, in her own way, I suppose, she believes that her salvation from the dread disease has stemmed the cancer of America as well.

But my father is not so easily persuaded. "I work with white people every day," he tells my mother. "Nothing has changed at all." But she thinks that the fact of his working with white people is the biggest change of all.

Every second or third Sunday, she dressed us all up and herded us down the highway for dinner at the Alcanthia Inn, where the white waitresses called us sir and ma'am and served us with a cordiality that my father and I openly suspected. But what was an ordeal for my father and me was a delight for my mother. She seemed to swell up like a balloon in the white atmosphere. Looking at her as she ate, it was impossible to detect that she was a hollowed-out woman. She was very light-skinned; and her cheeks turned rosy red as she stuffed them with roast pig and applesauce. The artificial breast she wore was smaller than her right one; she readjusted it from time to time as it slipped out of place from the energy of her eating. "I do *adore* pig," she said between mouthfuls. She dabbed her greasy lips with the edge of a paper napkin. "Homer, it'll soon be time to kill our pig, won't it?" My father nodded, picking at his food.

We had a white sow ready for killing this year. Since the farmers had gone to work in the factories at Dillwyn, hardly anyone kept livestock any more. But my mother had bought the white sow as a shoat and she had nursed it to a solid two hundred pounds by feeding it dinner scraps and grass. My father wasn't too happy about killing the pig. Although he did not say so, I think he had become attached to it and wanted to keep it as a pet. "There's no need to kill that sow," he said. "Maybe we can find a male somewhere and mate her with it."

Swallowing, my mother shook her head. "It's hard enough keeping one pig, much less a bunch of them. It's not like the old days, Homer. If we kill her now, we'll have pork for all winter and part of the spring. We've got to be realistic about this, honey. Do you know what pork chops cost in the supermarket?"

Glumly, my father shoved back his plate. "The price of meat is right high," he said.

"Indeed it is," my mother said. "You find out from George when he can kill the sow. Is he out there picketing at the factory today?" Her voice showed that she didn't approve of Uncle George's militancy. Although black and white men worked side by side at the factory in Dillwyn, blacks were denied equal opportunity and equal pay. Uncle George had called some of the black workers together to picket the factory that day.

"He's out there," my father said.

"Well, I'm glad you had sense enough not to go," my mother said. "That does nothing but destroy the balance of things." My father said nothing; and we went on with our dinner.

After peach cobbler and coffee for dessert, my mother paid the bill and left a large tip. The waitress thanked her and followed us to the door. "You all come back again, you hear? And tell your friends," she said.

"Indeed we will," my mother said. "I certainly did

enjoy that pork." That same night, I saw the ghost of Martin Luther King for the first time.

I had gone to Roberta Green's house down the road to play dominoes. She lives with her family at the old Willis place that her father rents for fifteen dollars a month. It is a shack, really, where all the Greens—there are nine of them—live together in three rooms in a kind of amiable disorder that I sometimes enjoyed being a part of. That night, one of the older girls was frying turnovers made from some apples that Mr. Green had brought home from Dillwyn. I played dominoes with him and Roberta. She kept her eyes downcast all through the game, her long lashes casting shadows on her thin cheeks. Mrs. Green, fat and lazy, sat in an armchair and ordered everyone around like some large black empress. When the turnovers were ready, we gulped them down sizzling hot and succulent with butter and cinnamon. It was a comfortable atmosphere and I thoroughly enjoyed myself, especially when Mr. Green put the dominoes away and started telling ghost stories that made my hair stand on end.

Then we heard a car screech to a stop outside, and almost immediatly afterward, Clay Green, the oldest boy, burst through the door. "Turn out the lights!" he cried. "I think I'm being followed!"

At first, no one moved. Then Mrs. Green repeated the order in a high, frightened voice. Someone clicked a switch, then another and a third; and the shack was plunged into darkness.

One of the children began whimpering and I heard Mrs. Green's chair creak as she moved to hush the child. The air was heavy with the odor of cinnamon; and the only light came through the grille of the kitchen stove. Roberta found my hand in the darkness and held it. None of us knew what was going on, which made the suspense almost unbearable. As for myself, I thought about movies I had seen on television of frightened Jews hiding from the Nazi terror; and I held Roberta's hand even harder.

Finally, Mr. Green cleared his throat. "Doggone it, Clay," he whispered, "what the hell's going on?"

"I thought the Sheriff and some of his deputies might have followed me," Clay whispered back. "There's been trouble at the factory. The Sheriff tried to break up the picket line. Some of the men started throwing stones."

"What happened then?" Mr. Green said impatiently.

"The Sheriff started hitting us with his billy club," Clay went on. His voice was low and hoarse. "Some of the men ran. But I stayed and stood my ground with the rest. Then one of the deputies fired his gun. That's when I ran. I got in the car and took off. Just when I was leaving, I saw them drag Mr. George Stapleton to the Sheriff's car. I think he was the only one they arrested."

Mr. Green got up and turned the light on. His face seemed drawn and gray. "I knew there was going to be trouble," he said. "That's why I didn't go when George asked me. Did your father go, David?"

"No, sir," I said. "We had dinner at the Alcanthia Inn."

Mr. Green nodded. "Well, you'd better go home and tell your Daddy that George is in jail. Maybe he can do something about it tomorrow morning. It's probably too late tonight."

I said good night to everybody and started for home. It was late October and the road that led to the high-

way was covered with leaves. There was a blob of a
moon in the sky, bright and misshapen, like a lopsided
pearl. A blanket of stars winked and glittered in a
dome of dark blue. The air was unusually chilly for
that time of year and I pulled my jacket collar up
around my ears and walked on to the highway. When
I was a child, this had been harvest weather, the time
of pumpkins and corn, of tobacco to be cut and cured
and sold, of walnuts, hazelnuts and chinquapins to be
hunted out in the golden woods. But now the land
went to waste while farmers became factory hands and
bought their food at the supermarket in Dillwyn. The
fields were stark under the hunched moon's glare, as
though the earth begged forgiveness for the evil that
man was doing to himself.

I was thinking about that and about what Clay had
said about the pickets. It made me feel strange, knowing that Uncle George was spending the night in jail
in Alcanthia Court House. He was bigger and bolder
than my own father; and I felt that he would be all
right until we could bail him out the next morning.
This was not his first time in jail. He had been locked
up during the early voter-registration drives and the
agitation for civil rights. And each time he had been
freed, he had gone home angrier than before and more
determined, as he put it, to get his rightful share of
things. I admired Uncle George, although the violence
in him frightened me sometimes, as I was sure it
frightened my father and mother.

From far away, I could hear the yelping of dogs;
and once again I thought about those movies I had
seen of Nazi Germany and the hounds of fear. It was
true, too, that in these same woods and fields, black
slaves had once made their desperate bid for freedom

in the years before the Civil War. There had been hounds then, too, slavering at the heels of frightened men.

Had so much changed since then? Was it true that America's Negroes had become the successors to Hitler's Jews? I walked on. The wind slid around my ankles and through the leaves, rustling and hissing like the angry sound of autumn snakes. I had come to the hickory grove where it forms a kind of arch over the road where it joins at right angles with the highway. And then I saw the ghost.

He was walking toward me, on the other side of the road. It was dark in the grove, with only a trace of moonlight falling through the trees; and at first I thought that the ghost was some neighbor carrying a lantern that illuminated him in a kind of ethereal light. But as he drew closer, I saw that it was Martin Luther King—the solid, almost portly build, the round head, thick lips, eyes cast down, with an expression of infinite sorrow on his face, as though he was looking for something on the way and not finding it. He was dressed in a black suit and white shirt, and he came down the road at a solemn pace. Walking with almost military precision, surrounded by unearthly light, he was as real as anything I had had ever seen.

My first impulse was to run. But the apparition did not seem to mean me any harm. It was deathly quiet in the hickory grove, as though all sound had been suspended inside a vacuum contained by the towering trees. But, from the fields around me, tree frogs and crickets raised a cacophony of song that accompanied the specter in his ghostly walk.

Just as he neared me, my legs came to life and I dived off the road into some bushes. But the ghost paid no attention to me at all. Looking neither left nor right, he proceeded down the road to the end of the grove. And where the moonlight fell, there in the open space beyond the last tree, he disappeared as completely as though he had not existed at all.

I walked the rest of the way home in a daze. All my life, I had heard stories about ghosts, but this was my first time actually seeing one. The apparition had not frightened me; in fact, it thrilled me with a sense of excitement and expectation that I had never experienced before. And I wondered what had called forth the ghost of Martin Luther King from his grave. What ominous events did his appearance foretell?

When I got home, I told my mother and father about Uncle George's being arrested. My father sat down and wrung his hands. "I knew it," he said. "I knew it would wind up like this."

My mother agreed with him. "I think you showed great sense in not going yourself," she said. "It never pays to rock the boat." Her artificial breast was hanging at a grotesque angle in her dress.

I did not tell them about the ghost that night, because they were too excited about Uncle George's being in jail. Next day, I went to school with Roberta. All the black students were abuzz about the events at the factory; and I did not tell any of them about the ghost, either.

When I got home from school, Uncle George was there drinking coffee with my mother. She had gone to Alcanthia Court House to bail him out, so that my father would not have to miss a day's work.

Uncle George winked at me when I went in. He was big and burly and very, very black. "Hi, David," he said. I told him hello. My mother told me to go change my clothes, which was her way of letting me know that she'd prefer me not to talk to Uncle George about yesterday. When I went back to the kitchen, Uncle George was ready to go. He thanked my mother for bailing him out. Before he left, she asked him if he'd kill the white sow for us come hog-killing time. "I'd be glad to," Uncle George said. He went down the road whistling.

In the weeks that followed, I saw the ghost of Martin Luther King several more times. After the second occasion, I told my mother and father and found my mother afraid to believe that the dead can return and my father wanting to believe but fearing some danger if he did. So I confided in Roberta; but she, like everyone else in Burnside, was stirred by the continual agitation at the factory in Dillwyn. Every day, it seemed, there was new trouble there—name calling, fist fights, long-simmering hostilities finally brought into the open as blacks tried to tear down the old barriers while whites did their utmost to maintain them. Then, near the middle of November, the blacks—who made up the majority of the work force at the factory— walked out in a general strike. The factory limped along for a few days, trying to stay open with a minority of white workers on the job; but finally it was forced to close down altogether.

Uncle George was elated. My own father, more through necessity than conviction, had joined the strikers; and he was somber and apprehensive, as was my mother. But it was clear that something more solid than Uncle George's rhetoric had fired the men and moved them to that drastic step. I went with my father to their meeting at May's, the black tavern; and underneath all their grumblings and protestations, as they bought beer with the last of their dwindling funds, it became apparent that their main complaint had to do with the fact that, at the factory, they were treated as less than men. Uncle George and other speakers warned them of the rough days ahead but exhorted them to stick to their guns. That day, the union representative, who was white, came to explain to the men that their strike was illegal and to plead with them to go back to work. Jeering, shouting, stomping their feet, they drowned him out. "What's going on at that factory is illegal, too!" some of them cried. "We won't go back there until things change!" At last, the union man left, red in the face and looking disgruntled by their surprising show of solidarity.

But, after the first heady days of excitement wore off, the hard reality of providing for ourselves set in. My mother had a few stores that she shared—somewhat begrudgingly, I must admit—with some of the other women. And there were a few gardens where collards and turnips grew in the November cold; these, too, were shared. We foraged in the woods for nuts and berries to keep going on. When some of the men went hunting and came back with an occasional wild turkey or quail or a brace of partridge, as many as possible shared in the meager supplies. We cleaned the fields and forest of all there was to eat. Our hunters stopped going to the woods for game, because there was no money with which to buy ammunition. Yet the strike lingered on. The earlier, boisterous acceptance was replaced by a kind of surly pride that worked as well to keep the men away from their jobs; and it was evident that hardship had only served to bring all of us together in a hard core of resistance to the injustices that had been practiced for so long at the factory. "Look at it this way," Uncle George told the men. "If we're suffering, it means that the white man is suffering more. Because there are fewer of them and they are less willing to share than we are."

One night near the end of November, I was going home from May's with my father and Uncle George. We were walking because there was no money to buy gas for the cars. Uncle George had made a peppery speech to the men at the tavern and he was still in a buoyant mood, bouncing along on the balls of his feet, waving his arms about. My father was hunched over, as though a pain had hit him in the gut. "Something's got to happen soon," he told Uncle George. It was clear that he was ready to go back to work. "We can't go on like this much longer."

"Would you go crawling back to the factory on your belly?" Uncle George said. "Would you have the white man laugh in your face? As for me, I'd rather die of starvation than take less than we deserve."

He kept trying to cheer up my father as we walked along the lonely road. From time to time, a car whizzed past us in the night. Then a car pulled up behind us and four hooded men jumped out. "Run, David!" my father cried at once. But the suddenness of the attack left me paralyzed. Uncle George stepped back, ready to fight; but two of the men grabbed him while a third went to work on him with his fists. The fourth man scrambled for my father, who turned to run and fell into a ditch. The fourth man laughed and came for me. I fought him as best I could, but it was no use. He clobbered me in the face with a hard fist and my head felt like it was coming off. When I hit the ground, he went to join his partners in the attack on Uncle George.

From the way they concentrated on him, it was obvious that he was their central target. They held him in the glare of the headlights while they beat him. Two men held his arms pinned behind his body, but still he fought with his feet, kicking at the other men as they circled him cautiously and tried to connect. When they did hit him, they smashed blows on his head, chest and belly. Finally, Uncle George sagged in their arms like a rag doll and they let him fall to the ground. They kicked him, one after another, then they piled into their car and pulled away. I thought at first they had run over Uncle George, but they had barely avoided him. The moon was shining brightly and I could see the blood on his face and clothes. "Uncle George! Uncle George!" He was breathing heavily and his body felt almost broken as I wrapped my arms around him and dragged him to the edge of the road.

"Is he all right?" It was my father, panting at my elbow. I was filled with disgust for him, the way he'd run like a coward and dived into that ditch.

"He's unconscious," I said. "I think they hurt him bad."

Suddenly, my father started to cry. "I think I sprained my ankle," he said. I had never heard him cry before. He sounded so weak and miserable that I had to bite my lips to keep from screaming at him.

"We've got to get Uncle George home," I told him. "Then we can worry about your leg."

We eventually got Uncle George revived. And somehow we got him home, half carrying him, dragging him sometimes. My father moaned and whined like a

woman and I think it was his weakness that gave me
strength. We must have made a strange sight, the three
of us stumbling along the road, Uncle George reel-
ing between me and my father in the white moonlight. There was no doubt in my mind that the hooded
men had beaten Uncle George so terribly because
he was the leader of the strike. That thought was in
my father's mind, too. "I knew something like this
would happen," he complained. "I just knew it."

Uncle George was almost completely revived by
then. "Homer, why don't you shut your damned
mouth?" he said thickly. "If you . . . if those men . . .
think this beating's going to drive me back to work,
you've all got another thought coming."

"We can't go on like this!" my father said, limping along.

"We've got to go on," Uncle George said. He shook
his broad shoulders. "Let me alone. I can walk by myself." Although he freed himself from my father, he
still walked with his arm around me. "Did they hurt
you, David?"

"Not much," I said. I was proud now that I hadn't
run, even though that man had hit me.

"I think I sprained my ankle," my father said. He
had stopped crying, but he was still limping badly.

"You'll live," Uncle George said. "We're all going
to live."

Still my father complained. "I'm hungry," he said.
It sounded so irrelevant that I almost laughed in
his face. "I haven't had a good meal in days."

Uncle George did laugh. And I loved him then for
the fact that he could laugh, beaten and broken as
he was. "I think it's time we killed that hog of yours,

Homer. She's about the only thing left in Burnside for us to eat."

Hungry as he was, my father didn't seem too happy at the idea. "There must be another way, George. I've grown kind of fond of that sow."

"Homer, you're a damned fool," Uncle George said with heavy contempt. "The whole community's starving and you're worried about saving a sow's life. If we kill that hog, that'll give us a little more time. If they sent those men out to beat me up, it means they're getting more desperate than we are. I'll kill that sow tomorrow."

We were nearing the house. "You think you'll be able to?" my father said.

"I'll be able to. It'll take more than a beating to stop me."

My mother almost fainted when she saw us. After she collected herself, she worked on Uncle George first, because he was our worst casualty. She gave me a cold rag to hold against my jaw. While she worked on my father, I went outside and sat on the porch with Uncle George. "Don't think too hard of your father," he told me. "Sometimes a man can't help being the way he is."

The night air was cold, but I sat on the porch with Uncle George in a warm glow of contentment. We had both been beaten by the hooded men and this made me feel closer to him than ever before. So I was sorry when he stood up to go. "You sure you well enough to go home, Uncle George? Why don't you spend the night?"

"I feel fine," he said. "Just a little bit sore. Come on and walk with me a way."

I walked with him to the highway. "Suppose those men come back?" I said.

But he said they wouldn't come back. "They've done enough damage for one night. Now they'll wait to see what we're going to do." I asked him what we would do. "Tomorrow we're going to butcher that hog of your Daddy's, so everybody can have a good meal. You want to help me?"

I had never helped butcher a hog before, and I felt very excited. "Sure. I'd like that." I tried to keep my voice calm, because he was treating me like we were equal men. He even clapped me on the shoulder when we got to the highway.

"I'll see you tomorrow," he said. I told him good night and watched him walk down the highway until he became a part of the moon mist and then disappeared.

On the way home, I saw the ghost again. It seemed to me that he was crying. While I did not see his tears, it was something that I felt intensely—a sense of his sorrow and his weeping. "What do you want?" I whispered. "Why are you crying?"

And then it came to me that I was special among all the people of Burnside, for the ghost of Martin Luther King apparently walked only for me. Whatever his message was, whatever the reason for his prowling these roads, it was meant only for me.

At the same time that I was gladdened, I also felt sad. The burden of being the only one to see the ghost was almost too much to bear. And it seemed to me then that all there was for me in life was to live a little, perhaps to love, and then to die as shamefully as that sow would die, shot in the head, her throat slit, then parceled out among the community to be eaten and soon forgotten.

Was that the message of Martin Luther King to me—how desperate and violent and fragile life is? I did not know. My jaw still hurt from where the white man had hit me. But my shoulder still felt warm from the memory of Uncle George's hand when he'd told me good night. Apparently unaware of all this, the ghost walked steadily on. Then the light around him seemed to flicker for a moment, like a candle flame that is about to go out. And then he disappeared.

When I got home, my mother announced that my father's ankle was, indeed, sprained. She had wrapped it in bandages and he was sitting before the fire with his injured leg stretched across a chair. "Good God," my mother said. "There's no money, there's no food. What are we going to do?"

My father looked like he might break out in tears again. "Don't worry. George is going to kill the sow tomorrow."

That seemd to calm my mother some. Still she wrung her hands. "What are we going to do after that?" she cried. I went to bed and left them both staring into the fire, as though they might find there the answers to our problem.

The next morning, nearly everyone in our community gathered for the killing of the white sow. Most of them were dressed in rags and they milled around my mother like hungry animals waiting to be fed. She had on one of my father's old jackets and she was trying, without much success, to make a list of the people there and the parts of the sow that they would get after killing. "Just be calm, now," my mother said.

"Please. There's going to be enough for everybody."
But the neighbors pressed in excitedly around her,
some of them reminding her of past favors in order
to get a preferred spot on her list.

"Let's get on with the killing," somebody said. "It
looks like it might snow before long." The sky did
look threatening and full. Crows were screaming down
in the field where the corn used to be.

The crowd moved away from my mother and over
to the grindstone, where Uncle George and I were
whetting the butcher knife. I was turning the wheel
for him and he was concentrating on getting the blade
honed to just the right point. In daylight, his bruises
from the night before were blue-black and ugly,
scabbing over on his cheeks. "We'll get going in a
minute," he told the crowd. My father nodded. He
was checking out the rifle that we were going to
shoot the sow with before cutting her throat. "That
seems to be a waste of good ammunition," Uncle
George told my father. "As scarce as shot is."

"It's the law, George," my father said. "We've got
to shoot the sow in the head before we cut her
throat. S.P.C.A. regulations say so."

Uncle George gave a nasty laugh. "I know that.
Somebody ought to start a society for the prevention
of cruelty to us niggers. That'll be the day."

Everybody laughed except my father. "George, please
don't start that kind of talk right now. My ankle's
hurting me and I'm not in the mood for that kind of
talk."

Uncle George was through sharpening the knife.
Expectant now, the crowd moved in closer around us.
But Uncle George waved them back. "Give me room,"

he said. "There's only two bullets here and I don't want to miss."

"Lawd, don't miss," somebody said. "As hungry as I am."

Now everybody laughed, but it was apparent that they were all thinking the same thing. You could see the hunger stamped on their faces.

Uncle George cocked the rifle almost disdainfully. "A waste of good lead, if you ask me."

"Maybe I'd better do the shooting, George," my father said. "This ankle ain't as bad as all that. Or let David do it. He's a good shot."

"If the white man says shoot her," Uncle George said, "then I'll shoot her. I always do what the white man says." He gave me the butcher knife. "David, you better hold this. Now go along and open the pen."

"Be sure to shoot her square in the head," my father said. "I don't want her to suffer."

The sow stood sniffing the boards of the pen with her pink snout. "Open the pen, David," Uncle George said.

I yanked up the slats over the opening of the pen. Then I prodded the sow with the knife handle until she came lumbering into the yard. She weighed over two hundred pounds by now, but she was still light and easy on her feet. Uncle George shouted as the rifle cracked and jerked in his hands. I closed my eyes then, because I didn't want to see the sow squealing and kicking about on the ground.

"Damn!" my father cried; and the crowd shouted in unison. I opened my eyes. Uncle George had missed the sow. She was loping down the hill where the pea patch used to be.

I took off after the sow, and so did everybody else. They went screaming like savages into the woods. But Uncle George and I were far ahead of them. And the white sow was a good hundred yards ahead of us. Uncle George ran beside me, holding the rifle up over his head. He was grinning.

As for the other people, they fanned out through the woods, shrieking, beating every bush as though they were looking for a fugitive slave. From time to time, someone caught sight of the sow and the crowd scrambled in that direction. But the sow was as fleet and as elusive as a ghost, moving through the woods like a fat wraith.

Finally, Uncle George put his hands to his mouth and hollered. "Everybody go back to the house!" he cried "We'll never catch her this way!" He yelled and cursed until the people turned and went back up the hill in small, disappointed groups.

When the woods were clear, he and I walked on. The trees around us were barren; the ground was covered with leaves. We tried to walk quietly, but the leaves kept up a constant crackling under our feet. High over the naked trees, the sun glimmered whitely.

Then I spotted the sow in a thicket in front of us. Uncle George was looking the other way and I tugged at his belt to get his attention. "There she is," I whispered. I still had the butcher knife. I rammed it into ground and closed my eyes as Uncle George brought the rifle to his shoulder. I waited a long time for the rifle to go off, but when it didn't, I opened my eyes.

Uncle George just stood there, squinting down the length of the rifle barrel. Ahead of us, the sow was munching acorns, rooting about with her wet snout and grunting. "Aren't you going to shoot her?" I said.

Uncle George handed me the gun. "Gimme that goddamned knife," he said. I gave him the knife, hilt first. His face was so black and ugly now, I wondered that I had ever liked him.

Crouching, he crept through the woods toward the sow. When she raised her head and looked at him, Uncle George stopped. The sow inspected Uncle George; then she took a step away and went on nuzzling the ground. Uncle George glided toward her like a big black snake, holding the butcher knife in his right fist. But before he could get to her, she wheeled and crashed off deeper into the woods.

"What you looking at me like that for?" Uncle George said. "What the hell you looking at me like that for?"

"Nothing." He seemed like a complete stranger now, his bruised face angry and streaked with sweat.

"Go find that sow! Goddamn you, go find her!"

Her trail was easy to follow. She had cut through the grove of pines near the old watering branch. There was a fresh pile of dung on the path and Uncle George laughed when he saw it. But I didn't laugh or say anything, because he seemed just mad enough to hit me.

The sky had been white before, but it turned very gray now, with heavy clouds hiding the sun. And there was a sharp chill in the air, like it really was going to snow. As quietly as we could, Uncle George and I followed the white sow.

We saw her as we rounded the bend in the creek. She was on the other side of the creek, her short legs and underbelly dripping wet. She was standing in a cone-shaped area where the skeletons of touch-me-nots and honeysuckle grew. In front of her, where we stood, was the creek. Behind her was a barbed-wire fence that curved around to the water's edge on both sides. She was trapped and she didn't seem to know it. She was sniffing at dead vines that grew all around her.

When Uncle George splashed into the creek and started across, the sow raised her head and looked at him. Uncle George stepped up onto the bank and slid the knife out of his belt. The sow just looked at him.

Uncle George beckoned to the sow with his left arm. "Come on, white baby." He held the butcher knife in his right fist. "You come on to your black Daddy." The sow took a step toward him. "Come on, baby," he coaxed. The sow took another step toward him and he smiled.

Something in me exploded then like an angry balloon. Uncle George was an expert shot—he had taught me how to use the rifle—and he had deliberately missed that sow back at the house. For some cruel reason, he wanted to cut her throat without shooting her first. At the same time I realized that, I also knew that I had to stop him somehow. "Uncle George!" I splashed across the creek. "Uncle George, I'm going to tell Daddy on you!"

The sow sprang into action then. She skittered past Uncle George and was halfway across the creek before he grabbed her by the ear. The sow squealed and Uncle George laughed. "Easy, baby. You take it easy, now."

"I'm going to tell Daddy," I said. I felt like crying, watching him as he yanked the sow's head up and back, throwing his thick legs around her at the same time. She floundered in the water, squealing to high heaven, her white body sliding up and down between Uncle

George's legs. Then she reared out of the water on her hind legs, slashing the air with her front feet. Uncle George tightened his legs around her sides. I could see the terror in her eyes as she fought for her life.

Then a strange thing happened. Thunder rolled in over our heads, shattering the air like a turmoil of kettledrums gone wild. There is often thunder here before a storm, because of the mountains around us. But this was deep-throated, primeval, heavier than any I had ever heard before. It startled Uncle George, too. He was looking up; his hand with the knife stopped a few inches from the sow's throat. And while we stood there, frozen in an incredible tableau, the ghost of Martin Luther King appeared beside me and walked across the creek.

I almost threw the rifle away and ran. The thunder rolled again and the sky grew nearly as dark as night. Uncle George could not see the ghost, for he readied himself again to cut the sow's throat. But I saw the ghost very clearly. He knelt beside the sow and laid his hand against her throat.

He was saying something to me so clearly, even as I heard the first snow filtering softly down through the trees. "Uncle George!" I called to warn him as I lifted the rifle to my shoulder. The ghost was pointing now at the sow's head, leaning in an attitude of near supplication over the struggling animal.

"Uncle George!" He was steadily pulling the sow's head back, about to cut her throat. The ghost pointed. I aimed very carefully. And fired. And caught the sow squarely in the head, where the ghost was pointing. The sow leaped once and died. The ghost disappeared.

Blood splashed on Uncle George. He dropped the

sow and started for me. But I held the rifle on him. "Don't come any closer," I said. The rifle was empty, but he didn't seem to realize that.

"You goddamn fool," he said harshly. "You could've shot me."

"I know," I said. I could hardly talk. My throat felt pinched together and my mouth was sour. The snow was falling hard around us now, whispering through the trees like cold secrets. "You wanted to kill her because she was white," I said. It seemed a strange thing to accuse him of. Yet I knew it was true. "You hated her because she was white."

"Well, didn't *you?*" Uncle George said. He seemed angry and bewildered at the same time. The sow formed an obscene white lump behind him. I didn't know what to say, so I turned and went back toward home.

Some of the men went down to help Uncle George bring the sow to the house. They had built a fire in the yard and were boiling water in a large steel barrel. First they hung the sow by her heels from a low tree. My father cut her throat and some of the neighbors caught the blood in pots. They would use that to make blood pudding.

Then they took the sow down and dipped her into the barrel of boiling water to loosen her hair. When they pulled her out, she was steaming; and they went to work on her with knives and pieces of tin can, scraping off the hair.

The snow was falling steadily and heavily now; and the people beat their arms and blew into their hands to keep warm. I went inside and watched through the window while they butchered the sow and portioned her out. When Roberta got her piece of meat, she came in and stood beside me at the window.

There was snow everywhere, choking the woods, the roads, beating down on the black people as they trudged home with their portion of the white sow. Uncle George was the last one to leave. I watched him through the window as he went up the road, bent over under the oppression of snow swirling around him. My mother and father came inside, beating the snow out of their clothes. "I'm glad that's over," my mother said. She invited Roberta to stay and share what we had for dinner.

The strike at the factory ended several days after that, with management making a few token concessions that the black men were eager to accept. It snowed off and on for a week, and when it ended, the world around us was almost completely white, ugly in some places, beautiful in others.

I have not seen the ghost of Martin Luther King since that day in the woods, although I have looked for him from time to time. But I have not seen him; and all there is to do now is to look at the snow and to wait, with whatever patience I am capable of, until the sun comes again to hammer it into the ground.

A Lot You Got to Holler

BY NELSON ALGREN

I think I started stealing right after the old man threw Aunt out of the house. I was about eight, and used to look forward to her visit all week. She would dangle me on her knee, kiss me, and give me small coins: pennies and nickels and dimes. I remember her smell, the leather touch of her purse, and the warm touch of her hand when she pressed the coins into my hand. That smell, that purse, those kisses, and those coins were all something that belonged peculiarly to her, as she belonged peculiarly to me; for I never received, nor ever expected, those things from anyone else.

The last time I heard her voice was in the hallway, and sensed that she was pleading to kiss me good night. But the old man was in a high-wheeled huff and made her leave without saying good-by. Years later I learned she didn't even have a place to stay that night.

It must have been the next morning that I saw a neighbor woman's purse on a dresser and put it down the front of my shirt without even opening it. They found me sleeping under the back porch with the purse under my cheek like a pillow.

The old man gave me a sound whaling for stealing; but all the while he was slapping me around I had the conviction that I hadn't really done what I was being slapped around for. I felt that, if Aunt were there, she would say I hadn't done anything wrong. I felt, for the first time, that everything was wrong, all wrong.

I first began to believe, about that time, that Aunt was really my mother. It was a screwy, kid's sort of hope, and a hope that finally came true: I must have been about twelve when I learned that the old man had left her and married her younger sister. Don't ask me what he was thinking of, but that's what he did. When I was born, and Aunt had no way of taking care of me, he and the younger sister took me in. I guess the old man figured that was the cheapest way out. He always figured the cheapest way, no matter how much it cost in the long run or who had to pay off. That's how it was that I grew up remembering my mother as "Aunt" and calling my aunt "Ma."

And everything, in remembering her, was hooked up with the smell of her purse and the small coins of love it had carried: I didn't grow up thinking of pennies and nickels and dimes as such; I thought of them always, without fully realizing it, as love-pennies, love-nickels, and love-dimes. When I saved them, as a kid, I wasn't really saving money. Because when I'd realize that money was all they came to I'd break the bank and get rid of them at the nearest candy store as fast as I could spend. If the candy store was closed I'd give them away.

It wasn't always stealing either. Once, when I was about nine, I was going down Division Street flipping a dime. It slipped through my fingers and rolled off the curb into the gutter. When I stooped to pick it up I saw a quarter lying beside it. I looked to see if it had

Aunt's picture on it: it was years before I really ceased to believe that the woman's head on a quarter wasn't hers.

And for the next two weeks all I did was walk down Division flipping that lucky dime. I couldn't tell you yet whether I was looking for Aunt or another quarter. When I didn't find either I tried new sidewalks and strange streets. I got to know the whole Near Northwest Side that way. Then I lost the dime. And that, in a small way, was like losing Aunt all over.

But I began dreaming up other ways of finding quarters. Toward spring I decided that lots of kids must have lost money skating on the pond at Eckert Park during the winter. I went over there on the first day that the ice was melting and surveyed the slush inch by inch, although the soles of my shoes were paper-thin. I found four pennies, three dice, and tin of Prince Albert tobacco. The tin was rusted but the tobacco tasted interesting.

I was sick by evening and, in a fever, confessed about chewing the tobacco. That's the only time I remember admitting doing something wrong without getting whipped. I was too sick to whip.

But sick as I was, I didn't squeal about the four pennies. They were hidden. I was going to return them to Aunt, and I would have died before telling. I remember having a vague and feverish conviction that they were hers, because all the pennies and nickels in the world, somehow, really belonged to her.

By evening the doctor had to come: it wasn't the Prince Albert entirely. I'd caught cold from wading in the slush and it had gone into flu. That was the epidemic of 1917, I guess. Something has always happened to ruin my get-rich-quick schemes.

nd you can guess the rest: as soon as she'd finished
nother strawberry double-header the Pinkerton raced
o Ma. "Augie steals money every day," she told th
ld lady.

"A lot you got to holler, Sissie," I told her. "You
elped me spend it." I knew it wasn't any use saying
'd earned it selling the *Blade*. It was a beating either
vay.

Every time I was whipped unjustly I became lonely
or Aunt, and the next morning I started out looking
or her, to tell her how it was that nobody bothered
ou when you spent stolen money, except to help you
pend it; but that the pay-off came when you were
aught spending money you'd earned honestly. I
ouldn't figure that out, beyond feeling that my mis
ake had been in going to work at all. If I'd gone
earching around that broken board in the coalyard
ence, it seemed to me, instead of fooling around with
he *Blade*, I might have done better. At least I
vouldn't have been licked.

I had no idea where she lived, and so just wandered
round looking at houses and occasionally ringing a
loorbell in some blind hope that that might be the
lace she lived. I knew better than to ask Ma where
unt lived, because all Ma did when I mentioned
unt was to bawl.

It got so late that I was afraid to go home without
ome excuse. I'd been up and down streets and alleys
he whole morning and most of the afternoon. And
ow the red headlines of the *Blade*, which had been
eaturing kidnap stories, came to my mind. Toward
ark I stopped in an alley, found a piece of glass, and
ave myself a long scratch down my right arm. The

Toward the end of that summer I was coming home
from a swimming pool in Little Italy, about a mile
away, where kids could swim for a penny. I remember
that my swimming suit was still wet under my clothes
and that I took a short cut across the Northwestern
tracks. There was a long board fence bounding the
coalyard there, in those years, and as I passed a place
where a board was missing a kid poked his head out
and hissed, "Hey, you, c'mere," as though he'd been
expecting me. I'd never seen the kid before. He was
about seven, I guess.

He squatted down in the weeds and came up with a
green bandanna in which lay eight singles and some
small change. "That's your part," he tells me, and gives
me half the bills and half the change. He'd taken it
all out of a Northwestern caboose, and he knew it was
stealing as well as I. That was why he'd called me: to
share his guilt.

Only, I didn't feel guilty. I'd already had my beating
for stealing so what I had in my hand had been well
paid for. I felt as though somebody, maybe God, had
owed me this for a long time and it was only in the
natural run of things that it should come my way at
last. And as I stood there the warmth of the coins,
that had been lying in summer sunlight, spread from
my palm through my whole body; for Aunt's warmth
was in all coins. When I closed my fist over them I was
enclosing her hand, and in that moment they became
so precious to me that my fingernails dug into the flesh
as if I never wanted to open my hand again. Then I
thought of the old man and flattened the bills and
stuffed them into my rolled sleeves. I don't know
where I got the idea to do that, but kids raised on
crowded corners get cunning pretty early.

I wandered around looking for kids I knew and found half a dozen ragged strays lagging beer corks on the corner of Allen Street. With a prissy-looking eleven-year-old blonde watching in solemn disapproval. I knew her. She lived next door and spent half her life, it seemed to me, on the alert for me to do something wrong in order to report it to the old man. If I spent a penny a mile away she'd learn of it and I'd become entangled in such a web of lies, trying to duck another beating, that I wouldn't know myself what the truth was.

So I stood there, with the most money I'd ever had in my life and just as unable to buy anything with it as though all the ice-cream parlors had closed for keeps. My bathing suit began to itch.

Kids are sly all right. There wasn't any use waiting for her to leave. She'd find out anyhow. So when no one was looking I dropped a dollar in the dirt and hollered, "Oh boy! Look what I found!" The lagging stopped.

"Augie found a dollar! We were all here'n nobody seen it but Augie! Augie the lucky eagle-eye!"

So here we all go to the ice-cream store, with the kids crowding around me and the prissy blonde following like a little Pinkerton. I bought two cones for myself first and alternated at licking them—one chocolate and one vanilla. I didn't like strawberry even then.

I don't think all the kids got cones, because there must have been at least forty swarming into the store by that time.

The blonde got one though. A strawberry double-header.

When the lagging was resumed and the excitement had subsided I felt a crying need for more ice cream.

It was getting toward suppertime but I hated home, even to rid myself of the itching bathing felt a couple more cones would keep me going hours.

This time I played it safe. I only used a half which seemed then only half as wrong.

"Look! A halfer! Am I lucky today you!"

"Is he lucky today you. Lucky Augie the eag And so back to the ice-cream store.

When I came out of the house the next half a dozen kids were waiting for me. Kids I' seen before from way over on Chicago Avenu didn't say anything, but they followed me so c was impossible to lose a penny without being the act. And, of course, the twenty-four-hour ton, the eye that never slept, a little taller th of the other kids, still shadowing me and still as ever.

The sprouts followed my very eyes: if I toward a telephone pole they would race th search the alley for yards around. The blond search. She was hep. She just watched my poc my hands.

It didn't do her any good, because I started beer corks with the other kids until her inte dered to other suspects on whom she was keep And that evening I earned seventy-five cents Saturday Evening Blade on the corner of Avenue and Ashland.

The same kids were waiting for me the ing, and I spent every dime of the Saturd Blade money on them before noon, to m far-flung reputation as an easy spender. S single morning broke all local records for

kidnapers had done that, I would tell Ma, when I was struggling to get away.

That's one you'll have to figure out for yourself; but I don't think I really did it to pass myself off as a kidnaped kid. Nor entirely to get out of a beating, either. I think that, at bottom, I had the hope of getting sympathy out of the old man.

It turned out to be the worst beating I'd ever had, and I know I never tried for anyone's sympathy again. After that, I'm sure, I was entirely on my own. After that, so far as myself and the old man were concerned, it was strictly warfare.

But I still feel that, if I could, somehow, have seen Aunt that day, things might have turned out different. I think she might have kept things from getting mixed up, at least until I was grown enough to figure them out for myself. But I didn't see her, and when things got mixed up that day they stayed mixed for keeps.

We grew out of the beer-cork stage into lagging for ten-a-penny pictures of baseball players. Like the beer corks, some of these had a larger value than others: I remember trading an entire strip of ten to get just one of Joe Jackson. And a month later, when Jackson had been kicked out of organized baseball, I had to give one of him, one of Buck Weaver, and two Happy Felschs just to get one Ray Schalk—who'd been on the original strip I'd traded for Shoeless Joe in the first place.

When we started lagging for pennies we forgot about the baseball players, and nobody cared any more whether Ray Schalk was a good guy or a bad guy anyhow. The feeling grew that he may have been a sucker.

Who'd gotten the pay roll? that's what we wanted to know now.

We drifted into the crap games behind the Anderson School, and when the cops started breaking them up the attraction became irresistible. Once a dozen of us spent an afternoon in the Racine Avenue Station because the kid we'd set up as a lookout had wandered off to match nickels with the corner newsie. It was a hot afternoon, and our numbers gave us courage. We heckled the cops, and were really proud of being jailbirds. How did we kill the afternoon when the cops ignored us? You guessed it again. I lost forty-six cents.

When I got home Sissie had already told my old man where I'd been. But the whipping was nothing at all compared to the sense of manhood attained by an afternoon in the clink. It was the most exciting thing that had ever happened to us. For days we bragged to each other about our various parts in the escapade: who was the most scared, who wasn't scared at all, and whose brother, right now, was doing ninety days in County. For us the kid whose brother was doing a stretch was as distinguished as a kid in another neighborhood whose brother was a college football star.

This was all in the days when newspapers were a penny apiece and we had a lot of dodges around the stands. When the race-track and baseball fans handed you a nickel, they'd grab the sheet and stare at the results, with one hand held out blindly for their change. The dodge was to lay a penny in the waiting hand, click a second penny on the first and the third on the second; but the last penny was just clicked, without dropping it. The fellow would shove the change in his pocket and never know he'd been gypped.

Sometimes, if a customer didn't have anything smaller than a nickel or a dime, we'd plead that we had no change and go into the nearest saloon to get it. Then we'd duck out the Ladies' Entrance, leaving the sucker waiting in front.

When the streetcar was waiting for a red light we'd run up alongside the car and some guy would stick his hand out for a paper. If he offered a nickel or a dime we'd fumble and dig for that change until the car started, and then run beside the car with the change trying to reach the fellow's hand but never, somehow, quite making it. That only failed me once. A guy got off at the next stop and came back for the change. A tinhorn.

Around Christmas the big paper guys had cards printed and sold them to us little paper guys for a nickel apiece. The cards read, if I remember rightly:

> *Christmas comes but once a year*
> *And when it comes it brings good cheer*
> *So open your purse without a tear*
> *And remember the newsboy standing here.*

Sometimes that one was good for as much as a quarter. But this was the pay-off: we had to ask for the card back, because it cost us a nickel, and the customer would be thinking it was his, that he'd bought it. We called the big paper guys the Knothole Wonders, I don't remember why.

There were no stands in those days; the papers were just piled on the corners with stones on them, and every corner pile was run by some big guy. If a little guy sold a paper, it had to be in the middle of the block. But I remember selling a paper to a woman on the corner of Robey and Division, right under a big guy's nose.

I never tried that again. I had to buy the paper back from the big guy—and got a kick that was positively terrific. It lifted me off the ground and scattered my papers for yards. I didn't even take time to howl while gathering them up in the rush of noontime traffic—I was so afraid of losing those papers. But when I got home it really began hurting, and I cried all night.

And every time I saw the big paper guy, for a year after, I would still feel that kick. Sometimes I can still feel it.

And sometimes one of the big guys would make a deal with one of the little guys. He would say, "Hey, sprout, you want to buy me out tonight?" That meant buying him out around midnight, when the final lull began, at the wholesale price.

I made a deal like that once, but along about 1 A.M. it turned bitterly cold, and I had more papers left than I could sell in a week of Saturday nights. I was stuck. So I started to bawl, too cold to stand still and too afraid to go home. Just wandered around, wiping my nose on my sleeve and bawling, making people pause to ask what the matter was. I sold out, bawling the whole time. And had enough tears left over to help one of the other kids get rid of his papers too. I must have been nine or ten by that time.

If there wasn't anything in the headlines to yell about we just hollered, "Big Whitehouse scandal! Big Whitehouse scandal!" I thought the Whitehouse was the Derby Hotel, where the big guys went to see the big girls. It had white doors and a long white marble desk.

One afternoon when I was about thirteen I delivered a couple papers up there, to the third floor, and saw a woman in a kimono come down the hall whom I took for Aunt. I said, "Hello, Aunt," with such a hope of happiness in me I've never felt since. I don't think I'll ever come that close again. But she didn't answer and she didn't look around, and I had to believe it wasn't her after all.

But in later years I figured it this way: if it really *hadn't* been her, she would have turned when I called. She would have turned her head to see who'd called her. I figure now she was afraid to turn her head.

I went up there a number of times after that, under the pretense of delivering a paper, and wandered the long plush-carpeted hall listening to the laughter of women behind many doors, hoping always to hear Aunt's laughter. It was dark in the hallway, that was why she hadn't recognized me, I had decided. It had been so long since I'd seen her, I'd grown so much taller, that was why she hadn't recognized me. I spent so much time up there that the desk man made me leave the papers at the desk. He thought I was up to something else.

That's how it's always been: I was always in the clear so long as I was truly guilty. But the minute my motives were honest someone would finger me.

Another way we used to raise money was to go to the market and get those big empty barrels—not the casks, the barrels. The bigger guys could carry them, but we little guys rolled them. They rolled easy, and the meat packers paid us a nickel each for them. We couldn't find enough of them, naturally; so we'd steal them from one packer and sell them to another.

I must have been about fourteen when I made sudden friends with a kid who had a nice home. I don't remember the kid, but I remember the home, which was clean and bright all day, and his mother, who was handsome. It was a third-floor flat somewhere, with lots of plants in the front room with the sunlight on them. He had a puppy and we used to play with it up there. It's the first memory I have of being happy, playing with that pup in that pleasant place.

We must have been making a lot of noise, because this kid's mother walked past and said jokingly, to make us be a little quiet, "Why don't you kids just throw that dog out of the window?" I was so happy at just being there, so overwhelmed with an eagerness to please, that I picked up the pup, walked to the window and threw it out. Just like that.

I can still see that poor damned pup sprawling and turning and pawing for a foothold in mid-air on its way down to the pavement. And felt, suddenly, that I was falling too.

I was falling all right. But I was sixteen before I hit the ground. It happened the week after the old man told me that Aunt was dead, and I guess a kid still has a right to tears at that age. But I didn't shed one. I had some twisted idea that that would give the old man some sort of satisfaction. I just dummied up on him.

He was so puzzled because I didn't bawl, or even look like I felt bad, that he followed me out of the room to tell me that she was really my mother.

"I knew that eight years ago," I told him straight. "I knew she was my old lady the night you threw her out. But you were never my old man." Of course he was all right. I was just trying to make him feel like he was trying to make me feel.

He started blowing up and told me to get out. I knew he didn't mean it, because I was bringing him the rent. "If I left now," I told him, "you'd have me locked up. I'll wait till I'm of age. Then I'll see you in hell with your back broke."

"I'll be glad to get rid of you now," he tells me. "You're going to go bad, you might as well go now and get a good start."

"And you won't have me locked up for running away?"

"Why should I?" he asks. "All you been to me is trouble."

"What do you think you've been to me?" I asked him then. "A father? A lot you got to holler." And I grabbed my cap and left.

I took a room with Little Johnny Polish over on Western Avenue. Johnny called himself a juke-box mechanic, and he had a car. We went around fixing jukes whenever we got on the shorts. We really fixed them, too. Only, sometimes we'd make a mistake and hit some juke we'd already fixed once. We did that once in a bookie, of all places.

A tavern with a bookie in the back. I thought it looked familiar, but Johnny didn't say anything so we went right ahead. On the way out the bartender, who knew Johnny, called him over and said something, looking a little white. When we got in the car Johnny looked white too and I really wheeled out of there.

"They're gettin' tired of us in there," Johnny said after a while. "That's a syndicate box."

We didn't go near that joint again and were more careful altogether. We operated out of the neighborhood until the syndicate cooled off. And sometimes we'd have so many dimes, nickels, and quarters up in the room that we wouldn't even bother to divide them. We got a scale and weighed them. I remember we figured eleven ounces to the dollar.

The first time I took a fall I was alone, having coffee at a restaurant on Damen and Division. They sat down, one on either side of me, and the first thing that popped into my head was that they were syndicate men dressed like coppers. Something like that had happened in the neighborhood before.

They were real cops though. I had to sweat it out at Eleventh and State overnight and stand the showup before I found out that all it was was the old man. He'd reneged on his word to me, just as he had with Aunt. He'd given me out as a runaway and I had to put in twenty days at Juvenile.

All I remember of that stretch is this: when we came in we were given a copy of the rules, told to make the best of things, and that was all the interest any of us received there.

The night I got out I slugged a peanut machine—one of those El platform jobs. It was in the dark, at the far end of the platform, and all I went up to the thing for was to get a handful of peanuts. But when I put my hand on the lever I felt the warmth of the day still trapped in the metal, and the warmth of Aunt's hand pressing pennies into my hand—before I knew what I was doing I'd slugged the glass with my naked fist.

It was absolutely crazy and I don't understand it myself to this day. I cut the hell out of my hand and a woman at the cashier's cage heard the tinkle of the glass. I would have been a lot smarter to have slugged her instead of the peanuts.

That was the only time I used raw-jaw methods. Rip-and-tear is all right for kids, but there's no future in it.

Johnny Polish laughed his head off over that one when he came up to see me at County. Then he had the ward superintendent put in the fix and all I got was thirty days. I was paroled to my old man. What a laugh.

I've never figured out to myself why I pinned everything onto the old man. Sometimes I think I started blaming him before I was born almost. It wasn't anything I tried figuring at all, it was just the way I *felt*, so deep down that it was beyond all figuring.

I used to wake up nights thinking of the night he'd given her the bum's rush when she didn't have a place to go. Except, perhaps, the Derby Hotel. When I thought of *that* I think I could have killed him as quick as stepping on a roach. And that easy.

And yet by that time it wouldn't have done me any more good than stepping on a roach. When I came out of County I had him where I could have stepped on him any time. Like it says in the song, I had him in the palm of my hand.

All I did was lay around the house smoking cigarettes and playing the radio loud and never letting the old man tune in the Polish hour, because that was the one program, I knew, which he understood and enjoyed. In fact it was the only thing he enjoyed and the one thing he'd bought the radio for. I'd turn on Spike Jones and he'd sit in the kitchen and drink and take it out on Ma. That was their business, so long as they stayed in the kitchen. He wanted me home, he'd told the police. So now he had me there. He wasn't in much of a position to tell them he'd changed his mind.

Some nights I'd have half the neighborhood in the front room. Little Johnny'd bring up a couple of neighborhood tramps and the joint would really jump. One night, just to get his goat, we started a strip-poker game. The old man lost his head and called the squad.

Little Johnny asked them in, and they saw who was there beside the tramps: the ward super, two precinct captains, Little Johnny, a Jew mouthpiece we called Noseberg O'Brien, and a bailiff from the Criminal Court. They asked us to be a little quiet about it and we slipped them a fin apiece, and they backed off. With all the writs and corpuses Noseberg O'Brien had in his hat, they were lucky to get out with their jobs, coming into a private home without a warrant like that.

After the party broke up I told the old man, polite-like, in Polish, that if he ever did a thing like that again they'd find him under the sink with his little toes turned up. Under the sink, with the rest of the pipes. But letting a roach go don't make you like him any more the next time you see him come crawlin'.

He *begged* me to leave then, and promised he wouldn't have me brought back.

"What's the use?" I said. "You'd have me locked up all over again is all."

"This time I won't," he said. And that time I knew he meant it at last. He had a stomachful of Little Augie by then.

I stayed home that night, and when I was packing, in the morning, he stuck his mug in the door and watched awhile, to see that I wasn't taking anything that belonged to him.

"You gonna die in jail, Augie," he tells me after a while, just to say something.

"You never cared where I lived," I told him, "a lot you got to holler where I die."

And I remembered how she had wanted to say good-by to me one night in this same house and he hadn't let her.

I didn't even say so long.

The Old Chief Mshlanga

BY DORIS LESSING

They were good, the years of ranging the bush over her father's farm which, like every white farm, was largely unused, broken only occasionally by small patches of cultivation. In between, nothing but trees, the long sparse grass, thorn and cactus and gully, grass and outcrop and thorn. And a jutting piece of rock which had been thrust up from the warm soil of Africa unimaginable eras of time ago, washed into hollows and whorls by sun and wind that had travelled so many thousands of miles of space and bush, would hold the weight of a small girl whose eyes were sightless for anything but a pale willowed river, a pale gleaming castle—a small girl singing: "Out flew the web and floated wide, the mirror cracked from side to side . . ."

Pushing her way through the green aisles of the mealie stalks, the leaves arching like cathedrals veined with sunlight far overhead, with the packed red earth underfoot, a fine lace of red starred witchweed would summon up a black bent figure croaking premonitions: the Northern witch, bred of cold Northern forests, would stand before her among the mealie fields, and it was the mealie fields that faded and fled, leaving her among the gnarled roots of an oak, snow falling thick and soft and white, the woodcutter's fire glowing red welcome through crowding tree trunks.

A white child, opening its eyes curiously on a sun-suffused landscape, a gaunt and violent landscape, might be supposed to accept it as her own, to take the msasa trees and the thorn trees as familiars, to feel her blood running free and responsive to the swing of the seasons.

This child could not see a msasa tree, or the thorn, for what they were. Her books held tales of alien fairies, her rivers ran slow and peaceful, and she knew the shape of the leaves of an ash or an oak, the names of the little creatures that lived in English streams, when the words "the veld" meant strangeness, though she could remember nothing else.

Because of this, for many years, it was the veld that seemed unreal; the sun was a foreign sun, and the wind spoke a strange language.

The black people on the farm were as remote as the trees and the rocks. They were an amorphous black mass, mingling and thinning and massing like tadpoles, faceless, who existed merely to serve, to say "Yes, Baas," take their money and go. They changed season by season, moving from one farm to the next, according to their outlandish needs, which one did not have to understand, coming from perhaps hundreds of miles North or East, passing on after a few months—where? Perhaps even as far away as the fabled gold mines of Johannesburg, where the pay was so much better than the few shillings a month and the double handful of mealie meal twice a day which they earned in that part of Africa.

The child was taught to take them for granted: the servants in the house would come running a hundred yards to pick up a book if she dropped it. She was called "Nkosikaas"—Chieftainess, even by the black children her own age.

Later, when the farm grew too small to hold her curiosity, she carried a gun in the crook of her arm and wandered miles a day, from vlei to vlei, from *kopje* to *kopje,* accompanied by two dogs: the dogs and the gun were an armor against fear. Because of them she never felt fear.

If a native came into sight along the kaffir paths half a mile away, the dogs would flush him up a tree as if he were a bird. If he expostulated (in his uncouth language which was by itself ridiculous) that was cheek. If one was in a good mood, it could be a matter for laughter. Otherwise one passed on, hardly glancing at the angry man in the tree.

On the rare occasions when white children met together they could amuse themselves by hailing a passing native in order to make a buffoon of him; they could set the dogs on him and watch him run; they could tease a small black child as if he were a puppy —save that they would not throw stones and sticks at a dog without a sense of guilt.

Later still, certain questions presented themselves in the child's mind; and because the answers were not easy to accept, they were silenced by an even greater arrogance of manner.

It was even impossible to think of the black people who worked about the house as friends, for if she talked to one of them, her mother would come running anxiously: "Come away; you mustn't talk to natives."

It was this instilled consciousness of danger, of something unpleasant, that made it easy to laugh out loud, crudely, if a servant made a mistake in his English or if he failed to understand an order—there is a certain kind of laughter that is fear, afraid of itself.

One evening, when I was about fourteen, I was walking down the side of a mealie field that had been newly ploughed, so that the great red clods showed fresh and tumbling to the vlei beyond, like a choppy red sea; it was that hushed and listening hour, when the birds send long sad calls from tree to tree, and all the colors of earth and sky and leaf are deep and golden. I had my rifle in the curve of my arm, and the dogs were at my heels.

In front of me, perhaps a couple of hundred yards away, a group of three Africans came into sight around the side of a big antheap. I whistled the dogs close in to my skirts and let the gun swing in my hand, and advanced, waiting for them to move aside, off the path, in respect for my passing. But they came on steadily, and the dogs looked up at me for the command to chase. I was angry. It was "cheek" for a native not to stand off a path, the moment he caught sight of you.

In front walked an old man, stooping his weight on to a stick, his hair grizzled white, a dark red blanket slung over his shoulders like a cloak. Behind him came two young men, carrying bundles of pots, assegais, hatchets.

The group was not a usual one. They were not natives seeking work. These had an air of dignity, of quietly following their own purpose. It was the dignity that checked my tongue. I walked quietly on, talking softly to the growling dogs, till I was ten paces away.

Then the old man stopped, drawing his blanket close.

"Morning, Nkosikaas," he said, using the customary greeting for any time of the day.

"Good morning," I said. "Where are you going?" My voice was a little truculent.

The old man spoke in his own language, then one of the young men stepped forward politely and said in careful English: "My Chief travels to see his brothers beyond the river."

A Chief! I thought, understanding the pride that made the old man stand before me like an equal— more than an equal, for he showed courtesy, and I showed none.

The old man spoke again, wearing dignity like an inherited garment, still standing ten paces off, flanked by his entourage, not looking at me (that would have been rude) but directing his eyes somewhere over my head at the trees.

"You are the little Nkosikaas from the farm of Baas Jordan?"

"That's right," I said.

"Perhaps your father does not remember," said the interpreter for the old man, "but there was an affair with some goats. I remember seeing you when you were . . ." The young man held his hand at knee level and smiled.

We all smiled.

"What is your name?" I asked.

"This is Chief Mshlanga," said the young man.

"I will tell my father that I met you," I said.

The old man said: "My greetings to your father, little Nkosikaas."

"Good morning," I said politely, finding the politeness difficult, from lack of use.

"Morning, little Nkosikaas," said the old man, and stood aside to let me pass.

I went by, my gun hanging awkwardly, the dogs sniffling and growling, cheated of their favorite game of chasing natives like animals.

Not long afterwards I read in an old explorer's book the phrase: "Chief Mshlanga's country." It went like this: "Our destination was Chief Mshlanga's country, to the north of the river and it was our desire to ask his permission to prospect for gold in his territory."

The phrase "ask his permission" was so extraordinary to a white child, brought up to consider all natives as things to use, that it revived those questions, which could not be suppressed: they fermented slowly in my mind.

On another occasion one of those old prospectors who still move over Africa looking for neglected reefs, with their hammers and tents, and pans for sifting gold from crushed rock, came to the farm and, in talking of the old days, used that phrase again: "This was the Old Chief's country," he said. "It stretched from those mountains over there way back to the river, hundreds of miles of country." That was his name for our district: "The Old Chief's Country"; he did not use our name for it—a new phrase which held no implication of usurped ownership.

As I read more books about the time when this part of Africa was opened up, not much more than fifty years before, I found Old Chief Mshlanga had been a famous man, known to all the explorers and prospectors. But then he had been young; or maybe it was his father or uncle they spoke of—I never found out.

During that year I met him several times in the part of the farm that was traversed by natives moving over the country. I learned that the path up the side of the big red field where the birds sang was the recognized highway for migrants. Perhaps I even haunted it in the hope of meeting him: being greeted by him, the exchange of courtesies, seemed to answer the questions that troubled me.

Soon I carried a gun in a different spirit; I used it for shooting food and not to give me confidence. And now the dogs learned better manners. When I saw a native approaching, we offered and took greetings; and slowly that other landscape in my mind faded, and my feet struck directly on the African soil, and I saw the shapes of tree and hill clearly, and the black people moved back, as it were, out of my life: it was as if I stood aside to watch a slow intimate dance of landscape and men, a very old dance, whose steps I could not learn.

But I thought: this is my heritage, too; I was bred here; it is my country as well as the black man's country; and there is plenty of room for all of us, without elbowing each other off the pavements and roads.

It seemed it was only necessary to let free that respect I felt when I was talking with old Chief Mshlanga, to let both black and white people meet gently, with tolerance for each other's differences: it seemed quite easy.

Then, one day, something new happened. Working in our house as servants were always three natives: cook, houseboy, garden boy. They used to change as the farm natives changed: staying for a few months, then moving on to a new job, or back home to their kraals. They were thought of as "good" or "bad" natives; which meant: how did they behave as servants? Were they lazy, efficient, obedient, or disrespectful? If the family felt good-humored, the phrase was: "What can you expect from raw black savages?" If we were angry, we said: "These damned niggers, we would be much better off without them."

One day, a white policeman was on his rounds of the district, and he said laughingly: "Did you know you have an important man in your kitchen?"

"What!" exclaimed my mother sharply. "What do you mean?"

"A Chief's son." The policeman seemed amused. "He'll boss the tribe when the old man dies."

"He'd better not put on a Chief's son act with me," said my mother.

When the policeman left, we looked with different eyes at our cook: he was a good worker, but he drank too much at week-ends—that was how we knew him.

He was a tall youth, with very black skin, like black polished metal, his tightly-growing black hair parted white man's fashion at one side, with a metal comb from the store stuck into it; very polite, very distant, very quick to obey an order. Now that it had been pointed out, we said: "Of course, you can see. Blood always tells."

My mother became strict with him now she knew about his birth and prospects. Sometimes, when she lost her temper, she would say: "You aren't the Chief yet, you know." And he would answer her very quietly, his eyes on the ground: "Yes, Nkosikiaas."

One afternoon he asked for a whole day off, instead of the customary half-day, to go home next Sunday.

"How can you go home in one day?"

"It will take me half an hour on my bicycle," he explained.

I watched the direction he took; and the next day I went off to look for this kraal; I understood he must be Chief Mshlanga's successor: there was no other kraal near enough our farm.

Beyond our boundaries on that side the country was new to me. I followed unfamiliar paths past *kopjes* that till now had been part of the jagged horizon, hazed with distance. This was Government land, which had never been cultivated by white men: at first I could not understand why it was that it appeared, in merely crossing the boundary, I had entered a completely fresh type of landscape. It was a wide green valley, where a small river sparkled, and vivid water-birds darted over the rushes. The grass was thick and soft to my calves, the trees stood tall and shapely.

I was used to our farm, whose hundreds of acres of harsh eroded soil bore trees that had been cut for the mine furnaces and had grown thin and twisted, where the cattle had dragged the grass flat, leaving innumerable criss-crossing trails that deepened each season into gullies, under the force of the rains.

This country had been left untouched, save for prospectors whose picks had struck a few sparks from the surface of the rocks as they wandered by; and for migrant natives whose passing had left, perhaps, a charred patch on the trunk of a tree where their evening fire had nestled.

It was very silent: a hot morning with pigeons cooing throatily, the midday shadows lying dense and thick with clear yellow spaces of sunlight between and in all that wide green park-like valley, not a human soul but myself.

I was listening to the quick regular tapping of a woodpecker when slowly a chill feeling seemed to grow up from the small of my back to my shoulders, in a constricting spasm like a shudder, and at the roots of my hair a tingling sensation began and ran down over the surface of my flesh, leaving me goosefleshed and cold, though I was damp with sweat. Fever? I thought; then uneasily, turned to look over my shoulder; and realized suddenly that this was fear. It was extraordinary, even humiliating. It was a new fear. For all the years I had walked by myself over this country I had never known a moment's uneasiness; in the beginning because I had been supported by a gun and the dogs, then because I had learnt an easy friendliness for the Africans I might encounter.

I had read of this feeling, how the bigness and silence of Africa, under the ancient sun, grows dense and takes shape in the mind, till even the birds seem to call menacingly, and a deadly spirit comes out of the trees and the rocks. You move warily, as if your very passing disturbs something old and evil, something dark and big and angry that might suddenly rear and strike from behind. You look at groves of entwined trees, and picture the animals that might be lurking there; you look at the river running slowly, dropping from level to level through the vlei, spreading into pools where at night the bucks come to drink, and the crocodiles rise and drag them by their soft noses into underwater caves. Fear possessed me. I found I was turning round and round, because of that shapeless menace behind me that might reach out and take me; I kept glancing at the files of *kopjes* which, seen from a different angle, seemed to change with every step so that even known landmarks, like a big mountain that had sentinelled my world since I first became conscious of it, showed an unfamiliar sun-lit valley among its foothills. I did not know where I was. I was lost. Panic seized me. I found I was spinning round and round, staring anxiously at this tree and that, peering up at the sun which appeared to have moved into an eastern slant, shedding the sad yellow light of sunset. Hours must have passed! I looked at my watch and found that this state of meaningless terror had lasted perhaps ten minutes.

The point was that it was meaningless. I was not ten miles from home: I had only to take my way back along the valley to find myself at the fence; away among the foothills of the *kopjes* gleamed the roof of a neighbor's house, and a couple of hours' walking would reach it. This was the sort of fear that contracts the flesh of a dog at night and sets him howling at the full moon. It had nothing to do with what I thought or felt; and I was more disturbed by the fact that I could become its victim than of the physical sensation itself: I walked steadily on, quietened, in a divided mind, watching my own pricking nerves and apprehensive glances from side to side with a disgusted amusement. Deliberately I set myself to think of this village I was seeking, and what I should do when I entered it—if I could find it, which was doubtful, since I was walking aimlessly and it might be anywhere in the hundreds of thousands of acres of bush that stretched about me. With my mind on that village, I realized that a new sensation was added to the fear: loneliness. Now such a terror of isolation invaded me that I could hardly walk; and if it were

not that I came over the crest of a small rise and saw
a village below me, I should have turned and gone
home. It was a cluster of thatched huts in a clearing
among trees. There were neat patches of mealies and
pumpkins and millet, and cattle grazed under some
trees at a distance. Fowls scratched among the huts,
dogs lay sleeping on the grass, and goats friezed a *kopje*
that jutted up beyond a tributary of the river lying
like an enclosing arm round the village.

As I came close I saw the huts were lovingly dec-
orated with patterns of yellow and red and ochre mud
on the walls; and the thatch was tied in place with
plaits of straw.

This was not at all like our farm compound, a dirty
and neglected place, a temporary home for migrants
who had no roots in it.

And now I did not know what to do next. I called
a small black boy, who was sitting on a lot playing
a stringed gourd, quite naked except for the strings of
blue beads round his neck, and said: "Tell the Chief
I am here." The child stuck his thumb in his mouth
and stared shyly back at me.

For minutes I shifted my feet on the edge of what
seemed a deserted village, till at last the child scuttled
off, and then some women came. They were draped
in bright cloths, with brass glinting in their ears and
on their arms. They also stared, silently; then turned
to chatter among themselves.

I said again: "Can I see Chief Mshlanga?" I saw
they caught the name; they did not understand what
I wanted. I did not understand myself.

At last I walked through them and came past the
huts and saw a clearing under a big shady tree, where
a dozen old men sat cross-legged on the ground, talk-

ing. Chief Mshlanga was leaning back against the tree, holding a gourd in his hand, from which he had been drinking. When he saw me, not a muscle of his face moved, and I could see he was not pleased: perhaps he was afflicted with my own shyness, due to being unable to find the right forms of courtesy for the occasion. To meet me, on our own farm, was one thing; but I should not have come here. What had I expected? I could not join them socially: the thing was unheard of. Bad enough that I, a white girl, should be walking the veld alone as a white man might: and in this part of the bush where only Government officials had the right to move.

Again I stood, smiling foolishly, while behind me stood the groups of brightly-clad, chattering women, their faces alert with curiosity and interest, and in front of me sat the old men, with old lined faces, their eyes guarded, aloof. It was a village of ancients and children and women. Even the two young men who kneeled beside the Chief were not those I had seen with him previously: the young men were all away working on the white men's farms and mines, and the Chief must depend on relatives who were temporarily on holiday for his attendants.

"The small white Nkosikaas is far from home," remarked the old man at last.

"Yes," I agreed, "it is far." I wanted to say: "I have come to pay you a friendly visit, Chief Mshlanga." I could not say it. I might now be feeling an urgent helpless desire to get to know these men and women as people, to be accepted by them as a friend, but the truth was I had set out in a spirit of curiosity: I had wanted to see the village that one day our cook, the reserved and obedient young man who got drunk on Sundays, would one day rule over.

"The child of Nkosi Jordan is welcome," said Chief Mshlanga.

"Thank you," I said, and could think of nothing more to say. There was a silence, while the flies rose and began to buzz around my head; and the wind shook a little in the thick green tree that spread its branches over the old men.

"Good morning," I said at last. "I have to return now to my home."

"Morning, little Nkosikaas," said Chief Mshlanga.

I walked away from the indifferent village, over the rise past the staring amber-eyed goats, down through the tall stately trees into the great rich green valley where the river meandered and the pigeons cooed tales of plenty and the woodpecker tapped softly.

The fear had gone; the loneliness had set into stiff-necked stoicism; there was now a queer hostility in the landscape, a cold, hard, sullen indomitability that walked with me, as strong as a wall, as intangible as smoke; it seemed to say to me: you walk here as a destroyer. I went slowly homewards, with an empty heart: I had learned that if one cannot call a country to heel like a dog, neither can one dismiss the past with a smile in an easy gush of feeling, saying: I could not help it, I am also a victim.

I only saw Chief Mshlanga once again.

One night my father's big red land was trampled down by small sharp hooves, and it was discovered that the culprits were goats from Chief Mshlanga's kraal. This had happened once before, years ago.

My father confiscated all the goats. Then he sent a

message to the old Chief that if he wanted them he would have to pay for the damage.

He arrived at our house at the time of sunset one evening, looking very old and bent now, walking stiffly under his regally-draped blanket, leaning on a big stick. My father sat himself down in his big chair below the steps of the house; the old man squatted carefully on the ground before him, flanked by his two young men.

The palaver was long and painful, because of the bad English of the young man who interpreted, and because my father could not speak dialect, but only kitchen kaffir.

From my father's point of view, at least two hundred pounds' worth of damage had been done to the crop. He knew he could not get the money from the old man. He felt he was entitled to keep the goats. As for the old Chief, he kept repeating angrily: "Twenty goats! My people cannot lose twenty goats! We are not rich, like the Nkosi Jordan, to lose twenty goats at once."

My father did not think of himself as rich, but rather as very poor. He spoke quickly and angrily in return, saying that the damage done meant a great deal to him, and that he was entitled to the goats.

At last it grew so heated that the cook, the Chief's son, was called from the kitchen to be interpreter, and now my father spoke fluently in English, and our cook translated rapidly so that the old man could understand how very angry my father was. The young man spoke without emotion, in a mechanical way, his eyes lowered, but showing how he felt his position by a hostile uncomfortable set of the shoulders.

It was now in the late sunset, the sky a welter of

colors, the birds singing their last songs, and the cattle, lowing peacefully, moving past us towards their sheds for the night. It was the hour when Africa is most beautiful; and here was this pathetic, ugly scene, doing no one any good.

At last my father stated finally: "I'm not going to argue about it. I am keeping the goats."

The old Chief flashed back in his own language: "That means that my people will go hungry when the dry season comes."

"Go to the police, then," said my father, and looked triumphant.

There was, of course, no more to be said.

The old man sat silent, his head bent, his hands dangling helplessly over his withered knees. Then he rose, the young men helping him, and he stood facing my father. He spoke once again, very stiffly; and turned away and went home to his village.

"What did he say?" asked my father of the young man, who laughed uncomfortably and would not meet his eyes.

"What did he say?" insisted my father.

Our cook stood straight and silent, his brows knotted together. Then he spoke. "My father says: All this land, this land you call yours, is his land, and belongs to our people."

Having made this statement, he walked off into the bush after his father, and we did not see him again.

Our next cook was a migrant from Nyasaland, with no expectations of greatness.

Next time the policeman came on his rounds he was told this story. He remarked: "That kraal has no right to be there; it should have been moved long ago. I don't know why no one has done anything about it.

I'll have a chat with the Native Commissioner next week. I'm going over for tennis on Sunday, anyway."

Some time later we heard that Chief Mshlanga and his people had been moved two hundred miles east, to a proper Native Reserve; the Government land was going to be opened up for white settlement soon.

I went to see the village again, about a year afterwards. There was nothing there. Mounds of red mud, where the huts had been, had long swathes of rotting thatch over them, veined with the red galleries of the white ants. The pumpkin vines rioted everywhere, over the bushes, up the lower branches of trees so that the great golden balls rolled underfoot and dangled overhead: it was a festival of pumpkins. The bushes were crowding up, the new grass sprang vivid green.

The settler lucky enough to be allotted the lush warm valley (if he chose to cultivate this particular section) would find, suddenly, in the middle of a mealie field, the plants were growing fifteen feet tall, the weight of the cobs dragging at the stalks, and wonder what unsuspected vein of richness he had struck.

Ball

BY SAM KOPERWAS

A flower grows for every drop of rain that falls. Don't tell me no. In the middle of the darkest night, there is still a candle that is glowing. This I believe. *Glowing.* If a lost person wanders in the street, somebody will come along to find the way for him. I would swear it on bibles. I *believe.*

It is my son who does not believe.

He stands in front of me, six-five. His arms hang down to his knees, to his ankles. You don't know how much I love him, my boy. I jump up to hug him. I press my face into his chest.

"You're a basketball player," I yell up to him. "Become a Knickerbocker, son. Listen to your father. Be a Piston, a Pacer."

I stuff vitamins into all his openings. In the house he has to wear lead weights under his socks if he wants to eat.

My son hates a basketball.

He reads books about blood circulation and heart conditions. Set shots he doesn't want to know from. I have to twist the boy's arm before he'll stand up straight.

"Floods wiped out a village in Pakistan," he cries to me. His shoulders slump like rooftops caving in.

"Puerto Ricans push carts in the gutter. Beaches are polluted. Where has the buffalo gone?"

"Grow up!" I shout. "What kind of talk is this from a boy? Play basketball and make money. Practice sky hooks. Forget floods, forget buffalo—you're not even a teen-ager yet. What I want from you are slam dunks. God made you tall. Run! Dribble!"

"Pop," he sobs to me.

"My boy," I say.

The kitchen tells the story. A history book of inches and feet is here. Growth is here, all the measurements right from the start.

"This is you," I holler. I point to pencil scratches on a leg of the kitchen table. "Right from the hospital I stood you up on those fabulous legs of yours."

I touch one mark after another. Tallness, like a beautiful beanstalk, climbs up the broom closet, up the refrigerator, a ladder of height. The inches add up, interest in the bank.

The boy stoops over. These measurements are making him sick. He takes his size like you take a ticket for speeding.

"I can't, Dad. Rapists and inflation and tumors are everywhere."

I grab the boy by the arm. I pull him to the refrigerator, push him against the door, stand him up tall. I point with a father's finger to faint key scratches on the door.

"Nursery school!" I scream. "Right here, son. What a smoothy you were, what a natural. Slop from the table you palmed with either hand. This is your father talking to you. When I cut your bites too big to finish, swish in the garbage bag you dunked them. I saw an athlete, son. I saw a millionaire."

My boy shuts his eyes. He sees stethoscopes behind them. I see basketballs.

The do-gooder, he refuses to shoot basketballs. Instead, he reaches for the encyclopedia. My son curls up to read.

Six-six, and growing every day like good stocks. This is an athlete. This is handsome, long and tall, and getting big and getting bigger.

I give him rabbit punches in the kidneys.

"Son," I explain to him.

"Dad," he mumbles.

I take my boy to the school yard. Above us is a basket. I point.

"Here is a ball. Shoot it!" I shout.

My son looks at the ball in his hands. Then he looks down at me.

"I can't, Pop."

Tears plip on his huge sneakers.

"I don't see little rubber bumps, Dad. I see faces of tiny orphans all over the world. Instead of black lines, I see segregation and the bald eagle that's becoming extinct. I see unhappiness and things that have to be stitched back together."

He drops the ball, klunk.

I chase after the ball. My boy runs next to me. Frazier does not run smoother, believe me. It breaks my heart.

I bounce the ball to my son and it hits his stomach. He doesn't move the hands that could squash watermelons.

"Wilt Chamberlain has a swimming pool in his house!" I scream up to the boy. "Your father is talking to you. In the *house!*"

Closer to six-eight than to six-seven and larger every

day, every day shooting up like the price of gold. I
need a chair to measure him.

"I won't play basketball," he cries to me. "I want to
be something. A heart surgeon. I have to help people.
How can I play basketball after what we've done to
the Navaho and the Cherokee?"

I reach up and grab the boy's ear. I drag him to
the basket. I shove the ball into his hands.

"Shoot!" I yell. "Stuff it in! Dribble like Maravich.
This is your father speaking to you. Spin the ball on a
finger. Make it roll down your arms and behind your
neck. Score baskets, son! Make money. Bring scouts.
Bring Red Holzman. I want contracts on the doorstep,
I want promises."

I stand toe to toe with the boy, nose to stomach.

I slam the ball into his belly.

"Son," I whisper.

"Pop," he moans.

You should eat an apple every day. This is a proven
fact. Every prayer that comes out of your mouth gets
listened to. This also is proven. Nobody can tell me
different. Somebody up there hears every single word.
Argue and I'll slap your eyes out. We live in the land
of opportunity.

My boy will be a basketball player.

I slip the ball into his bed at night. I put it on the
pillow next to his big sad face.

The boy opens his eyes. They are round, like hoops.

"Dad."

"Son."

Under his bed there are electric basketball games
covered with dust. Coloring books of basketball players turn yellow in his closet. Basketball pajamas the
boy has outgrown I will never throw away.

"Dad."

"Son."

I am with him at the table when he eats. I love the boy. I marvel at his appetite, whole shipments he packs away. My son can shovel it in. Lamb chops I set before him with gladness. My eyes are tears when he clears the table, the hamburgers and the shakes and the fries. I make him drink milk. Inside, he is oceans of milk.

"Eat!" I scream. "Get tall and taller. Grow to the skies."

My son rips through new sneakers every two weeks. Owners, managers, franchisers would kill for him right now.

"People starve," the boys says. "There are earthquakes in Peru that don't let me sleep nights. Squirrels are catching cold in the park. Drug addicts and retarded children walk the streets."

My flesh and blood weeps before me, my oil well. Cuffs never make it past the boy's ankles. In less than a week any sleeve retreats from his wrists.

"I'm not even thirteen," he sobs. "There's so much to do. Workers without unions gets laid off. Every day the earth falls a little closer into the sun. Kidneys fail. I don't know what to do, Pop. Mexicans get gassed. Puppies have to pick grapes."

I run over to the boy. He stoops to hug me.

"You're hot property," I shriek up to him. "Listen to your father. You're land in Florida, son. Scoop shots and pivots. I'm your father. Bounce passes and free throws. Listen to me."

I run to the bedroom. I drop the ball at his feet.

"Look, son. Red, white, and blue. What more could a boy ask for?"

He doesn't pick it up. I have to put the ball in his

arms. He cries. He lets the ball drop to the floor. Tears pour down on me from above.

"Son," I say.

"Pop," he says.

I lead my boy to a gymnasium. I push him under a basket.

"Turn-around jumpers and tip-ins," I shout up. "That's what I want from you. I want rebounds."

"Please, Pop."

"You're just a boy," I beg. "Listen to your father."

I hold the ball out for him to take.

"Pop," he says.

"Son," I say.

He takes the ball.

A baby cries and I am moved. A leaf gets touched and I melt. A son bends to take a ball from his father's hands, and . . . I . . . know . . . why . . . I . . . believe.

My son *spins* the ball. My son *eyes* the seams. My son *pats* the ball. My son *tests* the weight.

"I don't know, Pop."

I reach up a fatherly hand. I tap my boy on the chest.

"Factories murder the air. Russians steal fish."

"It was meant for you, son. Try it."

My son drops the ball with just a hint of English and it comes right back to him. He spins the ball again. It bounces back.

My son smiles.

He performs, he does tricks, he experiments. The kid is Benjamin Franklin with a kite, Columbus with a boat. Tears run from our eyes. This is an athlete in front of me. He is happy and tall.

My son is bouncing the ball.

I point to the net. He squeezes the ball. He shakes it. He shoots.

Swish.

My son makes baskets. Shot after shot, swish.

I love him. He sinks hook shots, jumpers from half court.

"Dad!" he shouts.

"My boy!" I scream.

He stands up tall. He tosses in baskets from everywhere. He reaches up and drops it through. He holds it with the fingertips of one hand. My six-tenner, he dunks it backward.

He runs, he jumps. He grows. His shoulders straighten, knees straighten. My son is a tree.

He zooms up taller, my seven-footer. I love him. He is enormous.

Buttons pop. The boy tears through his clothing. He grows taller. He throws it in with his eyes closed. His head grows over the rim, over the backboard. His fingers reach from one end of the court to the other.

"Son," I call up to him.

"Pop, Pop, Pop."

He grows taller still. He blasts through the ceiling. My son stands tall and naked. His head is in the sky. I love him, my monster.

He pushes himself up higher. He skyrockets above us. The boy is taller than buildings, bigger than mountains.

"Son," I call.

"Pop, Pop, Pop," he bellows from afar.

The boy is gigantic.

He pushes aside skyscrapers. He swallows clouds. He grows. He swats airplanes from the sky with either hand, crushes them between his fingers. He blots out the light.

My son keeps growing. There is thunder when he speaks, an earthquake when he moves. People die.

The boy grows and grows.

"Son," I sob.

"Pop, Pop, Pop!"

He grows in the sky. He stretches to the sun. My boy leaps past stars.

"Pop, Pop, Pop!"

But it is no longer a human voice I hear from the heavens. When my son speaks, it is the crashing of meteors, the four corners of the galaxy wheeling, wheeling, wheeling toward the outer horizon where the Titans themselves lob a furious ball in lethal play, and the score is always climbing. It is the playground where suns and moons careen in hopeless patterns. It is a void where victors hold frivolous service and cause thunder with tenpins, where old men shower the rain with unholy weeping, where solar systems are deployed in the secondary and every atom is a knuckle ball.

In this I sadly believe.

"Son," I say.

"Pop."

The boy is beside me. He is a good boy, a boy who wants to help people: he is young. This boy knows compassion, tenderness, genetics. His head is not in the clouds.

I buy microscope sets for him, medical journals. I bring home tongue depressors for the boy. We dissect frogs together. We cure diseases.

"I've seen things, Dad," he tells me. "My eyes have been opened."

"We'll make remedies, son. You'll heal the sick, comfort the needy."

"I can't explain it, Dad. It's all more than a basketball."

"You'll patch holes in the earth, son. You'll feed Biafrans, help birds fly south in winter. You'll bring peace to the Mideast, equal rights to women."

My son spins the ball in front of him. My son eyes the seams. My son pats the ball. My son tests the weight.

"You'll plug up radium leaks, son, solve busing problems. You'll put the business to venereal disease. You'll grow bananas that don't spoil. Listen to me. You'll invent cars that don't shrink, cotton goods that run on water. I am your father."

The boy does not hear. Nobody does. Babies are born every second and every one of them cries. Leaves by the million turn brown in the street. The sky is all poisonous particles.

"Son."

"Dad?"

He shoots the ball at a basket. *Swish*. He spins them in off the backboard. *Swish*. Flips from corners. *Swish*.

I clutch at my chest.

"Here comes a lefty hook, Pop."

Swish.

I collapse at his feet. The boy looms over me. Cancers strike at my vitals. Seizures grip me. Plagues and pestilence and uncertainty flood my veins. Pandora's box breaks open in my heart.

My son looks down at me. He twirls the ball on a

terrible finger. I look up at a son whose hands could cradle nations.

"Son," I beg.

"Not now, Pop."

He bounces the ball on my stomach. Once, twice, three times for luck. He dribbles between his legs, behind his back. My son flies to the basket. My son soars to his laurels over my dead body.

Barbed Wire

BY ROBERT CANZONERI

"An uncle would be the merest of appendages if there were something to be appended to." The boy read the sentence aloud to his mother from the letter he was holding. "Is that supposed to make sense?" he demanded.

"Your Uncle Royce never seemed to consider it important to make sense," his mother said.

The boy thought about it for a few minutes. He was sixteen and his face was fat and freckled. He was confident of becoming almost as good a journalist as his father would have been if he had lived. He was impatient of school, and he wanted to make a real start—perhaps the same one his father had made. Big words did not bother him. "I'm going anyway," he said.

"Well," his mother said doubtfully. "It's where you're from."

The boy had been two years old when his father was killed and his mother took him north to her home. Aunt Janey had visited them, but her husband, Uncle Royce, he could not envision at all.

Royce did not want the boy to come. He felt as if his life over the past several years had been composed

of trying to get around aging men who planted themselves unaccountably in his path and said to him with
eyes deliberately alight and faces expectant, "I believe
in living." He was certain the boy would be like
that—eyes alight and face expectant. Off and on all
summer Royce lay awake nights hoping the boy
wouldn't come.

It was a hot dry day in August when the boy arrived
on the bus from Indiana. There had been a long
drought, and now pasture grass was brown, dust was
thick on everything, and cow ponds were nothing but
crusted hoofprints down to the base of their dams,
where there was just about mud enough for a share-
cropper's pigpen. That was Royce's description in
his weekly paper. The boy got off the bus and felt
sweat pop out all over him. He was sore from sitting
so long and his seat was creased from the wrinkles
in his pants.

Aunt Janey looked just the same except smaller.
Now he had to lean down to let her kiss him, and
he could see to the roots of her fine hair which
used to float out against the light like a halo. She
was his father's sister.

The newspaper office had an old brick front. The boy
searched among the black-shaded gold letters on the
window for his father's name—left perhaps because
of laziness or perhaps out of sentiment or perhaps
as a tribute to his great contribution to the world
of journalism—but although the lettering was very old,
no trace of his father's name was visible:

THE SENTINEL
Lucius County's Oldest, Largest, Fatest Growing
and Only Newspaper
Royce Weatherly, Editor and Publisher

FOR SALE:
Typewriters, Office Supplies
The Whole Damn Paper including the Editor,
a few Books of doubtful value,
Pens, Pencils, new or used Paper

PRINTING

The *Sentinel* was not really for sale. When Royce had been approached about selling out—only twice in twenty-seven years—he had responded, "Every man has his price. Mine's just fifty cents higher than your highest offer." It was not because he was the third Weatherly to own the paper, nor was it because underneath his cynical exterior he was either sentimental about the newspaper or devoted to the community. It was rather, as Royce had written editorially, that he had

> *been around just enough to know that nowhere—not anywhere available to man—is there a truly better place to live, are there truly better people, is there possible a more meaningful existence than right here in Lucius County.*
>
> *No wonder the human race is trying to blow itself off this unstrung yo-yo we call Earth.*

It was also because Royce could say what he damn pleased. "'At's just old Royce," they'd say. "He's a caution though, ain't he?"

Once a minister had dropped by to enlist Royce on the side of the Lord. "Mr. Weatherly, you take some unpopular stands. But I wonder," he said, "if you wouldn't have more effect if you attacked specific local evils."

Royce broke in before he could name any. "Right, Preacher. I was just about to concoct an editorial on people who come around telling everybody else what to do."

The preacher blinked his eyes a couple of times and then said, "I feel it's my duty to indicate the Lord's will."

Royce had been sitting in a swivel chair with his green eyeshade on and his sleeves pulled up with garters, not altogether because it made him look quaint but because it shaded his eyes and saved his cuffs; now he stood up. "Preacher," he said, "you can't imagine what an infinitesimally minute fraction of an utterly casual goddamn I give what you feel."

If the boy had been old enough to remember such things, he might have noticed that Uncle Royce looked like a good clean stick of stovewood. As it was, he only noticed that his uncle was short and compact—straight up and down—with hard skin a few shades lighter than the red clay banks through which the country road cut.

"Well, boy?" Royce said to him. They were standing by Royce's old rolltop desk in the newspaper office. The boy saw an ancient typewriter that looked like an upright piano, spikes with haystacks of paper on them, pencils.

"Is this where my father worked?" The high school

newspaper office was neater and had newer equipment, but here there was the smell of the real thing and the boy breathed it the way he imagined a sailor would salt air after being long inland.

Royce sat in his swivel chair and put on his green eyeshade. "I reckon by now you've had pretty much of your boyhood. Played hooky so you could go to the ole swimmin' hole, where you shucked your clothes and dived in off the bank. Played baseball. You've gone fishing with overalls on and a rag around a sore toe, using a bent pin and worms to pull up old boots near a NO FISHING sign."

The boy shook his head. "I got my lifesaving badge in Scouts this summer. Is this where he worked?"

"You haven't done all those things? Then you can't live in the newspaper world." Royce paused. "That's where your father worked. In the newspaper world. He hung around here to do it, but this desk and the typewriter and pencils—those things weren't real. He believed what he read in the paper."

"Didn't he write it himself?" The boy was watching Uncle Royce closely. He was not sure he understood.

"Sure. Some of it. Even thought he was thinking it up." Royce reached into a pigeonhole and took out a half pint of whisky, unscrewed the cap and took what looked like a long drink, though the level seemed to be unchanged when he put the bottle back.

"Could you show me some of the things he wrote?"

Royce shook his head. "Could if I hadn't had to rewrite everything, I suppose. Couldn't pick them out, now."

The boy wandered around the big room and stopped at a table where ads had been cut out and were pasted onto another sheet of the newspaper. "What was it like?" he asked. He was trying to imagine into this office his father of the snapshot, the tall man with the smiling open mouth and the eyes cut aside. "I mean, I know how newspapers work, and how to write a story, and all that." He had written Uncle Royce that he was assistant editor of the school paper. "But what was it like here, back then?"

"Same old thing all the time," Royce said. "You're looking at it. Same old ads and the same old stories every week. Just paste it up out of an old copy, any date. When it's spring, you run in a cartoon of an editor trying to get finished at his desk because his rod and reel's right there waiting for him. Newspaper spring. Nothing to do with life. Down here you could go fishing almost any day of December or January— any time. I don't fish, myself."

"My father fished, didn't he?"

"Of course. And hunted and talked about baseball. Certainly. John Q. Public with the little mustache in a country that hates hair on the face. Uncle Sam with a white beard. Churches with little scrolls by them saying to go worship. Sure he did. He got married in the Society Pages and had you in the Birth Announcements and died as a contribution to the Obituary Column."

The boy looked at him. His mother had said he didn't make sense. She hadn't said that he would talk this way. "He was my father," the boy said.

"I never contracted with anybody," Royce replied, "to pretty up your old man to suit you and your mother and your Aunt Janey." He walked to the front window and looked out at the dusty street in the blinding sun.

The boy sat down carefully. He did not want his voice to shake. "That's just your opinion of him," he said.

Royce didn't move. "I can't spit anybody's spit but mine."

The boy and Aunt Janey had lunch together. She gave him a saucer of cold peach cobbler for dessert, and she talked while he ate.

"Of course your father was my younger brother, and when he married your mother he hadn't even finished his education—college, I mean—and he needed a job, so Royce had him helping on the paper. Oh, I reckon that was five or six years before you came along."

"Uncle Royce didn't like him, did he?" the boy said.

"Well," Aunt Janey said. Her face was smooth and she looked as if she had been kept in a glass case. The boy wondered how she had lived all these years with Uncle Royce. "Well," she said again, "of course he liked him, but you know how brother-in-laws are."

"I'm beginning to," the boy said.

"Well," she said, "soon as I've had my nap we'll go over and see where y'all used to live."

The house was small and white, set on tall brick foundations so that the bare ground beneath it looked cool. A rusty swing set was in the side yard. The lawn was withered, and the fig trees in the back looked limp.

"You used to crawl under the house," Aunt Janey said, "and your mother would have to go get you."

The boy could remember nothing about the house. Where were those first two years of his life? The house seemed as much an absurd concoction as did Uncle Royce's account of his father.

"We went by the house," Aunt Janey said when Royce came in.

Royce didn't respond. He stopped in the middle of the living room floor and looked directly at the boy. The boy looked back at him. He did not like Uncle Royce, and he was sure that his father hadn't liked Uncle Royce.

"I guess there's one more place you want to go," Royce said.

The boy was startled. He had not wanted to mention it—he wasn't sure it was at all the thing to do. "Yes, there is," he said finally.

"There's plenty of daylight left," Royce said.

Royce drove slowly with the windows open, and the hot air swirled up dust around their feet. They didn't speak for a long time, until once when they were driving alongside a field of brown-leafed cotton, with wads of white showing already.

"Cotton," the boy said, to show he was not totally ignorant.

"Old man Peeples' place," Royce said. "Nice white house, you see there now. But old man Peeples planted cotton and stayed broke all through the Depression and rayon and nylon and all those other things, and wore the land right down to the nub. So the county agent rebuilt his soil, and then some scientists figured out—somewhere else, not on old man Peeples' place— how to make a cotton shirt you can throw in the washing machine and take it out and wear it, and with that and the government old man Peeples has got some money at last. Downtown the other day he was bragging about his wisdom. Said he'd always told 'em a feller ought to stick with cotton. Them fellers they send out from the schools tried to tell him to plant something else, but he knowed better." After a moment Royce added, "Spent seventy-odd years broke. If he'd died at any normal retirement age, he wouldn't have had money for a coffin."

The boy shifted in his seat. Uncle Royce was probably getting at something, but he didn't know what. "Money's not everything," he said.

"True," Royce said. "There's all those blissful years of chopping cotton."

It seemed to the boy that the route they took was as devious as Uncle Royce's mind. After leaving the blacktop, they drove on three gravel roads and two dirt roads, with dust rolling up behind them so that the boy wondered if from an airplane it looked like a dirty jet trail. Finally they stopped at the edge of a field of brown sage grass.

"We can get there quicker by wading through," Royce said. The boy wondered what wading through was quicker than, but he did not ask. The sage came up to Royce's chest, but he plowed right on. In the distance was a solid wall of trees and before it pasture land lay flat like the front yard of a house.

"You wouldn't know about such things," Royce said, "but my mother used to cut swatches of sage grass like this and make her own brooms. She'd bind the stems into a handle. Swept everything in sight, but she wasn't much better off for it." His head and shoulders moved above the dry sage as if floating, hardly bobbing at all. The boy could imagine that that was all there was to him, a talking bust. "She believed that because she did her duty and was thrifty and kept a clean house, happiness was supposed to descend upon her like a dove. She was a bitter woman, always wondering why the Lord let her suffer. But she hung on 'til she died in her late seventies of a failure of the kidneys."

The boy was scarcely hearing. Heat radiated from the sky and the tall grass and the ground, and the sun was just low enough to be in his eyes. Uncle Royce's head was suspended on a bright brown haze, the voice continuing as if to no one, like the sound of bees.

"Watch out here for the fence," Royce said. The sage thinned slightly, and then they were in a narrow bare strip alongside a barbed-wire fence. Royce put his foot on the middle wire and pulled up the top one with his hand. "Crawl through," he said.

The boy wondered, but could not bring himself to ask, if this were *the* fence. He hesitated a moment. He would have preferred stepping over the top strand, anyway. He was tall enough; he would have to press it down only a couple of inches. But he stooped and went through and then held the wire for Uncle Royce.

"Nope," Royce said when he straightened up. "This is not the one. We've got to walk on over to the fence by the woods."

The pasture was dull yellow with bitterweeds; dust drifted from the flowers and puffed from the ground with every step the boy took. By the time they reached the other side of the pasture, Royce's shirt was wet and gray, clinging to his shoulders and to his undershirt. The boy's sight was blurred with sweat and his eyes and his face stung.

Royce put a hand on a post and said, "It was this

fence. It wasn't a day like today, though. It was late in November, during a frosty spell." He looked down along the fence as though he might point out something but then he said, "Let's get in the shade of a tree and cool off some."

Ths time the boy held the strands of wire apart to let his uncle go first. Royce bent over and was astraddle the middle strand when a voice shouted, "Hold on there!" from so nearby that Royce straightened and jabbed his back on the upper wire. The wire beneath him sprang up, too, and barbs scraped his thigh.

"Goddamn it," Royce said. He couldn't move either way.

"My foot slipped," the boy said. "I'm sorry." He was watching an old man in overalls approach from the woods with a long heavy stick, but he looked down and, as Royce removed the barbs from his trousers, pushed the wire down carefully with his foot. Then he worked a barb loose from the wet shirt back; it left a small metallic hole in the cloth which looked as if it ought to be made to bleed.

"Hold on there!" the old man shouted again.

"Hold on yourself!" Royce shouted back. He stood up beside the fence, his face dark red and running with sweat.

"This here's my land," the old man said, coming up to them. "Who is it?"

Royce wiped his face with his sleeve, violently. "Royce Weatherly," he said. "And this is my nephew."

The old man peered closely into Royce's face and said, as if the name had not just been told him, "Royce Weatherly, ain't it. Just didn't recognize the boy." He looked at the boy. "You don't live around here, I reckon."

"In Indiana," the boy said.

The old man looked at him, studied his face, saying, "Well, it's hot, ain't it?"

"Yes," the boy said, "it is."

The old man kept looking at him. "It's your daddy was killed out here four-five year ago, ain't it?"

"Fourteen years ago," the boy said.

The old man nodded. His face was coarse and brown; there were deep wrinkles at his eyes and beside his mouth. "I knew your daddy. He used to come hunting out here. Lots of squirrels before folks begun shooting them out of season. I figured maybe before I realized who it was that y'all was fixing to shoot a few."

Royce was trying to rub the sore place on his back. "With our bare hands," he said.

The old man nodded. "That's so," he said, but about what the boy could not be sure. "But your daddy and me used to talk now and then. He was a real smart man. Used to explain to me all about how to hunt scientific. Big man." He was looking at the boy. "You remember him?"

The boy shook his head.

"Worked for the newspaper, you know. Royce's here. He used to explain to me how a feller goes about it, starting out a piece in such and such a way, and all."

The boy wanted to quote, "Who, what, where . . ." but Royce spoke first.

"I could tell you in four minutes and you could talk about it the rest of your life," Royce said.

"Not me," the old man said. He was still looking at the boy. "It takes a smart man like your daddy for that. Educated, and all. Had some of them degrees, too."

"Ninety-eight and six-tenths," Royce said.

The old man nodded. "That's so. From some universities around over the country. Could of been called doctor in the phone book, I recollect he told me once, except folks would have thought he was a medical or a vetinary." The old man moved along the fence a little way. "You come to see where your daddy died?"

The boy nodded, although now the old man was not looking at him.

"Well, it was right along at this section, right here. He comes out alone without even a fice dog or anybody, and he was bent on getting in the woods before good daylight, and he forgot the rules of safety-first. Used to tell 'em to me, I bet fifty times."

The old man paused, taking his stick in both hands like a shotgun, to demonstrate. "Well," he said after a moment of thought, "I never seen him that many times. But he used to open the breech—he told me you never put a shell in 'til you're in the woods is a rule of safety-first. And then he'd put on the safety catch anyway and slide the gun real careful under the fence flat on the ground. And then he'd come over the fence himself and pick up his gun all safe and sound."

The old man straightened, still looking at the boy. The sun was still well above the tree tops and the boy felt as though his head would burst. "You come here to learn about your daddy now you've got to be a right smart sized boy yourself, ain't you?"

The boy nodded. For a moment he had a feeling of hot resentment, almost believing that Uncle Royce had planted the old man here—perhaps had invented him altogether.

"Well," the old man said. "That day he just forgot all them rules of safety-first he was so proud of. Pride goeth before a fall, it says in the Good Book, but that don't make it no easier, does it. Had a shell in the breech and the safety catch off and was putting the shotgun through the fence butt first when it went off in his face." The old man shook his head for a long time. "I never heard the shot. I was still in the barn. They come and got me, seeing as it was my place it was on."

The boy looked at the ground where his father must have fallen. The blood would have soaked in, been diluted with rain, washed down through the earth, filtered itself to water long ago. Grown up in bitterweeds. Popped out as sweat.

"I told 'em then," the old man said, "that he was as fine a man as ever I come acrost." He turned to Royce. "It's good cotton weather but hard on the cattle. Tell 'em"—he meant, Royce knew, the newspaper readers—"the signs is plow deep and plant shallow, come spring. My daddy knew about such things the way his daddy knew about newspaper writing and all."

It was not until the old man was gone that Royce and the boy realized they were standing on different sides of the fence.

"You want to come on over and find some shade, or go on back home?" Royce said.

The boy looked at the fence. "Is this really the place?"

"Close enough," Royce said. "It's hard to tell one post from another."

The boy stood a moment, not satisfied but unable to say why. Finally, without speaking, he held the fence and Royce carefully came through.

They walked in silence across half the pasture before

the boy stopped and looked back at the woods and the fence. "Was that the way it was?" he asked.

Royce took in a deep breath and let it out in a long sigh. "Who knows? You wouldn't remember about slop buckets any more than about sage brooms, but it used to be that everybody had a bucket in the kitchen to drop all the leftover food in, and when it got full you'd take it out and empty it in the pig trough, where it belonged."

The boy looked at him sharply. "And?" he said.

"It was just undigested scraps of stuff, all thrown together. And that's what I think of when I have to stand and listen to people like that old man talk. I feel like he's emptying the slop bucket in my face."

The boy didn't move. He found that he was breathing heavily through his mouth and could faintly taste the bitterweeds. "And you're saying my father was like that."

"Who knows how it was that morning?" Royce had never said it before, but it came as if he had written it as an editorial and memorized it. "Was he careless, or was it that he didn't care? Maybe he didn't have anybody to talk to but the barbed-wire fence, and the fence wouldn't put up with it and shot him with his own gun. Or maybe he got across to the fence what he couldn't say to any human being and it helped him pull the trigger, because it was himself and not the fence that had to stop the talk and couldn't do it any other way. Or maybe," Royce went on, wishing the boy would interrupt, would stop him, had stopped him before he got started, even, "or maybe it was the gun itself, talking back, showing him finally how to compress all banality into a single unanswerable sound and be done with it."

He stopped and the boy stood there flushed and sweating for a long time before they continue walking toward the car.

Royce didn't look at the boy when they got out of the car at home. He stretched and looked up. The red was going out of the sky, and everything seemed to focus directly overhead in a clear blue. "As easy as filling a slop bucket," Royce said, "and the pigs don't know the difference. But if you think that's what you want, you're welcome."

The boy realized after a moment that Uncle Royce was talking about the newspaper, and that earlier in the day that was what he would have wanted. Now he was not at all sure. Now he knew a little better who his father had been and what had happened; he had seen where and he had been told more about when. But without the why, what was the story? Was it merely an obituary? He did not know why, not only about his father, but about Uncle Royce, about himself. "I better get on through school," he said tentatively.

They crossed the yard and Royce paused with his hand on the screen. "Well," he said, "that's as good as anything, I reckon. If you just don't swallow too much."

A Temple of the Holy Ghost

BY FLANNERY O'CONNOR

All weekend the two girls were calling each other
Temple One and Temple Two, shaking with laughter and getting so red and hot that they were positively ugly, particularly Joanne who had spots on her
face anyway. They came in the brown convent uniforms they had to wear at Mount St. Scholastica but
as soon as they opened their suitcases, they took off
the uniforms and put on red skirts and loud blouses.
They put on lipstick and their Sunday shoes and
walked around in the high heels all over the house,
always passing the long mirror in the hall slowly
to get a look at their legs. None of their ways were
lost on the child. If only one of them had come, that
one would have played with her, but since there were
two of them, she was out of it and watched them
suspiciously from a distance.

They were fourteen—two years older than she was—
but neither of them was bright, which was why they
had been sent to the convent. If they had gone to a
regular school, they wouldn't have done anything but
think about boys; at the convent the sisters, her mother
said, would keep a grip on their necks. The child
decided, after observing them for a few hours, that
they were practically morons and she was glad to think

that they were only second cousins and she couldn't
have inherited any of their stupidity. Susan called
herself Su-zan. She was very skinny but she had a
pretty pointed face and red hair. Joanne had yellow
hair that was naturally curly but she talked through
her nose and when she laughed, she turned purple
in patches. Neither one of them could say an intelligent thing and all their sentences began, "You know
this boy I know well one time he . . ."

They were to stay all weekend and her mother said
she didn't see how she would entertain them since she
didn't know any boys their age. At this, the child,
struck suddenly with genius, shouted, "There's Cheat!
Get Cheat to come! Ask Miss Kirby to get Cheat
to come show them around!" and she nearly choked
on the food she had in her mouth. She doubled over
laughing and hit the table with her fist and looked
at the two bewildered girls while water started in her
eyes and rolled down her fat cheeks and the braces
she had in her mouth glared like tin. She had never
thought of anything so funny before.

Her mother laughed in a guarded way and Miss
Kirby blushed and carried her fork delicately to her
mouth with one pea on it. She was a long-faced blonde
schoolteacher who boarded with them and Mr.
Cheatam was her admirer, a rich old farmer who
arrived every Saturday afternoon in a fifteen-year-old
baby-blue Pontiac powdered with red clay dust and
black inside with Negroes that he charged ten cents
apiece to bring into town on Saturday afternoons. After
he dumped them he came to see Miss Kirby, always
bringing a little gift—a bag of boiled peanuts or a
watermelon or a stalk of sugar cane and once a wholesale box of Baby Ruth candy bars. He was bald-headed

except for a little fringe of rust-colored hair and his face was nearly the same color as the unpaved roads and washed like them with ruts and gulleys. He wore a pale green shirt with a thin black stripe in it and blue galluses and his trousers cut across a protruding stomach that he pressed tenderly from time to time with his big flat thumb. All his teeth were backed with gold and he would roll his eyes at Miss Kirby in an impish way and say, "Haw haw," sitting in their porch swing with his legs spread apart and his hightopped shoes pointing in opposite directions on the floor.

"I don't think Cheat is going to be in town this weekend," Miss Kirby said, not in the least understanding that this was a joke, and the child was convulsed afresh, threw herself backward in her chair, fell out of it, rolled on the floor and lay there heaving. Her mother told her if she didn't stop this foolishness she would have to leave the table.

Yesterday her mother had arranged with Alonzo Myers to drive them the forty-five miles to Mayville, where the convent was, to get the girls for the weeknd and Sunday afternoon he was hired to drive them back again. He was an eighteen-year-old boy who weighed two hundred and fifty pounds and worked for the taxi company and he was all you could get to drive you anywhere. He smoked or rather chewed a short black cigar and he had a round sweaty chest that showed through the yellow nylon shirt he wore. When he drove all the windows of the car had to be open.

"Well there's Alonzo!" the child roared from the floor. "Get Alonzo to show em around! Get Alonzo!"

The two girls, who had seen Alonzo, began to scream their indignation.

Her mother thought this was funny too but she said, "That'll be about enough out of you," and changed the subject. She asked them why they called each other Temple One and Temple Two and this sent them off into gales of giggles. Finally they managed to explain. Sister Perpetua, the oldest nun at the Sisters of Mercy in Mayville, had given them a lecture on what to do if a young man should—here they laughed so hard they were not able to go on without going back to the beginning—on what to do if a young man should—they put their heads in their laps—on what to do if—they finally managed to shout it out—if he should "behave in an ungentlemanly manner with them in the back of an automobile." Sister Perpetua said they were to say, "Stop sir! I am a Temple of the Holy Ghost!" and that would put an end to it. The child sat up off the floor with a blank face. She didn't see anything so funny in this. What was really funny was the idea of Mr. Cheatam or Alonzo Myers beauing them around. That killed her.

Her mother didn't laugh at what they had said. "I think you girls are pretty silly," she said. "After all, that's what you are—Temples of the Holy Ghost."

The two of them looked up at her, politely concealing their giggles, but with astonished faces as if they were beginning to realize that she was made of the same stuff as Sister Perpetua.

Miss Kirby preserved her set expression and the child thought, it's all over her head anyhow. I am a Temple of the Holy Ghost, she said to herself, and was pleased with the phrase. It made her feel as if somebody had given her a present.

After dinner, her mother collapsed on the bed and said, "Those girls are going to drive me crazy if I don't get some entertainment for them. They're awful."

"I bet I know who you could get," the child started.

"Now listen. I don't want to hear any more about Mr. Cheatam," her mother said. "You embarrass Miss Kirby. He's her only friend. Oh my Lord," and she sat up and looked mournfully out the window, "that poor soul is so lonesome she'll even ride in that car that smells like the last circle in hell."

And she's a Temple of the Holy Ghost too, the child reflected. "I wasn't thinking of him," she said. "I was thinking of those two Wilkinses, Wendell and Cory, that visit old lady Buchell out on her farm. They're her grandsons. They work for her."

"Now that's an idea," her mother murmured and gave her an appreciative look. But then she slumped again. "They're only farm boys. These girls would turn up their noses at them."

"Huh," the child said. "They wear pants. They're sixteen and they got a car. Somebody said they were both going to be Church of God preachers because you don't have to know nothing to be one."

"They would be perfectly safe with those boys all right," her mother said and in a minute she got up and called their grandmother on the telephone and after she had talked to the old woman a half an hour, it was arranged that Wendell and Cory would come to supper and afterwards take the girls to the fair.

Susan and Joanne were so pleased that they washed their hair and rolled it up on aluminum curlers. Hah, thought the child, sitting cross-legged on the bed to watch them undo the curlers, wait'll you get a load of Wendell and Cory! "You'll like these boys," she said. "Wendell is six feet tall ands got red hair. Cory

is six feet six inches talls got black hair and wears a
sport jacket and they gottem this car with a squirrel
tail on the front."

"How does a child like you know so much about
these men?" Susan asked and pushed her face up
close to the mirror to watch the pupils in her eyes
dilate.

The child lay back on the bed and began to count
the narrow boards in the ceiling until she lost her
place. I know them all right, she said to someone. We
fought in the world war together. They were under
me and I saved them five times from Japanese suicide
divers and Wendell said I am going to marry that
kid and the other said oh no you ain't I am and I
said neither one of you is because I will court marshall
you all before you can bat an eye. "I've seen them
around is all," she said.

When they came the girls stared at them a second
and then began to giggle and talk to each other about
the convent. They sat in the swing together and
Wendell and Cory sat on the banisters together. They
sat like monkeys, their knees on a level with their
shoulders and their arms hanging down between. They
were short thin boys with red faces and a high cheek-
bones and pale seed-like eyes. They had brought a
harmonica and a guitar. One of them began to blow
softly on the mouth organ, watching the girls over
it, and the other started strumming the guitar and
then began to sing, not watching them but keeping
his head tilted upward as if he were only interested
in hearing himself. He was singing a hillbilly song
that sounded half like a love song and half like a
hymn.

The child was standing on a barrel pushed into

some bushes at the side of the house, her face on a level with the porch floor. The sun was going down and the sky was turning a bruised violet color that seemed to be connected with the sweet mournful sound of the music. Wendell began to smile as he sang and to look at the girls. He looked at Susan with a dog-like loving look and sang,

> "I've found a friend in Jesus,
>   He's everything to me,
>   He's the lily of the valley,
>   He's the One who's set me free!"

Then he turned the same look on Joanne and sang,

> "A wall of fire about me,
>   I've nothing now to fear,
>   He's the lily of the valley,
>   And I'll always have Him near!"

The girls looked at each other and held their lips stiff so as not to giggle but Susan let out one anyway and clapped her hand on her mouth. The singer frowned and for a few seconds only strummed the guitar. Then he began. "The Old Rugged Cross" and they listened politely but when he had finished they said, "Let us sing one!" and before he could start another, they began to sing with their convent-trained voices,

> *"Tantum ergo Sacramentum*
> *Veneremur Cernui:*
> *Et antiquum documentum*

Novo cedat ritui:"

The child watched the boys' solemn faces turn with perplexed frowning stares at each other as if they were uncertain whether they were being made fun of.

"Præstet fides supplementum
Sensuum defectui.
Genitori, Genitoque
Laus et jubilatio

Salus, honor, virtus quoque . . ."

The boys' faces were dark red in the gray-purple light. They looked fierce and startled.

"Sit et benedictio;
Procedenti ab utroque
Compar sit laudatio.
Amen."

The girls dragged out the Amen and then there was a silence.

"That must be Jew singing," Wendell said and began to tune the guitar.

The girls giggled idiotically but the child stamped her foot on the barrel. "You big dumb ox!" she shouted. "You big dumb Church of God ox!" she roared and fell off the barrel and scrambled up and shot around the corner of the house as they jumped from the banister to see who was shouting.

Her mother had arranged for them to have supper in the back yard and she had a table laid out there under some Japanese lanterns that she pulled out for garden parties. "I ain't eating with them," the child said and snatched her plate off the table and carried it to the kitchen and sat down with the thin blue-gummed cook and ate her supper.

"Howcome you be so ugly sometime?" the cook asked.

"Those stupid idiots," the child said.

The lanterns gilded the leaves of the trees orange on the level where they hung and above them was black-green and below them were different dim muted colors that made the girls sitting at the table look prettier than they were. From time to time, the child turned her head and glared out the kitchen window at the scene below.

"God could strike you deaf dumb and blind," the cook said, "and then you wouldn't be as smart as you is."

"I would still be smarter than some," the child said.

After supper they left for the fair. She wanted to go to the fair but not with them so even if they had asked her she wouldn't have gone. She went upstairs and paced the long bedroom with her hands locked together behind her back and her head thrust forward and an expression, fierce and dreamy both, on her face. She didn't turn on the electric light but let the darkness collect and make the room smaller and more private. At regular intervals a light crossed the open window and threw shadows on the wall. She stopped and stood looking out over the dark slopes, past where the pond glinted silver, past the wall of woods to the speckled sky where a long finger of light was revolving up and around and away, searching the air as if it were hunting for the lost sun. It was the beacon light from the fair.

She could hear the distant sound of the calliope and she saw in her head all the tents raised up in a kind of gold sawdust light and the diamond ring of the ferris wheel going around and around up in the air and down again and the screeking merry-go-round going around and around on the ground. A fair lasted five or six days and there was a special afternoon for school children and a special night for niggers. She had gone last year on the afternoon for school children and had seen the monkeys and the fat man and had ridden on the ferris wheel. Certain tents were closed then because they contained things that would be known only to grown people but she had looked with interest at the advertising on the closed tents, at the faded-looking pictures on the canvas of people in tights, with stiff stretched composed faces like the faces of the martyrs waiting to have their tongues cut out by the Roman soldier. She had imagined that what was inside these tents concerned medicine and she had made up her mind to be a doctor when she grew up.

She had since changed and decided to be an engineer but as she looked out the window and followed the revolving searchlight as it widened and shortened and wheeled in its arc, she felt that she would have to be much more than just a doctor or an engineer. She would have to be a saint because that was the occupation that included everything you could know; and yet she knew she would never be a saint. She did not steal or murder but she was a born liar and slothful and she sassed her mother and was deliberately ugly to almost everybody. She was eaten up also with the sin of Pride, the worst one. She made fun of the Baptist preacher who came to the school at commencement to give the devotional. She would pull down her mouth and hold her forehead as if she were in agony and groan, "Fawther, we thank Thee," exactly the way he did and she had been told many times not to do it. She could never be a saint, but she thought she could be a martyr if they killed her quick.

She could stand to be shot but not to be burned in oil. She didn't know if she could stand to be torn to pieces by lions or not. She began to prepare her martyrdom, seeing herself in a pair of tights in a great arena, lit by the early Christians hanging in cages of fire, making a gold dusty light that fell on her and the lions. The first lion charged forward and fell at her feet, converted. A whole series of lions did the same. The lions liked her so much she even slept with them and finally the Romans were obliged to burn her but to their astonishment she would not burn down and finding she was so hard to kill, they finally cut off her head very quickly with a sword and she went immediately to heaven. She rehearsed this several times, returning each time at the entrance of Paradise to the lions.

Finally she got up from the window and got ready for bed and got in without saying her prayers. There were two heavy double beds in the room. The girls were occupying the other one and she tried to think of something cold and clammy that she could hide in their bed but her thought was fruitless. She didn't have anything she could think of, like a chicken carcass or a piece of beef liver. The sound of the calliope coming through the window kept her awake and she remembered that she hadn't said her prayers and got up and knelt down and began them. She took a running start and went through to the other side of the Apostle's Creed and then hung by her chin on the side of the bed, empty-minded. Her prayers, when she remembered to say them, were usually perfunctory but sometimes when she had done something wrong or heard music or lost something, or sometimes for no reason at all, she would be moved to fervor and would think of Christ on the long journey to Calvary, crushed three times on the rough cross. Her mind would stay on this a while and then get empty and when something roused her, she would find that she was thinking of a different thing entirely, of some dog or some girl or something she was going to do some day. Tonight, remembering Wendell and Cory, she was filled with thanksgiving and almost weeping with delight, she said, "Lord, Lord, thank You that I'm not in the Church of God, thank You Lord, thank You!" and got back in bed and kept repeating it until she went to sleep.

The girls came in at a quarter to twelve and waked her up with their giggling. They turned on the small blue-shaded lamp to see to get undressed by and their skinny shadows climbed up the wall and broke and continued moving about softly on the ceiling. The child sat up to hear what all they had seen at the fair. Susan had a plastic pistol full of cheap candy and Joanne a pasteboard cat with red polka dots on it. "Did you see the monkeys dance?" the child asked. "Did you see that fat man and those midgets?"

"All kinds of freaks," Joanne said. And then she said to Susan, "I enjoyed it all but the you-know-what," and her face assumed a peculiar expression as if she had bit into something that she didn't know if she liked or not.

The other stood still and shook her head once and nodded slightly at the child. "Little pitchers," she said in a low voice but the child heard it and her heart began to beat very fast.

She got out of her bed and climbed onto the footboard of theirs. They turned off the light and got in but she didn't move. She sat there, looking hard at them until their faces were well defined in the dark. "I'm not as old as you all," she said, "but I'm about a million times smarter."

"There are some things," Susan said, "that a child of your age doesn't know," and they both began to giggle.

"Go back to your own bed," Joanne said.

The child didn't move. "One time," she said, her voice hollow-sounding in the dark, "I saw this rabbit have rabbits."

There was a silence. Then Susan said, "How?" in an indifferent tone and she knew that she had them. She said she wouldn't tell until they told about the you-know-what. Actually she had never seen a rabbit have rabbits but she forgot this as they began to tell what they had seen in the tent.

It had been a freak with a particular name but they couldn't remember the name. The tent where it was had been divided into two parts by a black curtain, one side for men and one for women. The freak went from one side to the other, talking first to the men and then to the women, but everyone could hear. The stage ran all the way across the front. The girls heard the freak say to the men, "I'm going to show you this and if you laugh He may strike you the same way. The freak had a country voice, slow and nasal and neither high nor low, just flat. "God made me thisaway and if you laugh, God may strike you the same way." This is the way He wanted me to be and I ain't disputing His way. I'm showing you because I got to make the best of it. I expect you to act like ladies and gentlemen. I never done it to myself nor had a thing to do with it but I'm making the best of it. I don't dispute hit." Then there was a long silence on the other side of the tent and finally the freak left the men and came over onto the women's side and said the same thing.

The child felt every muscle strained as if she were hearing the answer to a riddle that was more puzzling than the riddle itself. "You mean it had two heads?" she said.

"No," Susan said, "it was a man and woman both. It pulled up its dress and showed us. It had on a blue dress."

The child wanted to ask how it could be a man and woman both without two heads but she did not. She wanted to get back into her own bed and think it out and she began to climb down off the footboard.

"What about the rabbit?" Joanne asked.

The child stopped and only her face appeared over the footboard, abstracted, absent. "It spit them out of its mouth," she said, "six of them."

She lay in bed trying to picture the tent with the freak walking from side to side but she was too sleepy to figure it out. She was better able to see the faces of the country people watching, the men more solemn than they were in church, and the women stern and polite, with painted-looking eyes, standing as if they were waiting for the first note of the piano to begin the hymn. She could hear the freak saying, "God made me thisaway and I don't dispute hit," and the people saying, "Amen. Amen."

"God done this to me and I praised Him."

"Amen. Amen."

"He could strike you thisaway."

"Amen. Amen."

"But he has not."

"Amen."

"Raise yourself up. A temple of the Holy Ghost. You! You are God's temple, don't you know? Don't you know? God's Spirit has a dwelling in you, don't you know?"

"Amen. Amen."

"If anybody desecrates the temple of God, God will bring him to ruin and if you laugh, He may strike you thisaway. A temple of God is a holy thing. Amen. Amen."

"I am a temple of the Holy Ghost."

"Amen."

The people began to slap their hands without making a loud noise and with a regular beat between the Amens, more and more softly, as if they knew there was a child near, half asleep.

The next afternoon the girls put on their brown convent uniforms again and the child and her mother took them back to Mount St. Scholastica. "Oh glory, oh Pete!" they said. "Back to the salt mines." Alonzo Myers drove them and the child sat in front with him and her mother sat in back between the two girls, telling them such things as how pleased she was to have had them and how they must come back again and then about the good times she and their mothers had had when they were girls at the convent. The child didn't listen to any of this twaddle but kept as close to the locked door as she could get and held her head out the window. They had thought Alonzo would smell better on Sunday but he did not. With her hair blowing over her face she could look directly into the ivory sun which was framed in the middle of the blue afternoon but when she pulled it away from her eyes she had to squint.

Mount St. Scholastica was a red brick house set back in a garden in the center of town. There was a filling station on one side of it and a firehouse on the other. It had a high black grillework fence around it and narrow bricked walks between old trees and japonica bushes that were heavy with blooms. A big moonfaced nun came bustling to the door to let them in and embraced her mother and would have done the same to her but that she stuck out her hand and preserved a frigid frown, looking just past the sister's shoes at the wainscoting. They had a tendency to kiss even homely children, but the nun shook her hand vigorously and even cracked her knuckles a little and said they must come to the chapel, that benediction was just beginning. You put your foot in their door and they got you praying, the child thought as they hurried down the polished corridor.

You'd think she had to catch a train, she continued in the same ugly vein as they entered the chapel where the sisters were kneeling on one side and the girls, all in brown uniforms, on the other. The chapel smelled of incense. It was light green and gold, a series of springing arches that ended with the one over the altar where the priest was kneeling in front of the monstrance, bowed low. A small boy in a surplice was standing behind him, swinging the censer. The child knelt down between her mother and the nun and they were well into the *"Tantum Ergo"* before her ugly thoughts stopped and she began to realize that she was in the presence of God. Hep me not to be so mean, she began mechanically. Hep me not to give her so much sass. Hep me not to talk like I do. Her mind began to get quiet and then empty but when the priest raised the monstrance with the Host shining ivory-colored in the center of it, she was thinking of the tent at the fair that had the freak in it. The freak was saying, "I don't dispute hit. This is the way He wanted me to be."

As they were leaving the convent door, the big nun swooped down on her mischievously and nearly smothered her in the black habit, mashing the side of her face into the crucifix hitched onto her belt and then holding her off and looking at her with little periwinkle eyes.

On the way home she and her mother sat in the back and Alonzo drove by himself in the front. The child observed three folds of fat in the back of his neck and noted that his ears were pointed almost like a pig's. Her mother, making conversation, asked him if he had gone to the fair.

"Gone," he said, "and never missed a thing and it was good I gone when I did because they ain't going to have it next week like they said they was."

"Why?" asked her mother.

"They shut it on down," he said. "Some of the preachers from town gone out and inspected it and got the police to shut it on down."

Her mother let the conversation drop and the child's round face was lost in thought. She turned it toward the window and looked out over a stretch of pasture land that rose and fell with a gathering greenness until it touched the dark woods. The sun was a huge red ball like an elevated Host drenched in blood and when it sank out of sight, it left a line in the sky like a red clay road hanging over the trees.

The Rocking-Horse Winner

BY D. H. LAWRENCE

There was a woman who was beautiful, who started with all the advantages, yet she had no luck. She married for love, and the love turned to dust. She had bonny children, yet she felt they had been thrust upon her, and she could not love them. They looked at her coldly, as if they were finding fault with her. And hurriedly she felt she must cover up some fault in herself. Yet what it was that she must cover up she never knew. Nevertheless, when her children were present, she always felt the center of her heart go hard. This troubled her, and in her manner she was all the more gentle and anxious for her children, as if she loved them very much. Only she herself knew that at the center of her heart was a hard little place that could not feel love, no, not for anybody. Everybody else said of her: "She is such a good mother. She adores her children." Only she herself, and her children themselves, knew it was not so. They read it in each other's eyes.

There were a boy and two little girls. They lived in a pleasant house, with a garden, and they had discreet servants, and felt themselves superior to anyone in the neighbourhood.

Although they lived in style, they felt always an

ánxiety in the house. There was never enough money. The mother had a small income, and the father had a small income, but not nearly enough for the social position which they had to keep up. The father went into town to some office. But though he had good prospects, these prospects never materialized. There was always the grinding sense of the shortage of money, though the style was always kept up.

At last the mother said: "I will see if I can't make something." But she did not know where to begin. She racked her brains, and tried this thing and the other, but could not find anything successful. The failure made deep lines come into her face. Her children were growing up, they would have to go to school. There must be more money, there must be more money. The father, who was always very handsome and expensive in his tastes, seemed as if he never would be able to do anything worth doing. And the mother, who had a great belief in herself, did not succeed any better, and her tastes were just as expensive.

And so the house came to be haunted by the unspoken phrase: There must be more money! There must be more money! The children could hear it all the time, though nobody said it aloud. They heard it at Christmas, when the expensive and splendid toys filled the nursery. Behind the shining modern rocking horse, behind the smart doll's-house, a voice would start whispering: "There must be more money! There must be more money!" And the children would stop playing, to listen for a moment. They would look into each other's eyes, to see if they had all heard. And each one saw in the eyes of the other two that they too had heard. "There must be more money! There must be more money!"

It came whispering from the springs of the still-swaying rocking horse, and even the horse, bending his wooden, champing head, heard it. The big doll, sitting so pink and smirking in her new pram, could hear it quite plainly, and seemed to be smirking all the more self-consciously because of it. The foolish puppy, too, that took the place of the Teddy bear, he was looking so extraordinarily foolish for no other reason but that he heard the secret whisper all over the house: "There must be more money!"

Yet nobody ever said it aloud. The whisper was everywhere, and therefore no one spoke it. Just as no one ever says: "We are breathing!" in spite of the fact that breath is coming and going all the time.

"Mother," said the boy Paul one day, "why don't we keep a car of our own? Why do we always use uncle's, or else a taxi?"

"Because we're the poor members of the family," said the mother.

"But why are we, mother?"

"Well—I suppose," she said slowly and bitterly, "it's because your father has no luck."

The boy was silent for some time.

"Is luck money, mother?" he asked, rather timidly.

"No, Paul. Not quite. It's what causes you to have money."

"Oh!" said Paul vaguely. "I thought when Uncle Oscar said filthy lucker, it meant money."

"Filthy lucre does mean money," said the mother. "But it's lucre, not luck."

"Oh!" said the boy. "Then what is luck, mother?"

"It's what causes you to have money. If you're lucky you have money. That's why it's better to be born lucky than rich. If you're rich, you may lose your money. But if you're lucky, you will always get more money."

"Oh! Will you? And is father not lucky?"

"Very unlucky, I should say," she said bitterly.

The boy watched her with unsure eyes.

"Why?" he asked.

"I don't know. Nobody ever knows why one person is lucky and another unlucky."

"Don't they? Nobody at all? Does nobody know?"

"Perhaps God. But He never tells."

"He ought to, then. And aren't you lucky either, mother?"

"I can't be, if I married an unlucky husband."

"But by yourself, aren't you?"

"I used to think I was, before I married. Now I think I am very unlucky indeed."

"Why?"

"Well—never mind! Perhaps I'm not really," she said.

The child looked at her, to see if she meant it. But he saw, by the lines of her mouth, that she was only trying to hide something from him.

"Well, anyhow," he said stoutly, "I'm a lucky person."

"Why?" said his mother, with a sudden laugh.

He stared at her. He didn't even know why he had said it.

"God told me," he asserted, brazening it out.

"I hope He did, dear!" she said, again with a laugh, but rather bitter.

"He did, mother!"

"Excellent!" said the mother, using one of her husband's exclamations.

The boy saw she did not believe him; or, rather,

that she paid no attention to his assertion. This angered him somewhat, and made him want to compel her attention.

He went off by himself, vaguely, in a childish way, seeking for the clue to "luck." Absorbed, taking no heed of other people, he went about with a sort of stealth, seeking inwardly for luck. He wanted luck, he wanted it, he wanted it. When the two girls were playing dolls in the nursery, he would sit on his big rocking horse, charging madly into space, with a frenzy that made the little girls peer at him uneasily. Wildly the horse careered, the waving dark hair of the boy tossed, his eyes had a strange glare in them. The little girls dared not speak to him.

When he had ridden to the end of his mad little journey, he climbed down and stood in front of his rocking horse, staring fixedly into its lowered face. Its red mouth was slightly open, its big eye was wide and glassy-bright.

"Now!" he would silently command the snorting steed. "Now, take me to where there is luck! Now take me!"

And he would slash the horse on the neck with the little whip he had asked Uncle Oscar for. He knew the horse could take him to where there was luck, if only he forced it. So he would mount again, and start on his furious ride, hoping at last to get there. He knew he could get there.

"You'll break your horse, Paul!" said the nurse.

"He's always riding like that! I wish he'd leave off!" said his elder sister Joan.

But he only glared down on them in silence. Nurse gave him up. She could make nothing of him. Anyhow he was growing beyond her.

One day his mother and his Uncle Oscar came in when he was on one of his furious rides. He did not speak to them.

"Hallo, you young jockey! Riding a winner?" said his uncle.

"Aren't you growing too big for a rocking horse? You're not a very little boy any longer, you know," said his mother.

But Paul only gave a blue glare from his big, rather close-set eyes. He would speak to nobody when he was in full tilt. His mother watched him with an anxious expression on her face.

At last he suddenly stopped forcing his horse into the mechanical gallop, and slid down.

"Well, I got there!" he announced fiercely, his blue eyes still flaring, and his sturdy long legs straddling apart.

"Where did you get to?" asked his mother.

"Where I wanted to go," he flared back at her.

"That's right, son!" said Uncle Oscar. "Don't you stop till you get there. What's the horse's name?"

"He doesn't have a name," said the boy.

"Gets on without all right?" asked the uncle.

"Well, he has different names. He was called Sansovino last week."

"Sansovino, eh? Won the Ascot. How did you know his name?"

"He always talks about horse races with Bassett," said Joan.

The uncle was delighted to find that his small nephew was posted with all the racing news. Bassett, the young gardener, who had been wounded in the left foot in the war and had got his present job through Oscar Cresswell, whose batman he had been, was a perfect blade of the "turf." He lived in the racing events, and the small boy lived with him.

Oscar Cresswell got it all from Bassett.

"Master Paul comes and asks me, so I can't do more than tell him, sir," said Bassett, his face terribly serious, as if he were speaking of religious matters.

"And does he ever put anything on a horse he fancies?"

"Well—I don't want to give him away—he's a young sport, a fine sport, sir. Would you mind asking him yourself? He sort of takes a pleasure in it, and perhaps he'd feel I was giving him away, sir, if you don't mind."

Bassett was serious as a church.

The uncle went back to his nephew, and took him off for a ride in the car.

"Say, Paul, old man, do you ever put anything on a horse?" the uncle asked.

The boy watched the handsome man closely.

"Why, do you think I oughtn't to?" he parried.

"Not a bit of it! I thought perhaps you might give me a tip for the Lincoln."

The car sped on into the country, going down to Uncle Oscar's place in Hampshire.

"Honor bright?" said the nephew.

"Honor bright, son!" said the uncle.

"Well, then, Daffodil."

"Daffodil! I doubt it, sonny. What about Mirza?"

"I only know the winner," said the boy. "That's Daffodil."

"Daffodil, eh?"

There was a pause. Daffodil was an obscure horse comparatively.

"Uncle!"

"Yes, son?"

"You won't let it go any further, will you? I promised Bassett."

"Bassett be damned, old man! What's he got to do with it?"

"We're partners. We've been partners from the first. Uncle, he lent me my first five shillings, which I lost. I promised him, honor bright, it was only between me and him; only you gave me that ten shilling note I started winning with, so I thought you were lucky. You won't let it go any further, will you?"

The boy gazed at his uncle from those big, hot, blue eyes, set rather close together. The uncle stirred and laughed uneasily.

"Right you are, son! I'll keep your tip private. Daffodil, eh? How much are you putting on him?"

"All except twenty pounds," said the boy. "I keep that in reserve."

The uncle thought it a good joke.

"You keep twenty pounds in reserve, do you, you young romancer? What are you betting, then?"

"I'm betting three hundred," said the boy gravely. "But it's between you and me, Uncle Oscar! Honor bright?"

The uncle burst into a roar of laughter.

"It's between you and me all right, you young Nat Gould," he said, laughing. "But where's your three hundred?"

"Bassett keeps it for me. We're partners."

"You are, are you! And what is Bassett putting on Daffodil?"

"He won't go quite as high as I do, I expect. Perhaps he'll go a hundred and fifty."

"What, pennies?" laughed the uncle.

"Pounds," said the child, with a surprised look at his uncle. "Bassett keeps a bigger reserve than I do."

Between wonder and amusement Uncle Oscar was silent. He pursued the matter no further, but he determined to take his nephew with him to the Lincoln races.

"Now, son," he said, "I'm putting twenty on Mirza, and I'll put five for you on any horse you fancy. What's your pick?"

"Daffodil, uncle."

"No, not the fiver on Daffodil!"

"I should if it was my own fiver," said the child.

"Good! Good! Right you are! A fiver for me and a fiver for you on Daffodil."

The child had never been to a race meeting before, and his eyes were blue fire. He pursed his mouth tight, and watched. A Frenchman just in front had put his money on Lancelot. Wild with excitement, he flayed his arms up and down, yelling "Lancelot! Lancelot!" in his French accent.

Daffodil came in first, Lancelot second, Mirza third. The child, flushed and with eyes blazing, was curiously serene. His uncle brought him four five-pound notes, four to one.

"What am I to do with these?" he cried, waving them before the boy's eyes.

"I suppose we'll talk to Bassett," said the boy. "I expect I have fifteen hundred now; and twenty in reserve; and this twenty."

His uncle studied him for some moments.

"Look here, son!" he said. "You're not serious about Bassett and that fifteen hundred, are you?"

"Yes, I am. But it's between you and me, uncle. Honor bright!"

"Honor bright all right, son! But I must talk to Bassett."

"If you'd like to be a partner, uncle, with Bassett and me, we could all be partners. Only, you'd have to promise, honor bright, uncle, not to let it go beyond us three. Bassett and I are lucky, and you must be lucky, because it was your ten shillings I started winning with . . ."

Uncle Oscar took both Bassett and Paul into Richmond Park for an afternoon, and there they talked.

"It's like this, you see, sir," Bassett said. "Master Paul would get me talking about racing events, spinning yarns, you know, sir. And he was always keen on knowing if I'd made or if I'd lost. It's about a year since, now, that I put five shillings on Blush of Dawn for him—and we lost. Then the luck turned, with that ten shillings he had from you, that we put on Singhalese. And since that time, it's been pretty steady, all things considering. What do you say, Master Paul?"

"We're all right when we're sure," said Paul. "It's when we're not quite sure that we go down."

"Oh, but we're careful then," said Bassett.

"But when are you sure?" smiled Uncle Oscar.

"It's Master Paul, sir," said Bassett, in a secret, religious voice. "It's as if he had it from heaven. Like Daffodil, now, for the Lincoln. That was as sure as eggs."

"Did you put anything on Daffodil?" asked Oscar Cresswell.

"Yes, sir, I made my bit."

"And my nephew?"

Bassett was obstinately silent, looking at Paul.

"I made twelve hundred, didn't I, Bassett? I told uncle I was putting three hundred on Daffodil."

"That's right," said Bassett, nodding.

"But where's the money?" asked the uncle.

"I keep it safe locked up, sir. Master Paul he can have it any minute he likes to ask for it."

"What, fifteen hundred pounds?"

"And twenty! and forty, that is, with the twenty he made on the course."

"It's amazing!" said the uncle.

"If Master Paul offers you to be partners, sir, I would, if I were you; if you'll excuse me," said Bassett.

Oscar Cresswell thought about it.

"I'll see the money," he said.

They drove home again, and sure enough, Bassett came round to the garden-house with fifteen hundred pounds in notes. The twenty pounds reserve was left with Joe Glee, in the Turf Commission deposit.

"You see, it's all right, uncle, when I'm sure! Then we go strong, for all we're worth. Don't we, Bassett?"

"We do that, Master Paul."

"And when are you sure?" said the uncle, laughing.

"Oh, well, sometimes I'm absolutely sure, like about Daffodil," said the boy; "and sometimes I have an idea; and sometimes I haven't even an idea, have I, Bassett? Then we're careful, because we mostly go down."

'You do, do you! And when you're sure, like about Daffodil, what makes you sure, sonny?"

"Oh, well, I don't know," said the boy uneasily. "I'm sure, you know, uncle; that's all."

"It's as if he had it from heaven, sir," Bassett reiterated.

"I should say so!" said the uncle.

But he became a partner. And when the Leger was coming on, Paul was "sure" about Lively Spark, which was a quite inconsiderable horse. The boy insisted on putting a thousand on the horse, Bassett went for five hundred, and Oscar Cresswell two hundred. Lively Spark came in first, and the betting had been ten to one against him. Paul had made ten thousand.

"You see," he said, "I was absolutely sure of him."

Even Oscar Cresswell had cleared two thousand.

"Look here, son," he said, "this sort of thing makes me nervous."

"It needn't, uncle! Perhaps I shan't be sure again for a long time."

"But what are you going to do with your money?" asked the uncle.

"Of course," said the boy. "I started it for mother. She said she had no luck, because father is unlucky, so I thought if I was lucky, it might stop whispering."

"What might stop whispering?"

"Our house. I hate our house for whispering."

"What does it whisper?"

"Why—why"—the boy fidgeted—"why, I don't know. But it's always short of money, you know, uncle."

"I know it, son, I know it."

"You know people send mother writs, don't you, uncle?"

"I'm afraid I do," said the uncle.

"And then the house whispers, like people laughing at you behind your back. It's awful, that is! I thought if I was lucky . . ."

"You might stop it," added the uncle.

The boy watched him with big blue eyes that had an uncanny cold fire in them, and he said never a word.

"Well, then!" said the uncle. "What are we doing?"

"I shouldn't like mother to know I was lucky," said the boy.

"Why not, son?"

"She'd stop me."

"I don't think she would."

"Oh!"—and the boy writhed in an odd way—"I don't want her to know, uncle."

"All right, son! We'll manage it without her knowing."

They managed it very easily. Paul, at the other's suggestion, handed over five thousand pounds to his uncle, who deposited it with the family lawyer, who was then to inform Paul's mother that a relative had put five thousand pounds into his hands, which sum was to be paid out a thousand pounds at a time, on the mother's birthday, for the next five years.

"So she'll have a birthday present of a thousand pounds for five successive years," said Uncle Oscar. "I hope it won't make it all the harder for her later."

Paul's mother had her birthday in November. The house had been "whispering" worse than ever lately, and, even in spite of his luck, Paul could not bear up against it. He was very anxious to see the effect of the birthday letter, telling his mother about the thousand pounds.

When there were no visitors, Paul now took his meals with his parents, as he was beyond the nursery control. His mother went into town nearly every day. She had discovered that she had an odd knack of sketching furs and dress materials, so she worked secretly in the studio of a friend who was the chief "artist" for the leading drapers. She drew the figures of ladies in furs and ladies in silk and sequins for the newspaper advertisements. This young woman artist earned several thousand pounds a year, but Paul's mother only made several hundreds, and she was again dissatisfied. She so wanted to be first in something, and she did not succeed, even in making sketches for drapery advertisements.

She was down to breakfast on the morning of her birthday. Paul watched her face as she read her letters. He knew the lawyer's letter. As his mother read it, her face hardened and became more expressionless. Then a cold, determined look came on her mouth. She hid the letter under the pile of others, and said not a word about it.

"Didn't you have anything nice in the post for your birthday, mother?" said Paul.

"Quite moderately nice," she said, her voice cold and absent.

She went away to town without saying more.

But in the afternoon Uncle Oscar appeared. He said Paul's mother had had a long interview with the lawyer, asking if the whole five thousand could be advanced at once, as she was in debt.

"What do you think, uncle?" said the boy.

"I leave it to you, son."

"Oh, let her have it, then! We can get some more with the other," said the boy.

"A bird in the hand is worth two in the bush, laddie!" said Uncle Oscar.

"But I'm sure to know for the Grand National; or the Lincolnshire; or else the Derby. I'm sure to know for one of them," said Paul.

So Uncle Oscar signed the agreement, and Paul's mother touched the whole five thousand. Then something very curious happened. The voices in the house suddenly went mad, like a chorus of frogs on a spring evening. There were certain new furnishings, and Paul had a tutor. He was really going to Eton, his father's school, in the following autumn. There were flowers in the winter, and a blossoming of the luxury Paul's mother had been used to. And yet the voices in the house, behind the sprays of mimosa and almond blossom, and from under the piles of iridescent cushions, simply trilled and screamed in a sort of ecstasy: "There must be more money! Oh-h-h, there must be more money. Oh, now, now-w! Now-w-w—there must be more money—more than ever! More than ever!"

It frightened Paul terribly. He studied away at his Latin and Greek with his tutors. But his intense hours were spent with Bassett. The Grand National had gone by: he had not "known," and had lost a hundred pounds. Summer was at hand. He was in agony for the Lincoln. But even for the Lincoln he didn't "know" and he lost fifty pounds. He became wild-eyed and srange, as if something were going to explode in him.

"Let it alone, son! Don't you bother about it!" urged Uncle Oscar. But it was as if the boy couldn't really hear what his uncle was saying.

"I've got to know for the Derby! I've got to know for the Derby!" the child reiterated, his big blue eyes blazing with a sort of madness.

His mother noticed how overwrought he was.

"You'd better go to the seaside. Wouldn't you like to go now to the seaside, instead of waiting? I think you'd better," she said, looking down at him anxiously, her heart curiously heavy because of him.

But the child lifted his uncanny blue eyes.

"I couldn't possibly go before the Derby, mother!" he said. "I couldn't possibly!"

"Why not?" she said, her voice becoming heavy when she was opposed. "Why not? You can still go from the seaside to see the Derby with your Uncle Oscar, if that's what you wish. No need for you to wait here. Besides, I think you care too much about these races. It's a bad sign. My family has been a gambling family, and you won't know till you grow up how much damage it has done. But it has done damage. I shall have to send Bassett away, and ask Uncle Oscar not to talk racing to you, unless you promise to be reasonable about it; go away to the seaside and forget it. You're all nerves!"

"I'll do what you like, mother, so long as you don't send me away till after the Derby," the boy said.

"Send you away from where? Just from this house?"

"Yes," he said, gazing at her.

"Why, you curious child, what makes you care about this house so much, suddenly? I never knew you loved it."

He gazed at her without speaking. He had a secret within a secret, something he had not divulged, even to Bassett or to his Uncle Oscar.

But his mother, after standing undecided and a little bit sullen for some moments, said:

"Very well, then! Don't go to the seaside till after the Derby, if you don't wish it. But promise me you won't let your nerves go to pieces. Promise you won't think so much about horse racing and events, as you call them!"

"Oh, no," said the boy casually. "I won't think much about them, mother. You needn't worry. I wouldn't worry, mother, if I were you."

"If you were me and I were you," said his mother, "I wonder what we should do!"

"But you know you needn't worry, mother, don't you?" the boy repeated.

"I should be awfully glad to know it," she said wearily.

"Oh, well, you can, you know. I mean, you ought to know you needn't worry," he insisted.

"Ought I? Then I'll see about it," she said.

Paul's secret of secrets was his wooden horse, that which had no name. Since he was emancipated from a nurse and a nursery-governess, he had had his rocking horse removed to his own bedroom at the top of the house.

"Surely, you're too big for a rocking horse!" his mother had remonstrated.

"Well, you see, mother, till I can have a real horse, I like to have some sort of animal about," had been his quaint answer.

"Do you feel he keeps you company?" she laughed.

"Oh, yes! He's very good, he always keeps me company, when I'm there," said Paul.

So the horse, rather shabby, stood in an arrested prance in the boy's bedroom.

The Derby was drawing near, and the boy grew more and more tense. He hardly heard what was spoken to him, he was very frail, and his eyes were really uncanny. His mother had sudden seizures of uneasiness about him. Sometimes, for half-an-hour, she would feel a sudden anxiety about him that was almost anguish. She wanted to rush to him at once, and know he was safe.

Two nights before the Derby, she was at a big party in town, when one of her rushes of anxiety about her boy, her first-born, gripped her heart till she could hardly speak. She fought with the feeling, might and main, for she believed in common sense. But it was too strong. She had to leave the dance and go downstairs to telephone to the country. The children's nursery-governess was terribly surprised and startled at being rung up in the night.

"Are the children all right, Miss Wilmot?"

"Oh, yes, they are quite all right."

"Master Paul? Is he all right?"

"He went to bed as right as a trivet. Shall I run up and look at him?"

"No," said Paul's mother reluctantly. "No! Don't trouble. It's all right. Don't sit up. We shall be home fairly soon." She did not want her son's privacy intruded upon.

"Very good," said the governess.

It was about one o'clock when Paul's mother and father drove up to their house. All was still. Paul's mother went to her room and slipped off her white fur coat. She had told her maid not to wait up for her. She heard her husband downstairs, mixing a whisky-and-soda.

And then, because of the strange anxiety at her heart, she stole upstairs to her son's room. Noiselessly she went along the upper corridor. Was there a faint noise? What was it?

She stood, with arrested muscles, outside his door, listening. There was a strange, heavy, and yet not loud noise. Her heart stood still. It was a soundless noise, yet rushing and powerful. Something huge, in violent, hushed motion. What was it? What in God's name was it? She ought to know. She felt that she knew the noise. She knew what it was.

Yet she could not place it. She couldn't say what it was. And on and on it went, like a madness.

Softly, frozen with anxiety and fear, she turned the door handle.

The room was dark. Yet in the space near the window, she heard and saw something plunging to and fro. She gazed in fear and amazement.

Then suddenly she switched on the light, and saw her son, in his green pyjamas, madly surging on the rocking horse. The blaze of light suddenly lit him up, as he urged the wooden horse, and lit her up, as she stood, blonde, in her dress of pale green and crystal, in the doorway.

"Paul!" she cried. "Whatever are you doing?"

"It's Malabar!" he screamed, in a powerful, strange voice. "It's Malabar."

His eyes blazed at her for one strange and senseless second, as he ceased urging his wooden horse. Then he fell with a crash to the ground, and she, all her tormented motherhood flooding upon her, rushed to gather him up.

But he was unconscious, and unconscious he remained, with some brain-fever. He talked and tossed, and his mother sat stonily by his side.

"Malabar! It's Malabar! Bassett, Bassett, I know it! It's Malabar!"

So the child cried, trying to get up and urge the rocking horse that gave him his inspiration.

"What does he mean by Malabar?" asked the heart-frozen mother.

"I don't know," said the father stonily.

"What does he mean by Malabar?" she asked her brother Oscar.

"It's one of the horses running for the Derby," was the answer.

And, in spite of himself, Oscar Cresswell spoke to

Bassett, and himself put a thousand on Malabar: at fourteen to one.

The third day of the illness was critical: they were waiting for a change. The boy, with his rather long, curly hair, was tossing ceaselessly on the pillow. He neither slept nor regained consciousness, and his eyes were like blue stones. His mother sat, feeling her heart had gone, turned actually into a stone.

In the evening, Oscar Cresswell did not come, but Bassett sent a message, saying could he come up for one moment, just one moment? Paul's mother was very angry at the intrusion, but on second thought she agreed. The boy was the same. Perhaps Bassett might bring him to consciousness.

The gardener, a shortish fellow with a little brown moustache, and sharp little brown eyes, tiptoed into the room, touched his imaginary cap to Paul's mother, and stole to the bedside, staring with glittering, small-ish eyes, at the tossing, dying child.

"Master Paul!" he whispered. "Master Paul! Malabar come in first all right, a clean win. I did as you told me. You've made over seventy thousand pounds, you have; you've got over eighty thousand. Malabar came in all right, Master Paul."

"Malabar! Malabar! Did I say Malabar, mother? Did I say Malabar? Do you think I'm lucky, mother? I knew Malabar, didn't I? Over eighty thousand pounds! I call that lucky, don't you, mother? Over eighty thousand pounds! I knew, didn't I know I knew? Malabar came in all right. If I ride my horse till I'm sure, then I tell you, Bassett, you can go as high as you like. Did you go for all you were worth, Bassett?"

"I went a thousand on it, Master Paul."

"I never told you, mother, that if I can ride my horse, and get there, then I'm absolutely sure—oh, absolutely! Mother, did I ever tell you? I'm lucky."

"No, you never did," said the mother.

But the boy died in the night.

And even as he lay dead, his mother heard her brother's voice saying to her: "My God, Hester, you're eighty-odd thousand to the good and a poor devil of a son to the bad. But, poor devil, poor devil, he's best gone out of a life where he rides his rocking horse to find a winner."

Samuel

BY GRACE PALEY

Some boys are very tough. They're afraid of nothing. They are the ones who climb a wall and take a bow at the top. Not only are they brave on the roof, but they make a lot of noise in the darkest part of the cellar where even the super hates to go. They also jiggle and hop on the platform between the locked doors of the subway cars.

Four boys are jiggling on the swaying platform. Their names are Alfred, Calvin, Samuel, and Tom. The men and the women in the cars on either side watch them. They don't like them to jiggle or jump but don't want to interfere. Of course some of the men in the cars were once brave boys like these. One of them had ridden the tail of a speeding truck from New York to Rockaway Beach without getting off, without his sore fingers losing hold. Nothing happened to him then or later. He had made a compact with other boys who preferred to watch: Starting at Eighth Avenue and Fifteenth Street, he would get to some specified place, maybe Twenty-third and the river, by hopping the tops of the moving trucks. This was hard to do when one truck turned a corner in the wrong direction and the nearest truck was a couple of feet too high. He made three or four starts before succeeding. He had gotten this idea from a film at school called *The Romance of Logging*. He had finished high school, married a good friend, was in a responsible job and going to night school.

These two men and others looked at the four boys jumping and jiggling on the platform and thought, It must be fun to ride that way, especially now the weather is nice and we're out of the tunnel and way high over the Bronx. Then they thought, These kids do seem to be acting sort of stupid. They *are* little. Then they thought of some of the brave things they had done when they were boys and jiggling didn't seem so risky.

The ladies in the car became very angry when they looked at the four boys. Most of them brought their brows together and hoped the boys could see their extreme disapproval. One of the ladies wanted to get up and say, Be careful you dumb kids, get off that platform or I'll call a cop. But three of the boys were Negroes and the fourth was something else she couldn't tell for sure. She was afraid they'd be fresh and laugh at her and embarrass her. She wasn't afraid they'd hit her, but she was afraid of embarrassment. Another lady thought, Their mothers never know where they are. It wasn't true in this particular case. Their mothers all knew that they had gone to see the missile exhibit on Fourteenth Street.

Out on the platform, whenever the train accelerated, the boys would raise their hands and point them up to the sky to act like rockets going off, then they rat-tat-tatted the shatterproof glass pane like machine guns, although no machine guns had been exhibited.

For some reason known only to the motorman, the train began a sudden slowdown. The lady who was

afraid of embarrassment saw the boys jerk forward
and backward and grab the swinging guard chains. She
had her own boy at home. She stood up with determination and went to the door. She slid it open
and said, "You boys will be hurt. You'll be killed.
I'm going to call the conductor if you don't just go
into the next car and sit down and be quiet."

Two of the boys said, "Yes'm," and acted as though
they were about to go. Two of them blinked their eyes
a couple of times and pressed their lips together. The
train resumed its speed. The door slid shut, parting
the lady and the boys. She learned against the side
door because she had to get off at the next stop.

The boys opened their eyes wide at each other and
laughed. The lady blushed. The boys looked at her
and laughed harder. They began to pound each other's
back. Samuel laughed the hardest and pounded Alfred's back until Alfred coughed and the tears came.
Alfred held tight to the chain hook. Samuel pounded
him even harder when he saw the tears. He said,
"Why you bawling? You a baby, huh?" and laughed.
One of the men whose boyhood had been more
watchful than brave became angry. He stood up
straight and looked at the boys for a couple of seconds. Then he walked in a citizenly way to the end
of the car, where he pulled the emergency cord. Almost at once, with a terrible hiss, the pressure of air
abandoned the brake and the wheels were caught
and held.

People standing in the most secure places fell forward, then backward. Samuel had let go of his hold
on the chain so he could pound Tom as well as Alfred. All the passengers in the cars whipped back and

forth, but he pitched only forward and fell head first to be crushed and killed between the cars.

The train had stopped hard, halfway into the station, and the conductor called at once for the trainmen who knew about this kind of death and how to take the body from the wheels and brakes. There was silence except for passengers from other cars who asked, What happened! What happened! The ladies waited around wondering if he might be an only child. The men recalled other afternoons with very bad endings. The little boys stayed close to each other, leaning and touching shoulders and arms and legs.

When the policeman knocked at the door and told her about it, Samuel's mother began to scream. She screamed all day and moaned all night, though the doctors tried to quiet her with pills.

Oh, oh, she hopelessly cried. She did not know how she could ever find another boy like that one. However, she was a young woman and she became pregnant. Then for a few months she was hopeful. The child born to her was a boy. They brought him to be seen and nursed. She smiled. But immediately she saw that this baby wasn't Samuel. She and her husband together have had other children, but never again will a boy exactly like Samuel be known.

Mr. Parker

BY LAURIE COLWIN

Mrs. Parker died suddenly in October. She and Mr. Parker lived in a Victorian house next to ours, and Mr. Parker was my piano teacher. He commuted to Wall Street, where he was a securities analyst, but he had studied at Juilliard and gave lessons on the side— for the pleasure of it, not for money. His only students were me and the church organist, who was learning technique on a double-keyboard harpsichord Mr. Parker had built one spring.

Mrs. Parker was known for her pastry; she and my mother were friends, after a fashion. Evey two months or so they spent a day together in the kitchen baking butter cookies and cream puffs, or rolling out strudel leaves. She was thin and wispy, and turned out her pastry with abstract expertness. As a girl, she had had bright-red hair, which was now the color of old leaves. There was something smoky and autumnal about her: she wore rust-colored sweaters and heather-colored skirts, and kept dried weeds in ornamental jars and pressed flowers in frames. If you borrowed a book fom her, there were petal marks on the back pages. She was tall, but she stooped as it she had spent a lifetime looking for something she had dropped.

The word "tragic" was mentioned in connection

with her death. She and Mr. Parker were in the middle of their middle age, and neither of them had ever been seriously ill. It was heart failure, and unexpected. My parents went to see Mr. Parker as soon as they got the news, since they took their responsibilities as neighbors seriously, and two days later they took me to pay a formal condolence call. It was Indian summer, and the house felt closed in. They had used the fireplace during a recent cold spell, and the living smelled faintly of ash. The only people from the community were some neighbors, the minister and his wife, and the rabbi and his wife and son. The Parkers were Episcopalian, but Mr. Parker played the organ in the synagogue on Saturday mornings and on High Holy Days. There was a large urn of tea, and the last of Mrs. Parker's strudel. On the sofa were Mrs. Parker's siters, and a man who looked like Mr. Parker ten years younger leaned against the piano, which was closed. The conversation was hushed and stilted. On the way out, the rabbi's son tried to trip me, and I kicked him in return. We were adolescent enemies of a loving sort, and since we didn't know what else to do, we expressed our love in slaps and pinches and other mild attempts at grievous bodily harm.

I loved the Parker's house. It was the last Victorian house on the block, and was shaped like a wedding cake. The living room was round, and all the walls curved. The third floor was a tower, on top of which sat a weathervane. Every five years the house was painted chocolate brown, which faded gradually to the color of weak tea. The front-hall window was a stained-glass picture of a fat Victorian baby holding a bunch of roses. The baby's face was puffy and neuter, and its eyes were that of an old man caught in a state of surprise. Its white dress was milky when the light shone through.

On Wednesday afternoons, Mr. Parker came home on an early train, and I had my lesson. Mr. Parker's teaching method never varied. He never scolded or corrected. The first fifteen minutes were devoted to a warmup in which I could play anything I liked. Then Mr. Parker played the lesson of the week. His playing was terrifically precise, but his eyes became dreamy and unfocused. Then I played the same lesson, and after that we worked on the difficult passages, but basically he wanted me to hear my mistakes. When we began a new piece, we played it part by part, taking turns, over and over.

After that, we sat in the solarium and discussed the next week's lesson. Mr. Parker usually played a record and talked in detail about the composer, his life and times, and the form. With the exception of Mozart and Schubert, he liked Baroque music almost exclusively. The lesson of the week was always Bach, which Mr. Parker felt taught elegance and precision. Mrs. Parker used to leave us a tray of cookies and lemonade, cold in the summer and hot in the winter, with cinnamon sticks. When the cookies were gone, the lesson was over and I left, passing the Victorian child in the hallway.

In the days after the funeral, my mother took several casseroles over to Mr. Parker and invited him to dinner a number of times. For several weeks he revolved between us, the minister, and the rabbi. Since neither of my parents cared much about music, except to hear my playing praised, the conversation at dinner was limited to the stock market and the blessings of country life.

In a few weeks, I got a note from Mr. Parker enclosed in a thank-you note to my parents. It said that piano lessons would begin the following Wednesday.

I went to the Parkers' after school. Everything was the same. I warmed up for fifteen minutes, Mr. Parker played the lesson, and I repeated it. In the solarium were the usual cookies and lemonade.

"Are they good, these cookies?" Mr. Parker asked.

I said they were.

"I made them yesterday," he said. "I've got to be my own baker now."

Mr. Parker's hair had once been blond, but was graying into the color of straw. Both he and Mrs. Parker seemed to have faded out of some bright time they once had lived in. He was very thin, as if the friction of living had burned every unnecessary particle off him, but he was calm and cheery in the way you expect plump people to be. On teaching days, he always wore a blue cardigan, buttoned, and a striped tie. Both smelled faintly of tobacco. At the end of the lesson, he gave me a robin's egg he had found. The light was flickering through the bunch of roses in the window as I left.

When I got home, I found my mother in the kitchen, waiting and angry.

"Where were you?" she said.

"At my piano lesson."

"What piano lesson?"

"You know what piano lesson. At Mr. Parker's."

"You didn't tell me you were going to a piano lesson," she said.

"I always have a lesson on Wednesday."

"I don't want you having lessons there now that Mrs. Parker's gone." She slung a roast into a pan.

I stomped off to my room and wrapped the robin's egg in a sweat sock. My throat felt shriveled and hot.

At dinner, my mother said to my father, "I don't want Jane taking piano lessons from Mr. Parker now that Mrs. Parker's gone."

"Why don't you want me to have lessons?" I said, close to shouting. "There's no reason."

"She can study with Mrs. Murchison." Mrs. Murchison had been my first teacher. She was a fat, myopic woman who smelled of bacon grease and whose repertoire was confined to "Little Classics for Children." Her students were mostly under ten, and she kept an asthmatic chow who was often sick on the rug.

"I won't go to Mrs. Murchison!" I shouted. "I've outgrown her."

"Let's be sensible about this," said my father. "Calm down, Janie."

I stuck my fork into a potato to keep from crying and muttered melodramatically that I would hang myself before I'd go back to Mrs. Murchison.

The lessons continued. At night I practiced quietly, and from time to time my mother would look up and say, "That's nice, dear." Mr. Parker had given me a Three-Part Invention, and I worked on it as if it were granite. It was the most complicated piece of music I had ever played, and I learned it with a sense of loss; since I didn't know when the ax would fall, I thought it might be the last piece of music I would ever learn from Mr. Parker.

The lessons went on and nothing was said, but when I came home after them my mother and I faced each other with division and coldness. Mr. Parker bought a kitten called Mildred to keep him company in the house. When we had our cookies and lemonade, Mildred got a saucer of milk.

At night, I was grilled by my mother as we washed the dishes. I found her sudden interest in the events of my day unnerving. She was systematic, beginning with my morning classes, ending in the afternoon. In the light of her intense focus, everything seemed wrong. Then she said, with arch sweetness, "And how is Mr. Parker, dear?"

"Fine."

"And how are the lessons going?"

"Fine."

"And how is the house now that Mrs. Parker's gone?"

"It's the same. Mr. Parker bought a kitten." As I said it, I knew it was betrayal.

"What kind of kitten?"

"A sort of pink one."

"What's its name?"

"It doesn't have one," I said.

One night she said, "Does Mr. Parker drink?"

"He drinks lemonade."

"I only asked because it must be so hard for him," she said in an offended voice. "He must be very sad."

"He doesn't seem all that sad to me." It was the wrong thing to say.

"I see," she said, folding the dish towel with elaborate care. "You know how I feel about this, Jane. I don't want you alone in the house with him."

"He's my *piano* teacher." I was suddenly in tears, so I ran out of the kitchen and up to my room.

She followed me up, and sat on the edge of my bed while I sat at the desk, secretly crying onto the blotter.

"I only want what's best for you," she said.

"If you want what's best for me, why don't you want me to have piano lessons?"

"I *do* want you to have piano lessons, but you're growing up and it doesn't look right for you to be in a house alone with a widowed man."

"I think you're crazy."

"I don't think you understand what I'm trying to say. You're not a little girl any more, Jane. There are privileges of childhood, and privileges of adulthood, and you're in the middle. It's difficult, I know."

"You don't know. You're just trying to stop me from taking piano lessons."

She stood up. "I'm trying to protect you," she said. "What if Mr. Parker touched you? What would you do then?" She made the word "touch" sound sinister.

"You're just being mean," I said, and by this time I was crying openly. It would have fixed things to throw my arms around her, but that meant losing, and this was war.

"We'll discuss it some other time," she said, close to tears herself.

I worked on the Invention until my hands shook. When I came home, if the house was empty, I practiced in a panic, and finally, it was almost right. On Wednesday, I went to Mr. Parker's and stood at the doorway, expecting something drastic and changed, but it was all the same. There were cookies and lemonade in the solarium. Mildred took a nap on my coat. My fifteen-minute warmup was terrible; I made mistakes in the simplest parts, in things I knew by heart. Then Mr. Parker played the lesson of the week and I tried to memorize his phrasing exactly. Before my turn came, Mr. Parker put the metronome on the floor and we watched Mildred trying to catch the arm.

I played it, and I knew it was right—I was playing music, not struggling with a lesson.

When I was finished, Mr. Parker grabbed me by the shoulders. "That's perfect! Really perfect!" he said. "A real breakthrough. These are the times that make teachers glad they teach."

We had lemonade and cookies and listened to some Palestrina motets. When I left, it was overcast, and the light was murky and green.

I walked home slowly, divided by dread and joy in equal parts. I had performed like an adult, and had been congratulated by an adult, but something had been closed off. I sat under a tree and cried like a baby. He had touched me after all.

The Deal

BY LEONARD MICHAELS

Twenty were jammed together on the stoop; tiers of
heads made one central head, and the wings rested
along the banisters: a raggedy monster of boys studying her approach. Her white face and legs. She passed
without looking, poked her sunglasses against the
bridge of her nose and tucked her bag between her
arm and ribs. She carried it at her hip like a rifle stock.
On her spine forty eyes hung like poison berries. Bone
dissolved beneath her lank beige silk, and the damp
circle of her belt cut her in half. Independent legs
struck toward the points of her shoes. Her breasts
lifted and rode the air like porpoises. She would cross
to the grocery as usual, buy cigarettes, then cross back
despite their eyes. As if the neighborhood hadn't
changed one bit. She slipped the bag forward to crack
it against her belly and pluck out keys and change.
In the gesture she was home from work. Her keys
jangled in the sun as if they opened everything and
the air received her. The monster, watching, saw the
glove fall away.

Pigeons looped down to whirl between buildings,
and a ten-wheel truck came slowly up the street. As it
passed she emerged from the grocery, then stood at
the curb opposite the faces. She glanced along the

street where she had crossed it. No glove. Tar reticulated between the cobbles. A braid of murky water ran against the curb, twisting bits of flotsam toward the drain. She took off her sunglasses, dropped them with her keys into the bag, then stepped off the curb toward the faces. Addressing them with a high, friendly voice, she said: "Did you guys see a glove? I dropped it a moment ago."

The small ones squinted up at her from the bottom step. On the middle steps sat boys fourteen or fifteen years old. The oldest ones made the wings. Dandies and introverts, they sprawled, as if with a common corruption in their bones. In the center, his eyes level with hers, a boy waited for her attention in the matter of gloves. To his right sat a very thin boy with a pocked face. A narrow-brimmed hat tipped toward his nose and shaded the continuous activity of his eyes. She spoke to the green eyes of the boy in the center and held up the glove she had: "Like this."

Teeth appeared below the hat, then everywhere as the boys laughed. Did she hold up a fish? Green eyes said: "Hello, Miss Calile."

She looked around at the faces, then laughed with them at her surprise. "You know my name?"

"I see it on the mailbox," said the hat. "He can't read. I see it."

"My name is Duke Francisco," said the illiterate.

"My name is Abbe Carlyle," she said to him.

The hat smirked. "His name Francisco Lopez."

Green eyes turned to the hat. "Shut you mouth, baby. I tell her my name, not you."

"His name Francisco Lopez," the hat repeated.

She saw pocks and teeth, the thin oily face and the hat, as he spoke again, nicely to her: "My name Francisco Pacheco, the Prince. I seen you name on the mailbox."

"Did either of you . . ."

"You name is shit," said green eyes to the hat.

"My name is Tito." A small one on the bottom step looked up for the effect of his name. She looked down at him. "I am Tito," he said.

"Did you see my glove, Tito?"

"This is Tomato," he answered, unable to bear her attention. He nudged the boy to his left. Tomato nudged back, stared at the ground.

"I am happy to know you, Tito," she said, "and you, Tomato. Both of you." She looked back up to green eyes and the hat. The hat acknowledged her courtesy. He tilted back to show her his eyes, narrow and black except for bits of white reflected in the corners. His face was thin, high-boned and fragile. She pitied the riddled skin.

"This guy," he said, pointing his thumb to the right, "is Monkey," and then to the left beyond green eyes, "and this guy is Beans." She nodded to the hat, then Monkey, then Beans, measuring the respect she offered, doling it out in split seconds. Only one of them had the glove.

"Well, did any of you guys see my glove?"

Every tier grew still, like birds in a tree waiting for a sign that would move them all at once.

Tito's small dark head snapped forward. She heard the slap an instant late. The body lurched after the head and pitched off the stoop at her feet. She saw green eyes sitting back slowly. Tito gaped up at her from the concrete. A sacrifice to the lady. She stepped back as if rejecting it and frowned at green eyes. He gazed indifferently at Tito, who was up, facing him with coffee-bean fists. Tito screamed, "I tell her you got it, dick-head."

The green eyes swelled in themselves like a light blooming in the ocean. Tito's fists opened, he turned, folded quickly and sat back into the mass. He began to rub his knees.

"May I have my glove, Francisco?" Her voice was still pleasant and high. She now held her purse in the crook of her arm and pressed it against her side.

Some fop had a thought and giggled in the wings. She glanced up at him immediately. He produced a toothpick. With great delicacy he stuck it into his ear. She looked away. Green eyes again waited for her. A cup of darkness formed in the hollow that crowned his chestbone. His soiled gray polo shirt hooked below it. "You think I have you glove?" She didn't answer. He stared between his knees, between heads and shoulders to the top of Tito's head. "Hey, Tito, you tell her I got the glove?"

"I didn't tell nothing," muttered Tito rubbing his knees harder as if they were still bitter from his fall.

"He's full of shit, Miss Calile. I break his head later. What kind of glove you want?"

"This kind," she said wearily, "a white glove like this."

"Too hot." He grinned.

"Yes, too hot, but I need it."

"What for? Too hot." He gave her full green concern.

"It's much too hot, but the glove is mine, mister."

She rested her weight on one leg and wiped her brow with the glove she had. They watched her do it, the smallest of them watched her, and she moved the glove slowly to her brow again and drew it down her cheek and neck. She could think of nothing to say, nothing to do without expressing impatience. Green eyes changed the subject. "You live there." He pointed toward her building.

"That's right."

A wooden front door with a window in it showed part of the shadowy lobby, mailboxes, and a second floor. Beyond her building and down the next street were warehouses. Beyond them, the river. A meat truck started toward them from a packing house near the river. It came slowly, bug-eyed with power. The driver saw the lady standing in front of the boys. He yelled as the truck went past. Gears yowled, twisting the sound of his voice. She let her strength out abruptly: "Give me the glove, Francisco."

The boy shook his head at the truck, at her lack of civilization. "What you give me?"

That tickled the hat. "*Vaya,* baby. What she give you, eh?" He spoke fast, his tone decorous and filthy.

"All right, baby," she said fast as the hat, "what do you want?" The question had New York and much man in it. The hat swiveled to the new sound. A man of honor, let him understand the terms. He squinted at her beneath the hat brim.

"Come on, Francisco, make your deal." She presented brave, beautiful teeth, smiling hard as a skull.

"Tell her, Duke. Make the deal." The hat lingered on "deal," grateful to the lady for this word.

The sun shone in his face and the acknowledged duke sat dull, green eyes blank with possibilities. Her question, not "deal," held him. It had come too hard, too fast. He laughed in contempt of something and glanced around at the wings. They offered nothing. "I want a dollar," he said.

That seemed obvious to the hat: he sneered, "He wants a dollar." She had to be stupid not to see it.

"No deal. Twenty-five cents." Her gloves were worth twenty dollars. She had paid ten for them at a sale. At the moment they were worth green eyes' life.

"I want ten dollars," said green eyes flashing the words like extravagant meaningless things; gloves of his own. He lifted his arms, clasped his hands behind his head and leaned against the knees behind him. His belly filled with air, the polo shirt rolled out on its curve. He made a fat man doing business. "Ten dollars." Ten fingers popped up behind his head like grimy spikes. Keeper of the glove, cocky duke of the stoop. The number made him happy: it bothered her. He drummed the spikes against his head: "I wan' you ten dol-lar." Beans caught the beat in his hips and rocked it on the stoop.

"Francisco," she said, hesitated, then said, "dig me, please. You will get twenty-five cents. Now let's have the glove." Her bag snapped open, her fingers hooked. stiffened on the clasp. Monkey leered at her and bongoed his knees with fists. "The number is ten dol-lar." She waited, said nothing. The spikes continued drumming, Monkey rocked his hips, Beans pummeled his knees. The hat sang sadly: "Twany fyiv not d'nummer, not d'nummer, not d'nummer." He made claves of his fingers and palms, tocked, clicked his tongue against the beat. "Twan-ny fyiv— na t'nomma." She watched green eyes. He was quiet now in the center of the stoop, sitting motionless, waiting, as though seconds back in time his mind still touched the question: what did he want? He seemed to wonder, now that he had the formula, what *did* he want? The faces around him, dopey in the music, wondered nothing, grinned at her, nodded, clicked, whined the chorus: "Twany-fyiv not t'nomma, twany fyiv not t'nomma."

Her silk blouse stained and stuck flat to her breasts and shoulders. Water chilled her sides.

"Ten dol-lar iss t'nomma."

She spread her feet slightly, taking better possession of the sidewalk and resting on them evenly, the bag held open for green eyes. She could see he didn't want that, but she insisted in her silence he did. Tito spread his little feet and lined the points of his shoes against hers. Tomato noticed the imitation and cackled at the concrete. The music went on, the beat feeding on itself, pulverizing words, smearing them into liquid submission: "Iss t'nomma twany fyiv? Dat iss not t'nomma."

"Twenty-five cents," she said again.

Tito whined, "Gimme twenty-five cents."

"Shut you mouth," said the hat, and turned a grim face to his friend. In the darkness of his eyes there were deals. The music ceased. "Hey, baby, you got no manners? Tell what you want." He spoke in a dreamy voice, as if to a girl.

"I want a kiss," said green eyes.

She glanced down with this at Tito and studied the small shining head. "Tell him to give me my glove, Tito," she said cutely, nervously. The wings shuffled and looked down bored. Nothing was happening. Twisting backwards Tito shouted up to green eyes, "Give her the glove." He twisted front again and crouched over his knees. He shoved Tomato for approval and smiled. Tomato shoved him back, snarled at the concrete and spit between his feet at a face which had taken shape in the grains.

"I want a kiss," said the boy again.

She sighed, giving another second to helplessness. The sun was low above the river and the street three quarters steeped in shade. Sunlight cut across the building tops where pigeons swept by loosely and and fluttered in to pack the stone foliage of the eaves. Her bag snapped shut. Her voice was business: "Come on, Francisco. I'll give you the kiss."

He looked shot among the faces.

"Come on," she said, "it's a deal."

The hat laughed out loud with childish insanity. The others shrieked and jiggled, except for the wings. But they ceased to sprawl, and seemed to be getting bigger, to fill with imminent motion. "Gimme a kiss, gimme a kiss," said the little ones on the lowest step. Green eyes sat with a quiet, open mouth.

"Let's go," she said. "I haven't all day."

"Where I go?"

"That doorway." She pointed to her building and took a step toward it. "You know where I live, don't you?"

"I don't want no kiss."

"What's the matter now?"

"You scared?" asked the hat. "Hey, Duke, you scared?"

The wings leaned toward the center, where green eyes hugged himself and made a face.

"Look, Mr. Francisco, you made a deal."

"Yeah," said the wings.

"Now come along."

"I'm not scared," he shouted and stood up among them. He sat down. "I don't want no kiss."

"You're scared?" she said.

"You scared chicken," said the hat.

"Yeah," said the wings. "Hey, punk. Fairy. Hey, Duke Chicken."

"Duke scared," mumbled Tito. Green eyes stood up again. The shoulders below him separated. Tito leaped clear of the stoop and trotted into the street. Green eyes passed through the place he had vacated and stood at her side, his head not so high as her shoulder. She nodded at him, tucked her bag up and began walking toward her building. A few others stood up on the stoop and the hat started down. She turned. "Just him." Green eyes shuffled after her. The hat stopped on the sidewalk. Someone pushed him forward. He resisted, but called after them, "He's my cousin." She walked on, the boy came slowly after her. They were yelling from the stoop, the hat yelling his special point, "He's my brother." He stepped after them and the others swarmed behind him down the stoop and onto the sidewalk. Tito jumped out of the street and ran alongside the hat. He yelled, "He's got the glove." They all moved down the block, the wings trailing sluggishly, the young ones jostling, punching each other, laughing, shrieking things in Spanish after green eyes and the lady. She heard him, a step behind her. "I give you the glove and take off."

She put her hand out to the side a little. The smaller hand touched hers and took it. "You made a deal."

She tugged him through the doorway into the tight, square lobby. The hand snapped free and he swung by, twisting to face her as if to meet a glow. He put his back against the second door, crouched a little. His hands pressed the sides of his legs. The front door shut slowly and the shadows deepened in the lobby. He crouched lower, his eyes level with her breasts, as she took a step toward him. The hat appeared, a black rock in the door window. Green eyes saw it, straightened up, one hand moving quickly toward his pants pocket. The second and third head, thick dark bulbs, lifted beside the hat in the window. Bodies piled against the door behind her. Green eyes held up the glove. "Here, you lousy glove."

She smiled and put out her hand. The hat screamed, "Hey, you made a deal, baby. Hey, you got no manners."

"Don't be scared," she whispered, stepping closer.

The glove lifted toward her and hung in the air between them, gray, languid as smoke. She took it and bent toward his face. "I won't kiss you. Run." The window went black behind her, the lobby solid in darkness, silent but for his breathing, the door breathing against the pressure of the bodies, and the scraping of fingers spread about them like rats in the walls. She felt his shoulder, touched the side of his neck, bent the last inch and kissed him. White light cut the walls. They tumbled behind it, screams and bright teeth. Spinning to face them she was struck, pitched against green eyes and the second door. He twisted hard, shoved away from her as the faces piled forward popping eyes and lights, their fingers accumulating in the air, coming at her. She raised the bag, brought it down swishing into the faces, and wrenched and twisted to get free of the fingers, screaming against their shrieks, "Stop it, stop it, stop it." The bag sprayed papers and coins, and the sunglasses flew over their heads and cracked against the brass mailboxes. She dropped amid shrieks, "Gimme a kiss, gimme a kiss," squirming down the door onto her knees to get fingers out from under her and she thrust up with the bag into bellies and thighs until a fist banged her mouth. She cursed, flailed at nothing.

There was light in the lobby and leather scraping on concrete as they crashed out the door into the street. She shut her eyes instantly as the fist came again, big as her face. Then she heard running in the street. The lobby was silent. The door shut slowly, the shadows deepened. She could feel the darkness getting thicker. She opened her eyes. Standing in front of her was the hat.

He bowed slightly. "I get those guys for you. They got no manners." The hat shook amid the shadows, slowly, sadly.

She pressed the smooth leather of her bag against her cheek where the mouths had kissed it. Then she tested the clasp, snapping it open and shut. The hat shifted his posture and waited. "You hit me," she whispered and did not look up at him. The hat bent and picked up her keys and the papers. He handed the keys to her, then the papers, and bent again for the coins. She dropped the papers into her bag and stuffed them together in the bottom. "Help me up!" She took his hands and got to her feet without looking at him. As she put the key against the lock of the second door she began to shiver. The key rattled against the slot. "Help me!" The hat leaned over the lock, his long thin fingers squeezing the key. It caught, angled with a click. She pushed him aside. "You give me something? Hey, you give me something?" The door shut on his voice.

Total Stranger

BY JAMES GOULD COZZENS

Clad in a long gray duster, wearing a soft gray cap, my father, who was short and strong, sat bolt upright. Stiffly, he held his gauntleted hands straight out on the wheel. The car jiggled scurrying along the narrow New England country road. Sometimes, indignant, my father drove faster. Then, to emphasize what he was saying, and for no other reason, he drove much slower. Though he was very fond of driving, he drove as badly as most people who had grown up before there were cars to drive.

"Well," I said, "I can't help it."

"Of course you can help it!" my father snorted, adding speed. His severe, dark mustache seemed to bristle a little. He had on tinted sunglasses, and he turned them on me.

"For heaven's sake, look what you're doing!" I cried. He looked just in time, but neither his dignity nor his train of thought was shaken. He continued: "Other boys help it, don't they?"

"If you'd just let me finish," I began elaborately: "If you'd just give me a chance to—"

"Go on, go on," he said. "Only don't tell me you can't help it! I'm very tired of hearing—"

"Well, it's mostly Mr. Clifford," I said. "He has it in

for me. And if you want to know why, it's because I'm not one of his gang of bootlickers who hang around his study to bum some tea, every afternoon practically." As I spoke, I could really feel that I would spurn an invitation so dangerous to my independence. The fact that Mr. Clifford rarely spoke to me except to give me another hour's detention because a point in my favor. "So, to get back at me, he tells the Old Man—"

"Do you mean Doctor Holt?"

"Everyone calls him that. Why shouldn't I?"

"If you were a little more respectful, perhaps you wouldn't be in trouble all the time."

"I'm not in trouble all the time. I'm perfectly respectful. This year I won't be in the dormitory any more, so Snifty can't make up a lot of lies about me."

My father drove dashing past a farmhouse in a billow of dust and flurry of panic-struck chickens. "Nonsense!" he said. "Sheer nonsense! Doctor Holt wrote that after a long discussion in faculty meeting he was satisfied that your attitude—"

"Oh, my attitude!" I groaned. "For heaven's sake, a fellow's attitude! Of course, I don't let Snifty walk all over me. What do you think I am? That's what that means. It means that I'm not one of Snifty's little pets, hanging around to bum some tea."

"You explained about the tea before," my father said. "I don't feel that it quite covers the case. How about the other masters? Do they also expect you to come around and take tea with them? When they tell the headmaster that you make no effort to do your work, does that mean that they are getting back at you?"

I drew a deep breath in an effort to feel less uncomfortable. Though I was experienced in defending myself, and with my mother, could do it very successfully, there was a certain remote solemnity about my father which made me falter. From my standpoint, talking to my father was a risky business, since he was only interested in proved facts. From his standpoint, I had reason to know, my remarks would form nothing but a puerile exhibition of sorry nonsense. The result was that he avoided, as long as he could, these serious discussions, and I avoided, as long as I could, any discussions at all.

I said laboriously, "Well, I don't think they told him that. Not all of them. And I can prove it, because didn't I get promoted with my form? What did I really flunk, except maybe algebra? I suppose Mr. Blackburn was the one who said it." I nodded several times, as though it confirmed my darkest suspicions.

My father said frigidly, "In view of the fact that your grade for the year was forty-four, I wouldn't expect him to be exactly delighted with you."

"Well, I can tell you something about that," I said, ill at ease, but sufficiently portentous. "You can ask anyone. He's such a bum teacher that you don't learn anything in his courses. He can't even explain the simplest thing. Why, once he was working out a problem on the board, and I had to laugh, he couldn't get it himself. Until finally one of the fellows who is pretty good in math had to show him where he made a mistake even a first former wouldn't make. And that's how good he is."

My father said, "Now, I don't want any more argument. I simply want you to understand that this fall term will be your last chance. Doctor Holt is disgusted with you. I want you to think how your mother would feel if you disgrace her by being dropped at Christmas. I want you to stop breaking rules and wasting time."

He let the car slow down for emphasis. He gave me a look, at once penetrating and baffled. He could see no sense in breaking the simple, necessary rules of any organized society; and wasting time was worse than wrong, it was mad and dissolute. Time lost, he very well knew, can never be recovered. Left to himself, my father's sensible impulse would probably have been to give me a thrashing I'd remember. But this was out of the question, for my mother had long ago persuaded him that he, too, believed in reasoning with a child.

Looking at me, he must have found the results of reasoning as unimpressive as ever. He said, with restrained grimness, "And if you're sent home, don't imagine that you can go back to the academy. You'll go straight into the public school and stay there. So just remember that."

"Oh, I'll remember all right," I nodded significantly. I had not spent the last two years without, on a number of occasions, having to think seriously about what I'd do if I were expelled. I planned to approach a relative of mine connected with a steamship company and get a job on a boat.

"See that you do!" said my father. We looked at each other with mild antagonism. Though I was still full of arguments, I knew that none of them would get me anywhere, and I was, as always, a little alarmed and depressed by my father's demonstrable rightness about everything. In my position, I supposed that he would always do his lessons, never break any rules, and probably end up a prefect, with his rowing colors and a football letter—in fact, with everything that I would like, if only the first steps toward them did not seem so dull and difficult. Since they did, I was confirmed in my impression that it was impossible to please him. Since it was impossible, I had long been resolved not to care whether I pleased him or not. Practice had made not caring fairly easy.

As for my father, surely he viewed me with much the same resentful astonishment. My mother was accustomed to tell him that he did not understand me. He must have been prepared to believe it; indeed, he must have wondered if he understood anything when he tried to reconcile such facts as my marks with such contentions as my mother's that I had a brilliant mind. At the moment he could doubtless think of nothing else to say, so he drove faster, as if he wanted to get away from the whole irksome matter; but suddenly the movement of the car was altered by a series of heavy, jolting bumps.

"Got a flat," I said with satisfaction and relief. "Didn't I tell you? Everybody knows those tires pick up nails. You can ask anybody."

My father edged the limping car to the side of the road. In those days you had to expect punctures if you drove any distance, so my father was not particularly put out. He may have been glad to get his mind off a discussion which was not proving very profitable. When we had changed the tire—we had demountable rims, which made it wonderfully easy, as though you were putting something over on a puncture—we were both in better spirits and could resume our normal, polite and distant attitudes. That is, what I said was noncommittal, but not impertinent; and what he said was perfunctory, but not hostile. We got into Sansbury at five o'clock, having covered one hundred and three miles, which passed at the time for a long, hard drive.

When my father drove me up to school, we always stopped at Sansbury. The hotel was not a good or comfortable one, but it was the only convenient place to break the journey. Sansbury was a fair-sized manu-facturing town, and the hotel got enough business from traveling salesmen—who, of course, traveled by train—to operate in a shabby way something like a metropolitan hotel. It had a gloomy little lobby with rows of huge armchairs and three or four imitation-marble pillars. There were two surly bellboys, one about twelve, the other about fifty. The elevator, al-ready an antique, was made to rise by pulling on a cable. In the dark dining room a few sad, patient, mid-dle-aged waitresses distributed badly cooked food, much of it, for some reason, served in separate little dishes of the heaviest possible china. It was all awful.

But this is in retrospect. At the time I thought the hotel more pleasant than not. My father had the habit, half stoical, half insensitive, of making the best of anything there was. Though he acted with promptness and decision when it was in his power to change cir-cumstances, he did not grumble when it wasn't. If the food was bad, favored by an excellent digestion, he ate it anyway. If his surroundings were gloomy and the company either boring to him or nonexistent, he did not fidget.

When he could find one of the novels at the mo-ment seriously regarded, he would read it critically. When he couldn't, he would make notes on business affairs in a shorthand of his own invention which nobody else could read. When he had no notes to make, he would retire, without fuss or regret, into whatever his thoughts were.

I had other ideas of entertainment. At home I was never allowed to go to the moving pictures, for my mother considered the films themselves silly and cheap, and the theaters likely to be infested with germs. Away from home, I could sometimes pester my father into taking me. As we moved down the main street of Sansbury—my father serenely terrorizing all the rest of the traffic—I was watching to see what was at the motion-picture theater. To my chagrin, it proved to be Annette Kellerman in *A Daughter of the Gods*, and I could be sure I wouldn't be taken to that.

The hotel garage was an old stable facing the kitchen wing across a yard of bare dirt forlornly stained with oil. My father halted in the middle of it and honked his horn until finally the fifty-year-old bellboy appeared, scowling. While my father had an argument with him over whether luggage left in the car would be safe, I got out. Not far away there stood another car. The hood was up, and a chauffeur in his shirt sleeves had extracted and spread out on a sheet of old canvas an amazing array of parts. The car itself was a big impressive landaulet with carriage lamps at the doorposts. I moved toward it and waited until the chauffeur noticed me.

"What's the trouble?" I inquired professionally.

Busy with a wrench, he grunted, "Cam shaft."

"Oh! How much'll she do?"

"Hundred miles an hour."

"Ah, go on!"

"Beat it," he said. "I got no time."

My father called me, and, aggrieved, I turned away,

for I felt sure that I had been treated with so little respect because I had been compelled to save my clothes by wearing for the trip an old knickerbocker suit and a gray cloth hat with the scarlet monogram of a summer camp I used to go to on it. Following the aged bellboy through the passage toward the lobby, I said to my father, "Well, I guess I'll go up and change."

My father said, "There's no necessity for that. Just see that you wash properly, and you can take a bath before you go to bed."

"I don't see how I can eat in a hotel, looking like this," I said. "I should think you'd want me to look halfway respectable. I—"

"Nonsense!" said my father. "If you wash your face and hands, you'll look perfectly all right."

The aged bellboy dumped the bags indignantly, and my father went up to the imitation-marble desk to register. The clerk turned the big book around and gave him a pen. I wanted to sign for myself, so I was standing close to him, watching him write in his quick, scratchy script, when suddenly the pen paused. He held his hand, frowning a little.

"Come on," I said, "I want to—"

"Now, you can just wait until I finish," he answered. When he had finished, he let me have the pen. To the clerk he said, "Curious coincidence! I used to know someone by that name." He stopped short, gave the clerk a cold, severe look, as though he meant to indicate that the fellow would be well advised to attend to his own business, and turned away.

The elevator was upstairs. While we stood listening to its creeping, creaky descent, my father said "Hm!" and shook his head several times. The lighted cage came into view. My father gazed at it a moment. Then he said "Hm!" again. It came shaking to a halt in front of us. The door opened, and a woman walked out. Her eyes went over us in a brief, impersonal glance. She took two steps, pulled up short, and looked at us again. Then, with a sort of gasp, she said, "Why, Will!"

My father seemed to have changed color a little, but he spoke with his ordinary equability: "How are you, May? I had an idea it might be you."

She came right up to him. She put her hand on his arm. "Will!" she repeated. "Well, now, honestly!" She gave his arm a quick squeeze, tapped it and dropped her hand. "Will, I can't believe it! Isn't it funny! You know, I never planned to stop here. If that wretched car hadn't broken down—"

I was looking at her with blank curiosity, and I saw at once that she was pretty—though not in the sense in which you applied pretty to a girl, exactly. In a confused way, she seemed to me to look more like a picture—the sort of woman who might appear on a completed jigsaw puzzle, or on the back of a pack of cards. Her skin had a creamy, powdered tone. Her eyes had a soft, gay shine which I knew from unconscious observation was not usual in a mature face. Her hair was just so. Very faint, yet very distinct, too, the smell of violets reached me. Although she was certainly not wearing anything resembling evening dress, and, in fact, had a hat on, something about her made me think of my mother when she was ready to go to one of the dances they called assemblies, or of the mothers of my friends who came to dinner looking not at all as they usually looked. I was so absorbed in this feeling of strangeness—I neither liked it nor disliked it;

it simply bewildered me—that I didn't hear anything until my father said rather sharply, "John! Say how do you do to Mrs. Prentice!"

"I can't get over it!" she was saying. She broke into a kind of bubbling laughter. "Why, he's grown up, Will! Oh, dear, doesn't it make you feel queer?"

Ordinarily, I much resented that adult trick of talking about you as if you weren't there, but the grown-up was all right, and she looked at me without a trace of the customary patronage; as though, of course, I saw the joke too. She laughed again. I would not have had the faintest idea why, yet I was obliged to laugh in response.

She asked brightly, "Where's Hilda?"

My father answered, with slight constraint, that my mother was not with us, that he was just driving me up to school.

Mrs. Prentice said, "Oh, that's too bad. I'd so like to see her." She smiled at me again and said, "Will, I can't face that dreadful dining room. I was going to have something sent up. They've given me what must be the bridal suite." She laughed. "You should see it! Why don't we all have supper up there?"

"Capital!" my father said.

The word astonished me. I was more or less familiar with most of my father's expressions, and that certainly was not one of them. I thought it sounded funny, but Mrs. Prentice said, "Will, you haven't changed a bit! But then, you wouldn't. It comes from having such a wonderful disposition."

The aged bellboy had put our luggage in the elevator and shuffled his feet beside it, glowering at us. "Leave the supper to me," my father said. "I'll see if something fit to eat can be ordered. We'll be down in about half an hour."

In our room, my father gave the aged bellboy a quarter. It was more than a bellboy in a small-town hotel would ever expect to get, and so, more than my father would normally give, for he was very exact in money matters and considered lavishness not only wasteful but rather common, and especially bad for the recipient, since it made him dissatisfied when he was given what he really deserved. He said to me, "You can go in the bathroom first, and see that you wash your neck and ears. If you can get your blue suit out without unpacking everything else, change to that."

While I was splashing around I could hear him using the telephone. It did not work very well, but he must eventually have prevailed over it, for when I came out he had unpacked his shaving kit. With the strop hung on a clothes hook, he was whacking a razor up and down. Preoccupied, he sang, or rather grumbled, to himself, for he was completely tone-deaf: "I am the monarch of the sea, the ruler of the Queen's—"

The room where we found Mrs. Prentice was quite a big one, with a large dark-green carpet on the floor, and much carved furniture, upholstered where possible in green velvet of the color of the carpet. Long full glass curtains and green velvet drapes shrouded the windows, so the lights—in brass wall brackets and a wonderfully coiled and twisted chandelier—were on. There was also an oil painting in a great gold frame showing a group of red-trousered French soldiers defending a farmhouse against the Prussians—the type of art I liked most. It all seemed to me tasteful and impressive, but Mrs. Prentice said, "Try not to look at it!" She and my father both laughed.

"I don't know what we'll get," my father said. "I did what I could."

"Anything will do," she said. "Will, you're a godsend! I was expiring for a cocktail, but I hated to order one by myself."

I was startled. My father was not a drinking man. At home I could tell when certain people were coming to dinner, for a tray with glasses and a decanter of sherry would appear in the living room about the time I was going upstairs, and a bottle of sauterne would be put in the icebox.

My mother usually had a rehearsal after the table was set, to make sure that the maid remembered how wine was poured.

Sometimes, when I was at the tennis club, my father would bring me into the big room with the bar and we would both have lemonades. I had never actually seen him drink anything else, so I had an impression that drinking was unusual and unnecessary. I even felt that it was reprehensible, since I knew that the man who took care of the garden sometimes had to be spoken to about it.

To my astonishment, my father said, as though it were the most natural thing in the world, "Well, we can't let you expire, May. What'll it be?"

She said, "I'd love a Clover Club, Will. Do you suppose they could make one?"

My father said, "We'll soon find out! But I think I'd better go down and superintend it myself. That bar looks the reverse of promising."

Left alone with Mrs. Prentice, my amazement kept me vaguely uncomfortable. I studied the exciting details of the fight for the farmhouse, but I was self-conscious, for I realized that she was looking at me. When I looked at her, she was lighting a gold-tipped cigarette which she had taken from a white cardboard box on the table. She seemed to understand something of my confusion. She said, "Many years ago your father and I were great friends, John. After I was married, I went to England to live—to London. I was there until my husband died, so we didn't see each other. That's why we were both so surprised."

I could not think of anything to say. Mrs. Prentice tried again. "You two must have wonderful times together," she said. "He's lots of fun, isn't he?"

Embarrassed, I inadvertently nodded; and thinking that she had found the right subject, she went on warmly, "He was always the most wonderful swimmer and tennis player, and a fine cyclist. I don't know how many cups he took for winning the century run."

Of course, I had often seen my father play tennis. He played it earnestly, about as well as a strong but short-legged amateur who didn't have much time for it could. He was a powerful swimmer, but he did not impress me particularly, even when he swam, as he was fond of doing, several miles; for he never employed anything but a measured, monotonous breast stroke which moved him through the water with unbending dignity. It was very boring to be in the boat accompanying him across some Maine lake. I had no idea what a century run was, but I guessed it meant bicycling, so my confusion and amazement were all the greater. The fad for bicycling wasn't within my memory. I could as easily imagine my father playing tag or trading cigarette pictures as riding a bicycle.

Mrs. Prentice must have wondered what was wrong with me. She could see that I ought to be past the stage when overpowering shyness would be natural. She must have known, too, that she had a more than ordinary gift for attracting people and putting them at ease. No doubt, her failure with me mildly vexed and amused her.

She arose, saying, "Oh, I forgot! I have something." She swept into the room beyond. In a moment she came back with a box in her hands. I had stood up awkwardly when she stood up. She brought the box to me. It was very elaborate. A marvelous arrangement of candied fruits and chocolates filled it. I said, "Thank you very much." I took the smallest and plainest piece of chocolate I could see.

"You mustn't spoil your appetite, must you?" she said, her eyes twinkling, "You take what you want. We won't tell your father."

Her air of cordial conspiracy really warmed me. I tried to smile, but I didn't find myself any more articulate. I said again, "Thank you. This is really all I want."

"All right, John," she said. "We'll leave it on the desk there, in case you change your mind."

The door, which had stood ajar, swung open. In came my father, carrying a battered cocktail shaker wrapped in a napkin. He headed a procession made up of the young bellboy, with a folding table; the old bellboy, with a bunch of roses in a vase; and a worried-looking waitress, with a tray of silver and glasses and folded linen.

"Why, Will," Mrs. Prentice cried, "it's just like magic!"

My father said, "What it will be just like, I'm afraid, is the old Ocean House."

"Oh, oh!" Mrs. Prentice laughed. "The sailing parties! You know, I haven't thought of those—and those awful buffet suppers!"

"Very good," my father said, looking at the completed efforts of his procession. "Please try to see that the steak is rare and gets here hot. That's all." He filled two glasses with pink liquid from the cocktail shaker. He brought one of them to Mrs. Prentice, and, lifting the other, said, "Well, May. Moonlight Bay!"

She looked at him, quick and intent. She began quizzically to smile. It seemed to me she blushed a little. "All right, Will," she said and drank.

They were both silent for an instant. Then, with a kind of energetic abruptness, she said, "Lottie Frazer! Oh, Will, do you know, I saw Lottie a month or two ago."

I sat quiet, recognizing adult conversation and knowing that it would be dull. I fixed my eyes on the battle picture. I tried to imagine myself behind the mottled stone wall with the French infantrymen, but constantly I heard Mrs. Prentice laugh. My father kept responding, but with an odd, light, good-humored inflection, as though he knew that she would laugh again as soon as he finished speaking. I could not make my mind stay on the usually engrossing business of thinking myself into a picture.

". . . you were simply furious," I heard Mrs. Prentice saying. "I didn't blame you."

My father said, "I guess I was."

"You said you'd break his neck."

They had my full attention, but I had missed whatever it was, for my father only responded, "Poor old

Fred!" and looked thoughtfully at his glass. "So you're going back?"

Mrs. Prentice nodded. "This isn't really home to me. Becky and I are—well, I can hardly believe we're sisters. She disapproves of me so."

"I don't remember Becky ever approving of anything," my father said. "There's frankness for you."

"Oh, but she approved of you!" Mrs. Prentice looked at him a moment.

"I never knew it," said my father. "She had a strange way of showing it. I had the impression that she thought I was rather wild, and hanging would be too good—"

"Oh, Will, the things you never knew!" Mrs. Prentice shook her head. "And of course, the person Becky really couldn't abide was Joe. They never spoke to each other. Not even at the wedding." Mrs. Prentice gazed at me, but abstractedly, without expression. She started to look back to my father, stopped herself, gave me a quick little smile, and then looked back. My father was examining his glass.

"Ah, well," he said, " 'there is a divinity that shapes our ends, rough-hew them—' "

Mrs. Prentice smiled. "Do you still write poetry?" she asked.

My father looked at her as though taken aback. "No," he said. He chuckled, but not with composure. "And what's more, I never did."

"Oh, but I think I could say some of it to you."

"Don't," said my father. "I'm afraid I was a very pretentious young man." At that moment, dinner arrived on two trays under a number of big metal covers.

* * *

I thought the dinner was good, and ate all that was offered me; yet eating seemed to form no more than a pleasant, hardly noticed undercurrent to my thoughts. From time to time I looked at the empty cocktail glasses or the great box of candied fruits and chocolates. I stole glances at Mrs. Prentice's pretty, lively face. Those fragments of conversation repeated themselves to me.

Intently, vainly, I considered "century run," "Ocean House," "Moonlight Bay." I wondered about Fred, whose neck, it seemed, my father thought of breaking; about this Becky and what she approved of; and about the writing of poetry. My mother had done a good deal to acquaint me with poetry. She read things like "Adonais," the "Ode to a Nightingale," "The Hound of Heaven" to me; and though I did not care much for them, I knew enough about poets to know that my father had little in common with pictures of Shelley and Keats. I had never seen a picture of Francis Thompson, but I could well imagine.

Thus I had already all I could handle; and though the talk went on during the meal, I hardly heard what they were saying. My attention wasn't taken until Mrs. Prentice, pouring coffee from a little pot, said something about the car.

My father accepted the small cup and answered. "I don't know that it's wise."

"But I've just got to," she said. "I can't make the boat unless—"

"Well, if you've got to you've got to," my father said. "Are you sure he knows the roads? There are one or two places where you can easily make the wrong turn. I think I'd better get a map I have and mark it for you. It will only take a moment."

"Oh, Will," she said, "that would be such a help."

My father set his cup down and arose with decision. When we were alone, Mrs. Prentice got up too. As I had been taught to, I jumped nervously to my feet. She went and took the box from the desk and brought it to me again. "Thank you very much," I stammered. I found another small plain piece of chocolate. "I'm going to put the cover on," she said, "and you take it with you."

I made a feeble protesting sound. I was aware that I ought not to accept such a considerable present from a person I did not know, but I realized that, with it, I was bound to be very popular on my arrival —at least, until the evening school meeting, when anything left would have to be turned in.

She could see my painful indecision. She set the box down. She gave a clear warm laugh, extended a hand and touched me on the chin. "John, you're a funny boy!" she said. My mother had sometimes addressed those very words to me, but with an air of great regret; meaning that the way I had just spoken or acted, while not quite deserving punishment, saddened her. Mrs. Prentice's tone was delighted, as though the last thing she meant to do was reprove me. "You don't like strangers to bother you, do you?"

The touch of her hand so astonished me that I hadn't moved a muscle. "I didn't think you were, at first," she said, "but you are! You don't look very much like him, but you can't imagine how exactly—" She broke into her delighted little laugh again. Without warning, she bent forward and kissed my cheek.

I was frightfully embarrassed. My instant reaction was a sense of deep outrage, for I thought that I had been made to look like a child and a fool. Collecting my wits took me a minute, however; and I found then that I was not angry at all. My first fear—that she might mean to imply that I was just a baby or a little boy—was too clearly unfounded. I was not sure just what she did mean, but part of it, I realized, was that I had pleased her somehow, that she had suddenly felt a liking for me, and that people she liked, she kissed.

I stood rigid, my face scarlet. She went on at once: "Will you do something for me, John? Run down and see if you can find my chauffeur. His name is Alex. Tell him to bring the car around as soon as he can. Would you do that?"

"Yes, Mrs. Prentice," I said.

I left the room quickly. It was only the second floor, so I found the stairs instead of waiting for the elevator. I went down slowly, gravely and bewildered, thinking of my father and how extraordinary it all was; how different he seemed, and yet I could see, too, that he really hadn't changed. What he said and did was new to me, but not new to him. Somehow it all fitted together. I could feel that.

I came into the lobby and went down the back passage and out to the yard. It was now lighted by an electric bulb in a tin shade over the stable door. A flow of thin light threw shadows upon the bare earth. The hood of the big landaulet was down in place, and the man was putting some things away. "Alex!" I said authoritatively.

He turned sharp, and I said, "Mrs. Prentice wants you to bring the car around at once." He continued to look at me a moment. Then he smiled broadly. He touched his cap and said, "Very good, sir."

When I got back upstairs, my father had returned. The old bellboy was taking out a couple of bags. After a moment Mrs. Prentice came from the other room with a coat on and a full veil pinned over her face and hat. "Thank you, John," she said to me. "Don't forget this." She nodded at the big box on the table. I blushed and took it.

"Aren't you going to thank Mrs. Prentice?" my father asked.

She said, "Oh, Will, he's thanked me already. Don't bother him."

"Bother him!" said my father. "He's not bothered. Why, I can remember my father saying to me, 'Step up here, sir, and I'll mend your manners!' And for less than not saying thank you. I'm slack, but I know my parental duties."

They both laughed, and I found myself laughing too. We all went out to the elevator.

In front of the hotel, at the bottom of the steps, the car stood. "Just see he follows the map," my father said. "You can't miss it." He looked at the sky. "Fine moonlit night! I wouldn't mind driving myself."

"Will," said Mrs. Prentice. "Will!" She took his hand in both of hers and squeezed it. "Oh, I hate to say good-bye like this! Why, I've hardly seen you at all!"

"There," said my father. "It's wonderful to have seen you, May."

She turned her veiled face toward me. "Well, John! Have a grand time at school!"

I said, "Good-by, Mrs. Prentice. Thank you very much for the—"

The chauffeur held the door open, and my father helped her in. There was a thick click of the latch closing. The chauffeur went around to his seat. We stood on the pavement, waiting, while he started the engine. The window was down a little, and I could hear Mrs. Prentice saying, "Good-by, good-by."

My father waved a hand, and the car drew away with a quiet, powerful drone. It passed, the sound fading, lights glinting on it, down the almost empty street.

"Well, that's that!" said my father. He looked at me at last and said, "I think you might send a post card to your mother to tell her we got here all right."

I was feeling strangely cheerful and obedient. I thought fleetingly of making a fuss about the movies, but I decided not to. At the newsstand inside, my father bought me a post card showing a covered bridge near the town. I took it to one of the small writing tables by the wall.

"Dear Mother," I wrote with the bad pen, "arrived here safely." I paused. My father had bought a paper and, putting on his glasses, had settled in one of the big chairs. He read with close, critical attention, light shining on his largely bald head, his mustache drawn down sternly. I had seen him reading like that a hundred times, but tonight he did not look quite the same to me. I thought of Mrs. Prentice a moment, but when I came to phrase it, I could not think of anything to say. Instead, I wrote: "We drove over this bridge." I paused again for some time, watching my father read, while I pondered. I wrote: "Father and I had a serious talk. Mean to do better at school—"

Unfortunately, I never did do much better at school. But that year and the years following, I would occasionally try to, for I thought it would please my father.

The Indian Feather

BY THOMAS DABNEY MABRY

"You may as well go on and go," his father said, sitting up a little and shoving another pillow behind him. "I'm not all that sick."

At the other end of the room his mother was pulling down the ivory-colored shades one by one. She looked at him over her shoulder and her eyes said he is very sick indeed and if you had any consideration for me you would not be going off somewhere.

"It's just for the afternoon," he said quickly, turning his face away from the tall windows that were closed against the spring sunshine. In the dimmed room his father's bed had resumed its consequential air. An extra quilt lay folded over the sturdy foot and the carvings of the high headboard twisted and turned in fixed and sculptured ambiguity.

His mother came back and stood beside the bed and her fingers smoothed a pillow's white monogram.

He watched her small hand finally come to rest on his father's arm. Then he said, "But I'll be glad to stay if you want me to . . . if there's anything you want me to do for you down at the factory."

His father smiled. "No sense in your sitting around down there on a sunny Saturday afternoon," he said, "without a blame thing to do."

The room's even light wanned, burgeoned to yellow and paused. It glowed intensely for a moment and sank back suddenly to grey again, and he felt the whole outside rush of shadow against the drawn shades. ". . . Besides," his father was saying, "Kirk is more likely to stay sober if he's with you. And I'll need him bad Monday if it rains and we have a good season."

"Yes sir," he said, and hoped the clouds he had noticed that morning were the usual kind, and not rain clouds.

Again the shades went luminous with the shifting sunlight and the walnut bed in front of him turned gold. Against the wall the sculptured wood shone for an instant in the travelling light like an ancient and beneficent face.

The smile lingered: "I'll need you too," his father said. "No telling how much tobacco'll come pouring in next week." The expression darkened. "But I'll be up from here by Monday," he added, and put his hand under the pillow for his watch. "Go on and have a good time."

His mother relaxed into her wicker rocking chair and looked forlornly at him through her glasses. He tried not to understand the look. From the distant dining-room he could hear Stella clearing off the table. He glanced at the tray of uneaten food that still weighted his father's legs into two straight sticks under the sheets.

He backed to the open door. Through his sneakers the sill was hard against the arch of his foot and from the hall floor behind him a coolness crept up under his pants and caressed the calves of his legs behind his knees. He kept his eyes on his father's face. "Are you sure there's nothing I can do for you?" he asked again, and when a faint "No" formed on the grey lips he said, "I hope you'll feel better, Father."

He let his foot slip off the sill into the hall, and backed away not looking at his mother. But from the closing crack of the door he saw her pretty arm reach out to the tray, saw his father turn his head toward the curtained windows and the unseen spring trees.

The front door was open; the May air filled the dark hall. He took his cap off the hat-rack—the one he called his hunting cap—and pulled his rifle out of the umbrella stand where he had stored it before lunch, took a handful of cartridges from the hat-rack drawer, and went out into the driveway and climbed into his old Ford.

Mr. Kirk was waiting outside the gate when he drove up, leaning against the wire fence in front of the one-story brick house that he rented from the boy's father for $10 a month. Mr. Kirk's wife and his three daughters were sitting on the porch silently looking out at the afternoon. He tipped his hat to them. The two younger girls and Mrs. Kirk were barefooted, but the eldest daughter wore high heeled shoes.

"How's J.J. today, J.D.?" Mr. Kirk asked, opening the car door.

"Better, I think," he said.

"Would you mind dropping my Ellen Alice up town?" Mr. Kirk asked. "It won't be out of our way none."

"Glad to," he said.

Mr. Kirk raised his voice and without looking back called out, "Come on here, girl."

She came running, her heels clicking on the brick walk. She opened the door and squeezed into the narrow space beside her father. "I don't want to crowd you," she said as the car moved forward. Her high smooth pompadour gleamed yellow like glue and the smell of her perfume filled the space between them, its heavy fugitive odor lingering in little waves even after the car had gathered speed.

At the corner of First and Franklin he slowed down and stopped at the newly installed traffic light in front of the Lillian Theatre. The electric bulbs that studded the theatre entrance and that at night seemed to pierce the sky with their brilliance now struggled weakly in the dry white sunlight. Ellen Alice leaned out to gaze. "I'll just get out here," she said, and got out. "I'm certainly much obliged."

The traffic light changed and he started to pull away from the curb.

"Hold on, J.D.," Mr. Kirk said suddenly in a low voice.

He put on the brakes again and as he did so a man in worn blue overalls and mud-dry shoes leaned into the car and slowly placed his hand over Mr. Kirk's knee.

"Hi, friend," Mr. Kirk said with composure.

The man stood waiting as if certain Mr. Kirk had more to say. Mr. Kirk looked up. "You class that tobacco clean before you bring it in to me, you hear?" he said, and felt in his coat pocket for a match and stuck the end of it in his ear. He twisted it around, pulled it out and threw it away. It landed at the feet of the man who still stood close beside him. "You class it clean, mister," Mr. Kirk said, thrusting his head out through the car door, "or I'll dock you so much you won't have enough gimmie left to take your old lady a sack of candy."

The man's lips smiled around his teeth that were clenched on a chew of tobacco. His eyes, under the red hairs of his eyebrows, narrowed in the sunlight. "You can't take nothing from nothing," he said, and turned away, still smiling, to touch the arm of another acquaintance and move with him slowly down the street.

Mr. Kirk spat on the curb and pulled his head back in.

"If I had half what that old feller's got salted away," he said, "I'd have me a Christmas dinner every Sunday. Let's go, J.D."

They rolled away from the curb and along Franklin and up to the Square. At the Square they turned down the rocky hill behind the tobacco warehouses. When they reached the bottom of the hill he drove across the Tennessee Central tracks (empty and abandoned except for a weekly freight from Kentucky) and parked on the cinder gravel in the hot treeless glare of the sun. Below them, forty feet down the sloping bank, stretched the river: silent and deep, shining with the pale yellow of suspended mud. At the water's edge a narrow unpainted skiff lay almost beached, dry at one end and half full of water at the other. It was tied to a stake and over the stake an upside-down tin can, glittering silver, jabbed their eyes as they walked down the steep incline.

"We'll have to bail her out," Mr. Kirk said.

"I'll do it," J.D. said, and knelt on the weathered board. An empty minnow bucket lay on its side and a dead minnow sloshed back and forth in the warm muddy water. A few dried fish scales speckled the narrow plank seats, and along the edges of the seats were black pencil-like scars where burning cigarettes had lain too long.

After a few minutes he said, "I'd like to have a boat like this."

Mr. Kirk was sitting down carefully on the bank. "We'll make you one out at the factory when things slow down," he said. "We'll get a nigger to help us and it won't take no time with all them hogshead staves lying around out there doing nobody no good."

"You mean you made this one?" he asked, and raised his head.

"Ten years ago," Mr. Kirk said, flipping away a cigarette butt and looking down at him from above, "and it's still holding up."

He dipped in the can and poured out the pale water—in and out, in and out. The smell filled him with a deep excitement: a smell of mud and warmth and wetness, a smell from the roots of plants.

"I'd sure appreciate your helping me build one," he said.

Mr. Kirk stood up and brushed the dust off his pants. "That'll do," he said. "Now you get up there in front."

J.D. sat down on the bow seat and they were quickly out in the middle of the river. Nothing was in sight on the smooth surface. The stiff moved silently with the unseen current. Above them, rich bottom land full of new corn stretched away on both sides until far, far down at the bend the river narrowed, and a line of bluff rose in chalky haze. From where he sat, close to the water, it looked a long way.

He hoped his father was asleep by now. He wondered if they would get back by dark. Maybe if Mr. Kirk didn't take too long they would get back in time for him to see his father a little while before supper. But the bluff was miles in the distance. They would hardly reach it much before sundown, and it might be night before Mr. Kirk got ready for the long pull home. If he could turn around now, immediately, and start back, before the current had carried them out of sight . . .

He heard Mr. Kirk say, "Well, how do you like the tobacco business, J.D.?"

"All right," he answered, "but I don't know much about it yet. But I like it fine."

"You've learned a lot for a young feller that just works in the afternoons after school," Mr. Kirk said.

He looked back toward town. Most of it had already disappeared. Even the high courthouse tower had sunk below the green crowning tree-tops, and the Presbyterian Church steeple as well. Only the tall smoke-stacks of the outlying water-works rose in lonely isolation against the cloudless sky and he could still tell, by the sprinkling of tiny white dots far out on the edge of town, where a corner of the City Graveyard came over the hill. He turned and faced forward, and the sun glistened on the water in front of him.

"I told J.J. the other day," Mr. Kirk was saying. "I said, 'J.J., you've got a boy what'll make a better to-bacco man than you and me both.'"

"Did you, sure enough?" he said.

"Yes sir, I did. And you know what J.J. said? He said, 'Well, Kirk, teach him all you know. I'm building it up so he can take it over.'"

"Did he, sure enough?" he said, and shivered and suddenly felt warm again.

The banks of the river were thick with willows. The green spears of canes grew rank close to the water's edge, but between the canes and the river lay a narrow band of cracked mud, treacherous and barren, a place for cottonmouths to lie in the sun and shed their last year's skins. He was surprised to see how wide the river was, now that the small boat was out in the middle of it. It occurred to him that he couldn't have recognized anybody standing on the bank. His fingers closed over the rifle across his knees.

The soft thrust of Mr. Kirk's paddle sent them forward at a good speed. Alone in the low flat trough of water they smelled but could not see the new corn in the endless fields above them. It was a little after two o'clock and no shade anywhere. But the bend of the river was getting nearer. By the time they would reach it there would be shade close to the bluff side.

"Yes sir," Mr. Kirk said, "you'll be better'n your daddy and me both if you keep on like you started. You're a pretty good judge of tobacco already." The skiff slowed for a moment while he lit a cigarette. "You have to watch them farmers, though."

"Why?" he asked.

"They'll cheat you every time if you give them half a chance."

He was silent for a minute. Then he said, "How can they cheat you?"

"They'll class their lugs with their seconds and their seconds with their prime leaf," Mr. Kirk said. "Then they'll wet it all down till it looks like first-class tobacco." He jabbed his paddle deep into the yellow water. "And what's more," he said, "they'll set up nights thinking up new ways to skin you."

He made no reply to this but kept his eyes on the smooth expanse in front of them. He doubted if he'd ever be able to dock a farmer the way Mr. Kirk could do it. His mind went back to the long line of wagons at the factory door, the four-mule team wagons standing all day in line, waiting to be unloaded. His job had been to help unload, and he remembered how often he had climbed up on the wagon and knelt on the great mound of tobacco—his knees crowding those of the farmer and of the farmer's sons and his Negro sharecroppers, lifting it down to the waiting dollies at the door—he remembered how Mr. Kirk would step up and pull out from the middle of the load below them an armful of the sweet odorous leaf. He would hold it up to the light in brief and critical appraisal, the farmer meanwhile still kneeling on the unloaded part, darting a quick glance down at Mr. Kirk, who, turning round and jerking his chin up in a beckoning command, would say, "Come here, my friend. Let me see you a minute, please sir." The crouched figure would rise, wordless, and slide down from the top of the load, hands slowly falling to his sides, and Mr. Kirk would look at him for a minute in thoughtful silence. "I can't accept this, my friend," he would then say with soft solicitude. "Here, feel this here. It's as wet as a new-born kitten. Smell it," and Mr. Kirk would stick it under his nose. "It's as high as a kite; I can't bulk it in this condition, and it will cost me big money to spread it out. Twon't be no good anyhow after what you done to it. I'll have to dock you." And the farmer would stand silently waiting, or maybe would say in a low whispering voice, "It warn't wet none when we loaded up last night," while above on the brown piled wagon the other faces stared down, the hands having slowed and come to a hesitant stop. "Well, boys, what do you want to do?" the farmer would say. "Take it back home?" And finally out of the silence the muttered reply would come: "Reckon he might as well take it on off the wagon. Ain't no place else to carry it." And the hands would begin again, now moving more slowly, moving this time in bitterness and hate.

The bluff rose in rocky layers above them on their left. Oaks and hickories leaned out along the ledges. Now and then a small spring trickled over the moss and slid without noise from one ledge to another and vanished into the river. This was the place where Mr. Kirk shot squirrels.

"Be right quiet now, J.D.," he said, and headed the boat toward the bluff. He laid his paddle down and they drifted slowly inward, and as the skiff moved noiselessly over the opaque surface of the water he picked up his rifle. "There's plenty of squirrels in them trees," Mr. Kirk said, and raised the rifle to his shoulder.

Almost instantly he fired, and a furry body fell from a high limb, hit another lower one, bounced among still lower branches, and thumped to a rocky slab near the water's edge.

"We'll drift a little farther down now, and pick him up on our way back," Mr. Kirk said.

"I don't see how you'll remember where he is," he said.

Mr. Kirk laughed. "Boy, what are you talking about! I never lost no squirrel yet."

At last there was shade in front of them. They slipped into it and at once the air from the water was cool and fresh. They were so close to the rocks that he could see the maiden's hair fern and the wild sweet-william and the yellow violets that grew in the earthy crevices. Mounting overhead, the arching trees hung out, while the boat, undirected by Mr. Kirk, was pulled fitfully onward by deep and invisible strings. Mr. Kirk fired again: a second squirrel fell upon a mossy ledge, crawled a few feet and was still.

"There's another little bastard; get it, boy, quick!"

"Where?" he asked, looking up into the green forest, turning his head this way and that, his hands gripping his rifle. For answer, Mr. Kirk's shot splintered the air behind him and he was aware of its brittle echo darting back from across the river.

"We might as well pick them two up now," Mr. Kirk said, and laid his gun down on the middle plank and made a few quick thrusts of the paddle.

The skiff nosed the bank and J.D. jumped out and scrambled over the rocks. He picked up one squirrel and shoved it in his pants pocket. He moved up the bank toward the second squirrel. It lay full length yet seemed to crouch a little, its open sightless eyes fixed on something bright caught under the outstretched claws. He paused, curious, and bending over saw that the object was only a feather. Yet it looked as if the squirrel's last faint throb of energy had been spent to reach the bright immaculate blue. He picked up the body by the tail, and as he did so the feather swung in the air, suspended by a single claw. Suddenly it fell; he caught it with his hand as it floated downward, and stuck it in his cap and climbed back into the boat and sat facing Mr. Kirk.

Mr. Kirk winked at him and said, "I used to play with them things when I was a kid. I called them Indian feathers. I'd get me a couple of bluebirds and make a whole Indian hat out of them. Yes sir. . . ." He leaned back, "Youngsters will do anything."

J.D. pulled the feather from his cap and held it in his fingers. The color lifted with the river breeze. Mr.

Kirk stopped paddling. "It's right pretty," he said, smiling. Then, as J.D. was about to drop it into the water, he added, "Why don't you keep it?"

J.D. looked up, and thrust the feather back under the band of his cap.

The current, stronger at the bend, caught at the skiff and bore them out toward the middle once more.

"Your daddy likes squirrel meat, don't he?" Mr. Kirk asked suddenly.

"Yes sir, I think so," he said.

"Well, I'll tell you what to do. You give them squirrels to your mamma and tell her to cook them for your daddy's supper."

"Thank you, sir, that's mighty nice," he said, "but I don't think Father could eat but one of them."

"Go ahead and take them," Mr. Kirk said. "Maybe he'll eat with a growing appetite. Besides which," he added, "there ain't nothing I wouldn't do for your daddy."

"Well, I certainly do thank you," he said.

Mr. Kirk looked at the sky. "I guess by the time we pick up that first one it'll be time to start moving along home."

With a deft twist of the paddle he turned the skiff round and they moved with stealth back along the way they'd come, keeping far enough away from the bank to see the tree-tops easily: maybe he would get another shot. But all unkilled squirrels on that part of the bluff had fled, and presently Mr. Kirk bore toward the bank.

The bow of the little boat was like a telescope. Perched in the center of its expanding eye, he watched earth, sky and water shift, blur, turn and focus again; watched gradually appear a fern or flower or fallen rock, a single blade of grass or wandering butterfly. The bluff was thirty feet away but seemed so close he might have touched it with his hand.

"I don't see how you remember the place," he said.

"I mark it with my eyes," said Mr. Kirk. "That little cedar yonder, sticking out crooked from the bluff, you see where it is?"

"Yes sir," he said.

"Well, that's the place."

They reached the spot and J.D. jumped again upon the land, upon the protruding rock, and Mr. Kirk sat in the skiff waiting. The squirrel lay only a few yards away on the flat ledge where it had fallen.

"Do you see him?" Mr. Kirk asked.

He walked forward, stooped and stretched out his hand, and on the instant his exploding heart froze him to stillness.

The dead squirrel lay on its side, its mouth slightly open and its teeth exposed. A little blood had dripped from the nostrils and congealed into a red button on the rock. Just beyond—a foot away—disturbed, jerked crookedly back, and rigid in sunlight, was a copperhead.

"Don't you see the squirrel, J.D.?"

He stood unable to open his lips, his knees half bent and his thin arm aching in slow spasms of recoiling blood. This noiseless confrontation was the evil so often warned against, the dream now suddenly become more real than all the hideous nights of dreaming ever made it.

Back in town, behind the closed windows, his father would be turning his head in restless sleep upon the walnut bed and his mother, opening doors softly, would softly close them and go upstairs and sit whispering in the dark corner at the telephone, and outside, above the roof, the maples would stir and lean against the house, and blocks away the courthouse clock would strike the slow deliberate hour. But here . . . but here . . . the ancient head, the dusty obsidian stare, that long ago had marked his fear and doomed his warm and vulnerable flesh.

If he could cry out through the dry erasure of his lips. If he could cry, "Help me, Help me! . . ." But the cry remained a voiceless echo in the back of his head and, acknowledging already the stinging venomous blow, he fell backward, as the rifle shot cracked behind him, spinning the raised snake in the air, knocking it across the rock where it lay and twisted in harmless subsiding grace. He snatched up the squirrel and ran back down to the river's edge.

Mr. Kirk was standing in the middle of the skiff, still holding his rifle up. His hat had fallen into the water and was floating a few feet from the bank.

"You have to watch out for them copperheads," he said, frowning hard at him. "I should of recollected this old bluff."

Mr. Kirk reached over with his paddle and pulled in his hat and then held the skiff steady while J.D. climbed in. He sat down in the bow as before, his rifle across his knees. He had not had a shot all afternoon. "I guess I'm not much good at shooting squirrels from a boat," he said.

"It's a lazy man's way," said Mr. Kirk.

"Don't you want me to paddle some?" he asked, turning his head back and looking into Mr. Kirk's grey-blue eyes. "I'll be glad to."

"Naw, son, naw. You just set there. I need the exercise."

By this time the whole length of the river was in shade and the drops of water from the paddle that touched his face now and then were cooler than they had been before. A few birds were starting up. Crows called to one another from the invisible corn fields, and a kingfisher spread its wings high over their heads, gently banking against the motionless air.

Mr. Kirk stopped paddling and glanced up toward the sky. "Looking for his supper," he said.

The river still belonged to them. No other craft was in sight. Behind, the bluff was gradually sinking, and far ahead he could just make out the distant smokestacks of the town water-works. In the late high afterlight of the sun, between and all around, the water was turning a pale green. From beyond the new corn, at the edge of an unseen woods, there came three falling singsong notes, the long seductive drawn-out call of a Negro, walking across the fields to supper and to sleep, the warm-throated sound at the end of day. He shut his eyes and saw the little line of dust rising behind in the path, smelled the supper smell of wood smoke as he neared the cabin, saw the bare feet and beaten ground, and now saw the smoke itself lift above the chimney, stretch out in horizontal veil and fade upward into sky. . . . You couldn't thank anybody for maybe saving your life. You couldn't thank a marksman for his aim. You couldn't thank him for the casual tone, for the grey embracing eyes. All you could do was to swear a silent oath to learn to shoot like that, to train your eye and your hand; to stand beside him in any danger, to be ready if he should ever, someday, need you. . . .

* * *

The roofs of the buildings on the Square were still touched with amber light. They climbed up the long bank and as he opened the car door the metal was warm under his hand. He could see the flame now as Mr. Kirk struck a match when he lit a cigarette. He looked down toward the water and as he turned it seemed to him that they had brought a little of the river air back up the hill with them. Mr. Kirk threw the three squirrels on the floor of the car.

"I'll ride on out to the house with you for a minute," Mr. Kirk said, "and see how J.J.'s coming along."

"All right, sir," he said.

The afternoon had altogether faded now. The streets were vacant and only a few empty cars were nosed to the curb. The Capitol Café's neon sign and the bubbling electric spelling of LILLIAN announced the end of the day to silent pavements. The town was briefly at supper, and its country visitors, scattered over the roads and hunched together on seats, were heading homeward through the rising dew.

In front of his house they saw the doctor's car. "Aw-aw," said Mr. Kirk, "ain't that Dr. Dan's car?"

"Yes sir, but that don't necessarily mean anything. Uncle Dan is just as liable to be coming to supper as anything else," he said, feeling a glow of family importance: his uncle, so desperately, so constantly sought by the rest of the town, often came to sit and talk and eat the evening meal at his house.

Dr. Dan was standing just inside the screen door in the unlighted hall, holding his black satchel and talking in a low voice. Mr. Kirk took off his hat and stood at the bottom of the porch steps. "You got all three of them squirrels, J.D.?" he whispered.

"Yes sir," he said, and turned toward the half open door, waiting. Presently his uncle came down the steps. "Aren't you going to stay to supper, Uncle Dan?" he said.

"Not tonight, young feller. I've got to go clear to Kentucky and back before suppertime."

"How's Mr. Bradbury, Doctor?" asked Mr. Kirk.

"Mr. Bradbury's right bad off, Kirk, right bad off."

"I'm mighty sorry to hear that, Doctor," said Mr. Kirk.

His mother did not open the screen door.

"Well, I'll be going on home," said Mr. Kirk. "You give them squirrels to your mamma, J.D., and tell her what I told you."

"All right," he said, hoping his mother was going to open the door and speak to Mr. Kirk. He started up the steps, stopped and turned round. Mr. Kirk was halfway to the street. "Mr. Kirk," he called out, "don't you want me to run you home?"

"You get them squirrels started, J.D. And telephone me if you need me, you hear?"

"Yes sir, I will," he called back, and went on up the steps.

He pushed the screen door open and entered the hall. His mother's hand reached out in the gloom and closed over his bare arm. She stood for a moment leaning silently upon him before she looked up.

"Uncle Dan says John is not going to get well," she whispered.

He glanced beyond her through the dark hallway toward the closed door. "No," he said.

She bent her head again, her soft hair brushing his cheek. "Yes," she said. "Yes, Son."

The blood pumped cold and sodden under his chest,

and he tried to swallow the dry pain in his throat. He backed against the doorframe, but she followed and pressed close to him. Pinning his arms at his sides, she leaned out and away to look up into his face, at the hair falling over his forehead, at his flushed cheeks, his eyes, at his open lips. "You will have to take over responsibilities," she said in the same intimate whisper.

He met her gaze at last. "What responsibilities, Mother?" he asked. And when she did not answer he repeated the question. "What responsibilities do you mean?"

She was looking at him in a way he had never seen her look before.

"What responsibilities, Mother?"

Her nails tightened on his flesh. "Many," she said.

He pulled away from her and had got as far as the stairs.

"Son!"

He turned round. She was still standing by the door.

"How can you treat me this way? How can you?" she said in a low vibrant voice.

He went back and picked up his rifle that he had left leaning against the wall beside the screen door, and turned without speaking and went up the stairs and into his room and hung the rifle on the nail above his bureau. He washed his face and combed his wet hair straight back over his forehead. The little mole on his cheek, just under his eye, was surrounded by the pink glow that shone through his smooth, tan skin. He still had the squirrels with him, so he went downstairs again and into the dining-room where he stood looking at the waiting supper table. The swinging door pushed open and Stella put her head in. "Tell your mamma supper's ready," she said.

"Here's some squirrels for Father," he said, holding them out to her. "Mr. Kirk shot them for him."

"Who's gonna clean um for him?" she said, and closed the door.

He followed her out into the kitchen. "I'll leave them here," he said, and laid them tenderly on the marble top of the beaten-biscuit table.

Stella glanced at him and suddenly the kitchen was filled with the sound of her voice: "Don't you leave them things on my table!"

He picked them up and held them to his chest.

"You ought to knowed better than to bring them things home with all I got to do."

She paused, straightened up and turned to stare at him as though she had never seen him before.

"Put um there on the drain board."

He went back into the dining-room and began to eat his supper. After a while his mother came in and sat down at the end of the table. She put her elbows on the white cloth and covered her face with her hands. The coils of her brown, voluptuous hair tilted forward.

He kept his eyes on his plate, and after he had finished eating he rose and went to his father's room. He opened the door gently into the darkness.

"Are you asleep, Father?" he asked in a low voice.

"Come in, Son," his father said, and roused himself to receive the guest. "Glad to see you."

He felt his way over and sat down in his mother's small rocking chair, his knees wedged tight against the hard side of the bed. In the subdued light its massive frame seemed to fill the long room.

"Well, Son," his father said, "it looks like you're going to have to take charge of things for a while."

"Yes sir," he said.

His father reached out and touched him with his hand. After a minute he said, "Your mother forgot to turn on the light. Switch it on, will you, Son?"

He got up and walked to the door, turned on the light and came back to the rocking chair.

"You can ask Kirk anything you want to know," his father said, as if at the end of a long conversation. "He's a right good judge of tobacco. He'll be a help to you."

"Yes sir," he said. He was conscious of a knot under his right buttock, and felt back and pulled his hunting cap out of his back pocket. The feather was bent but still sticking under the band. He smoothed out the rumpled blue.

"You'll make a good tobacco man, Son, if you keep on like you started," he heard his father say.

He looked up. "Yes sir," he said again.

"I wish Kirk was a little more dependable, though," his father said, and laid a strange white hand on the sheet.

"He shot three squirrels this afternoon, Father."

His father closed his eyes.

He leaned closer. "And, Father, besides that, Father, he killed . . ." But his father's eyes had opened again at the sound of the door, and his mother came in carrying a cup on a tray.

"Here's some freshly made chicken broth," she said. "I asked Stella to make it especially for you."

"Thank you," his father said, "I'm not hungry."

"You must try to eat something," his mother said.

He stood up and watched her come over to the

chair. She waited to sit down until he held it steady for her. She sat far forward and pushed the cup toward the bed.

He looked over her head at his father's face. "I think I'll walk down to the factory, Father, and see if the doors are locked up all right," he said.

"That's a good idea, Son," his father said. "The keys are there on the bureau."

He went over to the bureau and separated the keys from his father's watch, a thin gold watch with a black silk watch-fob to which was attached a gold pendant. He put the keys in his pocket.

Out on the porch he sat for a moment on the steps and looked down the street. He could not see any farther than the haw tree in the edge of the yard, but the corner street lights, marking the blocks, disappeared in the distance, telling him like a familiar code of all the houses between his own and town. He was still holding his cap so he put it on, spreading out the feather again, and slid down the steps.

From across the black grass, lights gleamed from the houses, and at the edges of the yards the night-filled trees made a dark and fragrant tunnel. He moved through it along the pavement, and as he walked fallen maple wings broke with occasional sound beneath the soles of his sneakers.

He crossed to Commerce Street and stopped at the top of the hill. Halfway down on the right the black expanse of the factory roof reflected the night sky. Low, one-story Negro cabins surrounded the large frame building. From where he stood the roof was a dim lake of tar whose obscure shores twinkled smokily from flickering lamps lit in the single rooms.

His feet lifted with pleasure at the answering movements of his ankles down the long slope. And as he moved the factory took form and shape: the roof disappeared, the clapboard walls appeared; and then he was standing at the office door next to the overhanging roofs of the sheds above the big doors where load after load of tobacco had been handed down, and weighed and wheeled away to bulks and handed up again to mountainous piles, built carefully, a handful at a time.

The factory loomed close above him like a benevolent monster, dark, inactive, silent: its deep interiors bulging with the brown sweet-smelling leaf. He leaned against the door, his hand on the knob, inhaling the smell.

He turned the key and stepped inside and walked through the office to the inner door that opened into the huge storage space. He held this door open and listened. Here the stronger odor of tobacco made his nostrils tingle. He heard nothing except from high overhead the faint cracking of the tin roof, cooling in the night. He smiled in the aromatic darkness. Things would be taken care of properly. He and Mr. Kirk would see to that.

He was about to switch on the lights to find the wooden steps that led to the floor below, but he decided to reach the lower floor from outside, down the hill in the rear. So he went back through the office and out into the street again. It was cool after the close heat of the factory. He stood, feeling the air around him, and heard the courthouse clock strike nine. He looked overhead. There were no stars. Heavy clouds had come up since supper.

He walked along the front of the building until he reached the alley that led to the rear. He turned down into this passage on the right and walked somewhat hesitantly until he came to the back corner where he turned right again and passed the big shipping door which opened waist high from the ground. It seemed to be pulled tightly shut so far as he could tell. This was the door where the hogsheads, full of the steamed and packed tobacco and weighing two thousand pounds each, were loaded behind mule teams and hauled to distant warehouses. Oh, the whole intricate process was there in his mind. He would surprise even Mr. Kirk with his knowledge.

The last thing to check was the small glass door of the prizing-room where during the day Negro girls stood at long tables under the horizontal windows, classing the different grades—the leaf, the seconds, and the lugs—all into three neat piles.

He put his hand on the doorknob and pressed his face close against the glass of the door. For an instant he thought he was looking at his own reflection. But the face shifted, its luminous head took form, moved forward, floating, swelling out toward him until, nose pressed to nose and eyes to eyes, it peered out through the vague light with only the thin dirty panes between them.

He could not move, transfixed, turned to stone by the same fetal stare, poised but this time, closer, closer, boring into the center of his brain. And surrounding his skull the tender skin, exposed, began to edge in inmemorial response, and his ears pounded with the trebled beating of his heart. Then the door opened and a voice, embarrassed, a new voice, spoke.

"That you, J.D.?"

The fear subsided, leaving him chill. "You kind of scared me," he said.

The door opened wider. "Come on in."

He stepped inside. "Sir?" he asked. "Is anything the matter?"

Mr. Kirk's grey hair was neatly parted and brushed flat slick on his large round head. Even in the dim light that filtered through the prizing-room windows his shirt looked white and clean, his trousers sleekly pressed.

"Ain't nothing the matter," he said, and paused: "I just thought for a minute you was that little gal. . . ."

"Sir?" he said.

Mr. Kirk spat noiselessly into the soft tobacco trash on the floor. ". . . that little high yaller I'm waiting for—the one what classes next to Aunt Emma." He nodded toward the empty classing tables. "Yes, sir," he said, laughing, "I sure thought for a minute you was that little gal."

His father's keys were heavy in his pocket. "I was just seeing if everything was locked up," he said, and glanced at the door.

Mr. Kirk sat down on one of the empty dollies. "Well, now you're here," he said, "set down and rest yourself."

"Father says we'll have to attend to things for a while," he said.

"Unh huh," Mr. Kirk said.

J.D. walked beyond Mr. Kirk and leaned against a tobacco bulk, his shoulder making a burrow in the soft leaf.

"Father said what you said, Mr. Kirk. He said I'd make a good tobacco man if I keep on like I started."

He paused, and swallowed. Then he said, "I've already been upstairs to see if the doors were all locked."

Mr. Kirk struck a match. "That so?" he said, and held out his hand. In the small flare he was holding an object, a Gargantuan rod of rounded, smoothed tobacco, skillfully, unmistakably shaped. He looked up inquiringly, his eyes yellow in the matchlight. "Ever see one of these here things, J.D.?"

Slowly the hot blood climbed all the way up to his cheeks. "No," he said.

The match went out. In the black silence there came from somewhere in the rear the soft swish of falling tobacco, inexpertly bulked, sliding to the floor. It would be stepped on Monday morning probably and the good cigar leaf crushed and ruined.

"Them gals are always making these things," Mr. Kirk said, and struck another match.

"Father doesn't want any doors left unlocked," he said slowly, starring at Mr. Kirk's hand.

There was a pause. Mr. Kirk stood up, thrust the brown rod in his pocket and pinched out the flame. He walked rapidly to the door and stuck his head out.

"What time is it?" he demanded, peeing out into the alley.

J.D. followed him to the door. "I just heard the courthouse clock strike nine a few minutes ago," he said. The outside air was soft with the coming rain. It sucked past him into the prizing-room, and he could almost hear the thousands of leaves relaxing from its dampness. His father had been right. Next week would be a good tobacco season. By Monday the leaves would be pliable and easy to work with.

Mr. Kirk stood in the door and looked up at the

sky. "It's on the way all right," he said, and pulled a handkerchief from his pocket and blew his nose, and as he flipped the white square back into a neat cone there rose from it an odor of perfume, filling the air between them as it had filled the car that afternoon, yet now mixing also with a faint and acrid smell of whiskey. He turned back into the prizing-room. "Damn that gal," he muttered, and went over to one of the classing-tables where his coat lay folded as neatly as if upon a bed.

A sudden swirl of cinder dust swept in upon them from the path, and the first heavy rain drops clicked against the long rows of window panes that lined the wall above the tables.

Mr. Kirk picked up his coat and looked at the boy. From across the room the words cut through the quiet air: "You're in a pretty big hurry, ain't you, Mister J.D., to close things up?" He paused, and tenderly unfolded his coat. Then he said: "I guess you sort of think you're looking after things around here now."

He met Mr. Kirk's stare. "I just promised Father I'd see if the doors were all locked," he said once more.

Mr. Kirk was shoving his arms into his coat sleeves. "Sure," he said. "Yes siree. And while you're at it you better take a look at all them windows."

"Windows?" J.D. asked.

"Sure," Mr. Kirk said. "Windows need locks, don't they?"

"Father didn't say anything. . . ."

"He must of forgot, then," Mr. Kirk said. "They been needing locks bad all year."

The grey light darkened, and the rain wavered and slowed against the glass and settled to a more regular beat. In the open doorway the form of a woman appeared. It paused for an instant before it slipped into the deeper shadow of the tobacco bulks.

Mr. Kirk's arms stopped in mid air, his sleeves dangling, and the coat slid back and fell to the floor. He leaned over slowly and picked it up, brushed it off with deliberate care and folded it over his arm.

"Sure," he said again, in a different tone. "Sure. . . ."

Then he was hurrying over to J.D. his eyes glittering with impatience. ". . . but them windows can wait now, Son," he whispered hoarsely. "I'll take care of them. And the doors too."

The boy turned and stared at the man. Even in the faint light he could see that Mr. Kirk was queerly smiling. He looked away, toward the waiting tables and the vacant dollies, toward the half-filled hogsheads and shadowy mounds of tobacco, and still turning, his gaze shifted to the door where outside the sharp rain was rapidly changing the cinder path to mud. It was raining harder now. It was raining on the Negro houses across the alley, and on the yard at home. It was raining on the whole town, raining on the little skiff tied at the dark water's edge and on the twisting glassy river itself. And far away, down at the river's bend, it was raining on the long bluff.

He roused himself and turned to speak again to Mr. Kirk. But Mr. Kirk had already disappeared among the bulks of tobacco. He took a step forward and hesitated. Then, as he stood trying to see through the dim light, he heard Mr. Kirk's voice call out to him softly.

"J.D. . . ."

And suddenly, from somewhere back in the shadows,

a long sibilant sound that must have been laughter filled the low room.

A second gust of wind swept through the doorway, billowing his shirt and almost lifting his cap from his head. His hand flew up to catch too late at the falling feather. He stooped down in the gloom and felt around him on the littered floor. He leaned farther over to reach a wider circle but his searching fingers still touched only nails and bits of wood and broken tobacco stalks, and he heard again the sound of his name called softly before the door banged shut, closing him into the black and pungent room.

Black Boy

BY KAY BOYLE

At that time, it was the forsaken part, it was the other end of the city, and on early spring mornings there was no one about. By soft words, you could woo the horse into the foam, and ride her with the sea knee-deep around her. The waves came in and out there, as indolent as ladies, gathered up their skirts in their hands and, with a murmur, came tiptoeing in across the velvet sand.

The wooden promenade was high there, and when the wind was up the water came running under it like wild. On such days, you had to content yourself with riding the horse over the deep white drifts of dry sand on the other side of the walks, the horse's hoofs here made no sound and the sparks of sand stung your face in fury. It had no body to it, like the mile or two of sand packed hard that you could open out on once the tide was down.

My little grandfather, Puss, was alive then, with his delicate gait and ankles, and his belly pouting in his dove-gray clothes. When he saw from the window that the tide was sidling out, he put on his pearl fedora and came stepping down the street. For a minute, he put one foot on the sand, but he was not at ease there. On the boardwalk over our heads was some other kind of life in progress. If you looked up, you could see it in motion through the cracks in the timber: rolling chairs, and women in high heels proceeding, if the weather were fair.

"You know," my grandfather said, "I think I might like to have a look at a shop or two along the boardwalk." Or: "I suppose you don't feel like leaving the beach for a minute," or: "If you would go with me, we might take a chair together, and look at the hats and the dress and roll along in the sun."

He was alive then, taking his pick of the broad easy chairs and the black boys.

"There's a nice skinny boy," he'd say. "He looks as though he might put some action into it. Here you are, sonny. Push me and the little girl down to the Million Dollar Pier and back."

The cushions were red velvet with a sheen of dew over them. And Puss settled back on them and took my hand in his. In his mind there was no hesitation about whether he would look at the shops on one side, or out on the vacant side where there was nothing shining but the sea.

"What's your name, Charlie?" Puss would say without turning his head to the black boy pushing the chair behind our shoulders.

"Charlie's my name, sir," he'd answer with his face dripping down like tar in the sun.

"What's your name, sonny?" Puss would say another time, and the black boy answered:

"Sonny's my name, sir."

"What's your name, Big Boy?"

"Big Boy's my name."

He never wore a smile on his face, the black boy. He was thin as a shadow but darker, and he was pushing and sweating, getting the chair down to the Million Dollar Pier and back again, in and out through the people. If you turned toward the sea for a minute, you could see his face out of the corner of your eye, hanging black as a bat's wing, nodding and nodding like a dark heavy flower.

But in the early morning, he was the only one who came down onto the sand and sat under the beams of the boardwalk, sitting idle there with a languor fallen on every limb. He had long bones. He sat idle there, with his clothes shrunk up from his wrists and his ankles, with his legs drawn up, looking out at the sea.

"I might be a king if I wanted to be," was what he said to me.

Maybe I was twelve years old, or maybe I was ten when we used to sit eating dog biscuits together. Sometimes when you broke them in two, a worm fell out and the black boy lifted his sharp finger and flecked it carelessly from off his knee.

"I seen kings," he said, "with a kind of cloth over they heads, and kind of jewels-like around here and here. They weren't any blacker than me, if as black," he said. "I could be almost anything I made up my mind to be."

"King Nebuchadnezzar," I said. "He wasn't a white man."

The wind was off the ocean and was filled with alien smells. It was early in the day, and no human sign was given. Overhead were the green beams of the boardwalk and no wheel or step to sound it.

"If I was a king," said the black boy with his biscuit in his fingers, "I wouldn't put much stock in hanging around here."

Great crystal jelly beasts were quivering in a hundred different colors on the wastes of sand around us. The dogs came, jumping them, and when they saw me still sitting still, they wheeled like gulls and sped back to the sea.

"I'd be traveling around," he said, "here and there. Now here, now there. I'd change most of my habits."

His hair grew all over the top of his head in tight dry rosettes. His neck was longer and more shapely than a white man's neck, and his fingers ran in and out of the sand like the blue feet of a bird.

"I wouldn't have much to do with pushing chairs around under them circumstances," he said. "I might even give up sleeping out here on the sand."

Or if you came out when it was starlight, you could see him sitting there in the clear white darkness. I could go and come as I liked, for whenever I went out the door, I had the dogs shouldering behind me. At night, they shook the taste of the house out of their coats and came down across the sand. There he was, with his knees up, sitting idle.

"They used to be all kinds of animals come down here to drink in the dark," he said. "They was a kind of a mirage came along and gave that impression. I seen tigers, lions, lambs, deer; I seen ostriches drinking down there side by side with each other. They's the Northern Lights gets crossed some way and switches the wrong picture down."

It may be that the coast has changed there, for even then it was changing. The lighthouse that had once stood far out on the white rocks near the outlet was standing then like a lighted torch in the heart of the town. And the deep currents of the sea may have altered so that the clearest water runs in another direction, and houses may have been built down as far as where the brink used to be. But the brink was so perilous then that every word the black boy spoke seemed to fall into a cavern of beauty.

"I seen camels; I seen zebras," he said. "I might have caught any of one of them if I'd felt inclined."

The street was so still and wide then that when Puss stepped out of the house, I could hear him clearing his throat of the sharp salty air. He had no intention of soiling the soles of his boots, but he came down the street to find me.

"If you feel like going with me," he said, "we'll take a chair and see the fifty-seven varieties changing on the electric sign."

And then he saw the black boy sitting quiet. His voice drew up short on his tongue and he touched his white mustache.

"I shouldn't think it a good idea," he said, and he put his arm through my arm. "I saw another little oak not three inches high in the Jap's window yesterday. We might roll down the boardwalk and have a look at it. You know," said Puss, and he put his kid gloves carefully on his fingers, "that black boy might do you some kind of harm."

"What kind of harm could he do me?" I said.

"Well," said Puss with the garlands of lights hanging around him, "he might steal some money from you. He might knock you down and take your money away."

"How could he do that?" I said. "We just sit and talk there." Puss looked at me sharply.

"What do you find to sit and talk about?" he said.

"I don't know," I said. "I don't remember. It doesn't sound like much to tell it."

The burden of his words was lying there on my heart when I woke up in the morning. I went out by myself to the stable and led the horse to the door and put the saddle on her. If Puss were ill at case for a day or two, he could look out the window in peace and see me riding high and mighty away. The day after tomorrow, I thought, or the next day, I'll sit down on the beach again and talk to the black boy. But when I rode out, I saw him seated idle there, under the boardwalk, heedless, looking away to the cool wide sea. He had been eating peanuts and the shells lay all around him. The dogs came running at the horse's heels, nipping the foam that lay along the tide.

The horse was as shy as a bird that morning, and when I drew her up beside the black boy, she tossed her head on high. Her mane went back and forth, from one side to the other, and a flight of joy in her limbs sent her forelegs like rockets into the air. The black boy stood up from the cold smooth sand, unsmiling, but a spark of wonder shone in his marble eyes. He put out his arm in the short tight sleeve of his coat and stroked her shivering shoulder.

"I was going to be a jockey once," he said, "but I changed my mind."

I slid down on one side while he climbed up the other.

"I don't know as I can ride him right," he said as I held her head. "The kind of saddle you have, it gives you nothing to grip your heels around. I ride them with their bare skin."

The black boy settled himself on the leather and put his feet in the stirrups. He was quiet and quick with delight, but he had no thought of smiling as he took the reins in his hands.

I stood on the beach with the dogs beside me, looking after the horse as she ambled down to the water. The black boy rode easily and straight, letting the horse stretch out and sneeze and canter. When they reached the jetty, he turned her casually and brought her loping back.

"Some folks licks hell out of their horses," he said. "I'd never raise a hand to one, unless he was to bite me or do something I didn't care for."

He sat in the saddle at ease, as though in a rocker, stroking her shoulder with his hand spread open, and turning in the stirrups to sooth her shining flank.

"Jockeys made a pile of money," I said.

"I wouldn't care for the life they have," said the black boy. "They have to watch their diet so careful."

His fingers ran delicately through her hair and laid her mane back on her neck.

When I was up on the horse again, I turned her toward the boardwalk.

"I'm going to take her over the jetty," I said. "You'll see how she clears it. I'll take her up under the boardwalk to give her a good start."

I struck her shoulder with the end of my crop, and she started toward the tough black beams. She was under it, galloping, when the dogs came down the beach like mad. They had chased a cat out of cover and were after it, screaming as they ran, with a wing of sand blowing wide behind them, and when the horse saw them under her legs, she jumped sidewise in sprightliness and terror and flung herself against an iron arch.

For a long time I heard nothing at all in my head except the melody of someone crying, whether it was my dead mother holding me in comfort, or the soft wind grieving over me where I had fallen. I lay on the sand asleep; I could feel it running with my tears through my fingers. I was rocked in a cradle of love, cradled and rocked in sorrow.

"Oh, my little lamb, little lamb pie!" Oh, sorrow, sorrow, wailed the wind, or the tide, or my own kin about me. "Oh, lamb, oh, lamb!"

I could feel the long swift fingers of love untying the terrible knot of pain that bound my head. And I put my arms around him and lay close to his heart in comfort.

Puss was alive then, and when he met the black boy carrying me up to the house, he struck him square across the mouth.

Man and Daughter in the Cold

BY JOHN UPDIKE

"Look at that girl ski!" The exclamation arose at Ethan's side as if, in the disconnecting cold, a rib of his had cried out; but it was his friend, friend and fellow-teacher, an inferior teacher but superior skier, Matt Langley, admiring Becky, Ethan's own daughter. It took an effort, in this air like slices of transparent metal interposed everywhere, to make these connections and to relate the young girl, her round face red with windburn as she skimmed down the run-out slope, to himself. She was his daughter, age thirteen. Ethan had twin sons, two years younger, and his attention had always been focussed on their skiing, on the irksome comedy of their double needs—the four boots to lace, the four mittens to find—and then their cute yet grim competition as now one and now the other gained the edge in the expertise of geländesprungs and slalom form. On their trips north into the mountains, Becky had come along for the ride. "Look how solid she is," Matt went on. "She doesn't cheat on it like your boys—those feet are absolutely together." The girl, grinning as if she could hear herself praised, wiggle-waggled to a flashy stop that sprayed snow over the men's ski tips.

"Where's Mommy?" she asked.

Ethan answered, "She went with the boys into the lodge. They couldn't take it." Their sinewy little male bodies had no insulation; weeping and shivering, they had begged to go in after a single T-bar run.

"What sissies," Becky said.

Matt said, "This wind is wicked. And it's picking up. You should have been here at nine; Lord, it was lovely. All that fresh powder, and not a stir of wind."

Becky told him, "Dumb Tommy couldn't find his mittens, we spent an *hour* looking, and then Daddy got the Jeep stuck." Ethan, alerted now for signs of the wonderful in his daughter, was struck by the strange fact that she was making conversation. Unafraid, she was talking to Matt without her father's intercession.

"Mr. Langley was saying how nicely you were skiing."

"You're Olympic material, Becky."

The girl perhaps blushed; but her cheeks could get no redder. Her eyes, which, were she a child, she would have instantly averted, remained a second on Matt's face, as if to estimate how much he meant it. "It's easy down here," Becky said. "It's babyish."

Ethan asked, "Do you want to go up to the top?" He was freezing standing still, and the gondola would be sheltered from the wind.

Her eyes shifted to his, with another unconsciously thoughtful hesitation. "Sure. If you want to."

"Come along, Matt?"

"Thanks, no. It's too rough for me; I've had enough runs. This is the trouble with January—once it stops snowing, the wind comes up. I'll keep Elaine company in the lodge." Matt himself had no wife, no children. At thirty-eight, he was as free as his students, as light on his skis and as full of brave know-how. "In case of frostbite," he shouted after them, "rub snow on it."

Becky effortlessly skated ahead to the lift shed. The encumbered motion of walking on skis, not natural to him, made Ethan feel asthmatic: a fish out of water. He touched his parka pocket, to check that the inhalator was there. As a child he had imagined death as something attacking from outside, but now he saw that it was carried within; we nurse it for years, and it grows. The clock on the lodge wall said a quarter to noon. The giant thermometer read two degrees above zero. The racks outside were dense as hedges with idle skis. Crowds, any sensation of crowding or delay, quickened his asthma; as therapy he imagined the emptiness, the blue freedom, at the top of the mountain. The clatter of machinery inside the shed was comforting, and enough teen-age boys were boarding gondolas to make the ascent seem normal and safe. Ethan's breathing eased. Becky proficiently handed her poles to the loader points up; her father was always caught by surprise, and often as not fumbled the little maneuver of letting his skis be taken from him. Until, five years ago, he had become an assistant professor at a New Hampshire college an hour to the south, he had never skied; he had lived in those Middle Atlantic cities where snow, its moment of virgin beauty by, is only an encumbering nuisance, a threat of suffocation. Whereas his children had grown up on skis.

Alone with his daughter in the rumbling isolation of the gondola, he wanted to explore her, and found her strange—strange in her uninquisitive child's silence, her accustomed poise in this ascending egg of metal. A dark figure with spreading legs veered out of control beneath them, fell forward, and vanished. Ethan cried out, astonished, scandalized; he imagined the man had buried himself alive. Becky was barely amused, and looked away before the dark spots struggling in the drift were lost from sight. As if she might know, Ethan asked, "Who was that?"'

"Some kid." Kids, her tone suggested, were in plentiful supply; one could be spared.

He offered to dramatize the adventure ahead of them: "Do you think we'll freeze at the top?"

"Not exactly."

"What do you think it'll be like?"

"Miserable."

"Why are we doing this, do you think?"

"Because we paid the money for the all-day lift ticket."

"Becky, you think you're pretty smart, don't you?"

"Not really."

The gondola rumbled and lurched into the shed at the top; an attendant opened the door, and there was a howling mixed of wind and of boys whooping to keep warm. He was roughly handed two pairs of skis, and the handler, muffled to the eyes with a scarf, stared as if amazed that Ethan was so old. All the others struggling into skis in the lee of the shed were adolescent boys. Students: after fifteen years of teaching, Ethan tended to flinch from youth—its harsh noises, its cheerful rapacity, its cruel onward flow as one class replaced another, ate a year of his life, and was replaced by another.

Away from the shelter of the shed, the wind was a high monotonous pitch of pain. His cheeks instantly ached, and the hinges linking the elements of his face seemed exposed. His septum tingled like glass—the rim of a glass being rubbed by a moist finger to produce a note. Drifts ribbed the trail, obscuring Becky's ski tracks seconds after she made them, and at each push through the heaped snow his scope of breathing narrowed. By the time he reached the first steep section, the left half of his back hurt as it did only in the panic of a full asthmatic attack, and his skis, ignored, too heavy to manage, spread and swept him toward a snowbank at the side of the trail. He was bent far forward but kept his balance; the snow kissed his face lightly, instantly, all over; he straightened up, refreshed by the shock, thankful not to have lost a ski. Down the slope Becky had halted and was staring upward at him, worried. A huge blowing feather, a partition of snow, came between them. The cold, unprecedented in his experience, shone through his clothes like furious light, and as he rummaged through his parka for the inhalator he seemed to be searching glass shelves backed by a black wall. He found it, its icy plastic the touch of life, a clumsy key to his insides. Gasping, he exhaled, put it into his mouth, and inhaled; the isoproterenol spray, chilled into drops, opened his lungs enough for him to call to his daughter, "Keep moving! I'll catch up!"

Solid on her skis, she swung down among the moguls and wind-bared ice, and became small, and again waited. The moderate slope seemed a cliff; if he fell and sprained anything, he would freeze. His entire body would become locked tight against air and light and thought. His legs trembled; his breath moved in and out of a narrow slot beneath the pain in his back. The cold and blowing snow all around him constituted an immense crowding, but there was no way out of this white cave but to slide downward toward the dark spot that was his daughter. He had forgotten all his lessons. Leaning backward in an infant's tense snowplow, he floundered through alternating powder and ice.

"You O.K., Daddy?" Her stare was wide, its fright underlined by a pale patch on her cheek.

He used the inhalator again and gave himself breath to tell her, "I'm fine. Let's get down."

In this way, in steps of her leading and waiting, they worked down the mountain, out of the worst wind, into the lower trail that ran between birches and hemlocks. The cold had the quality not of absence but of force: an inverted burning. The last time Becky stopped and waited, the colorless crescent on her scarlet cheek disturbed him, reminded him of some injunction, but he could find in his brain, whittled to a dim determination to persist, only the advice to keep going, toward shelter and warmth. She told him, at a division of trails, "This is the easier way."

"Let's go the quicker way," he said, and in this last descent recovered the rhythm—knees together, shoulders facing the valley, weight forward as if in the moment of release from a diving board—not a resistance but a joyous acceptance of falling. They reached the base lodge, and with unfeeling hands removed their skis. Pushing into the cafeteria, Ethan saw in the momentary mirror of the door window that his face was a spectre's; chin, nose, and eyebrows had retained the snow from that near-fall near the top. "Becky, look," he said, turning in the crowded warmth and clatter inside the door. "I'm a monster."

"I know, your face was absolutely white, I didn't know whether to tell you or not. I thought it might scare you."

He touched the pale patch on her cheek. "Feel anything?"

"No."

"Damn. I should have rubbed snow on it."

Matt and Elaine and the twins, flushed and stripped of their parkas, had eaten lunch; shouting and laughing with a strange guilty shrillness, they said that there had been repeated loudspeaker announcements not to go up to the top without face masks, because of frostbite. They had expected Ethan and Becky to come back down on the gondola, as others had, after tasting the top. "It never occurred to us," Ethan said. He took the blame upon himself by adding, "I wanted to see the girl ski."

Their common adventure, and the guilt of his having given her frostbite, bound Becky and Ethan together in complicity for the rest of the day. They arrived home as sun was leaving even the tips of the hills; Elaine had invited Matt to supper, and while the windows of the house burned golden Ethan shovelled out the Jeep. The house was a typical New Hampshire farmhouse, less than two miles from the college, on the side of a hill, overlooking what had been a pasture, with the usual capacious porch running around three sides, cluttered with cordwood and last summer's lawn furniture. The woodsy sheltered scent of these porches, the sense of rural waste space, never failed to please Ethan, who had been raised in a Newark half-house, then a West Side apartment, and just before college a row house in Baltimore, with his grandparents. The wind had been left behind in the mountains. The air was as still as the stars. Shovelling the light dry snow became a lazy dance.

But when he bent suddenly, his knees creaked, and his breathing shortened so that he paused. A sudden rectangle of light was flung from the shadows of the porch. Becky came out into the cold with him. She was carrying a lawn rake.

He asked her, "Should you be out again? How's your frostbite?" Though she was a distance away, there was no need, in the immaculate air, to raise his voice.

"It's O.K. It kind of tingles. And under my chin. Mommy made me put on a scarf."

"What's the lawn rake for?"

"It's a way you can make a path. It really works."

"O.K., you make a path to the garage and after I get my breath I'll see if I can get the Jeep back in."

"Are you having asthma?"

"A little."

"We were reading about it in biology. Dad, see, it's kind of a tree inside you, and every branch has a little ring of muscle around it, and they tighten." From her gestures in the dark she was demonstrating, with mittens on.

What she described, of course, was classic unalloyed asthma, whereas his was shading into emphysema, which could only worsen. But he liked being lectured to—preferred it, indeed, to lecturing—and as the minutes of companionable silence with his daughter passed he took inward notes on the bright quick impressions flowing over him like a continuous voice. The silent cold. The stars. Orion behind an elm. Minute scintillae in the snow at his feet. His daughter's strange black bulk against the white; the solid grace that had stolen upon her. The conspiracy of love. His father and he shovelling the car free from a sudden unwelcome storm in Newark, instantly gray with soot, the undercurrent of desperation, his father a salesman and must get to Camden. Got to get to Camden, boy, get to Camden or bust. Dead of a heart attack at forty-seven. Ethan tossed a shovelful into the air so the scintillae flashed in the steady golden chord from the house windows. Elaine and Matt sitting flushed at the lodge table, parkas off, in deshabille, as if sitting up in bed. Matt's way of turning a half circle on the top of a mogul, light as a diver. The cancerous unwieldiness of Ethan's own skis. His jealousy of his students, the many-headed immortality of their annual renewal. The flawless tall cruelty of the stars. Orion intertwined with the silhouetted elm. A black tree inside him. His daughter, busily sweeping with the rake, childish yet lithe, so curiously demonstrating this preference for his company. Feminine of her to forgive him her frostbite. Perhaps, flattered on skis, felt the cold her element. Her womanhood soon enough to be smothered in warmth. A plow a mile away painstakingly scraped. He was missing the point of the lecture. The point was unstated: an absence. He was looking upon his daughter as a woman but without lust. The music around him was being produced, in the zero air, like a finger on crystal, by this hollowness, this generosity of negation. Without lust, without jealousy. Space seemed love, bestowed to be free in, and coldness the price. He felt joined to the great dead whose words it was his duty to teach.

The Jeep came up unprotestingly from the fluffy snow. It looked happy to be penned in the garage with Elaine's station wagon, and the skis, and the oiled chain saw, and the power mower dreamlessly waiting for spring. Ethan was happy, precariously so, so that rather than break he uttered a sound: "Becky?"

"Yeah?"

"You want to know what else Mr. Langley said?"

"What?" They trudged toward the porch, up the path the gentle rake had cleared.

"He said you ski better than the boys."

"I bet," she said, and raced to the porch, and in the precipitate way, evasive and female and pleased, that she flung herself to the top step he glimpsed something generic and joyous, a pageant that would leave him behind.

Outstanding Laurel-Leaf Fiction for Young Adult Readers

☐ **A LITTLE DEMONSTRATION OF AFFECTION**
Elizabeth Winthrop $1.25
A 15-year-old girl and her older brother find themselves turning to each other to share their deepest emotions.

☐ **M.C. HIGGINS THE GREAT**
Virginia Hamilton $1.50
Winner of the Newbery Medal, the National Book Award and the Boston Globe-Horn Book Award, this novel follows M.C. Higgins' growing awareness that both choice and action lie within his power.

☐ **PORTRAIT OF JENNIE**
Robert Nathan $1.25
Robert Nathan interweaves touching and profound portraits of all his characters with one of the most beautiful love stories ever told.

☐ **THE MEAT IN THE SANDWICH**
Alice Bach $1.50
Mike Lefcourt dreams of being a star athlete, but when hockey season ends, Mike learns that victory and defeat become hopelessly mixed up.

☐ **Z FOR ZACHARIAH**
Robert C. O'Brien $1.50
This winner of an Edgar Award from the Mystery Writers of America portrays a young girl who was the only human being left alive after nuclear doomsday—or so she thought.

At your local bookstore or use this handy coupon for ordering:

Dell | **DELL BOOKS**
P.O. BOX 1000, PINEBROOK, N.J. 07058

Please send me the books I have checked above. I am enclosing $_____ (please add 75¢ per copy to cover postage and handling). Send check or money order—no cash or C.O.D.'s. Please allow up to 8 weeks for shipment.

Mr/Mrs/Miss_____

Address_____

City_____ State/Zip_____